SARAH

FOREVER MATES

CLAWS AND FANGS BOOK 3

Copyright © 2021 by Sarah Spade

All rights reserved.

No part of this book may be reproduced in any form or by any electronic or mechanical means, including information storage and retrieval systems, without written permission from the author, except for the use of brief quotations in a book review.

Cover by Zeki of Phoenix Design Studio

CHAPTER 1

I swear to the Luna, if I don't go from skin to fur and run off some of this aggression and *soon*, I'm going to go feral on the first packmate that so much as looks at me funny. And, yeah, it's probably not the best thing to admit, especially given my recent bump in status, but I can't help it.

To make my pissy mood worse, I'd put money down that they would just let me do it, too. As an alpha wolf, my off-the-charts dominance would have any lower-ranked shifters showing their throat in submission, but as their Alpha's newly bonded mate? There isn't a single wolf in Accalia that would dare lift a claw against me.

Damn it.

I know what's got my wolf on edge, too. Even if we weren't dealing with a monumental threat to the Mountainside Pack—a threat that I'm directly responsible for—the urge to tear off across the terrain isn't all that unusual for my kind of supe, especially given my rank.

The moon calls to me. She's *always* called to me. As a wolf shifter, the Luna is irresistible during the full moon, but even when she's barely a sliver, like now, it's almost impossible to escape her pull.

For the last year, I had to put on my big girl panties and figure out how to. Surprisingly, the secret turned out to be a half-gallon of Breyer's and binging mindless TV in my pajamas. Made sense, after all. What's the moon's effect on a shifter but just a different type of cycle?

It shouldn't be this bad tonight. It's only been two weeks since the last full moon. Two weeks since I claimed Ryker Wolfson as my bonded mate, and I allowed him to mark me as his. Two weeks since I came for what was supposed to be a short stay in Accalia—a short stay that became frustratingly open-ended as soon as my birth father decided to make his latest daring move against us.

Just remembering his nerve has my wolf snarling, desperate to lash out at someone. And though my human side is short with everyone in Accalia lately, both me and my wolf are in agreement that there's really only one target that I have in mind: Jack "Wicked Wolf" Walker, who not only made an informal challenge of my new mate, but who also did the impossible.

He made me willing to risk anything in the name of Trish freaking Danvers, even push my furious mate to his breaking point before he used our bond to convince me to sit tight until Ryker could figure out *our* next move.

That was a week ago. One week since the Wicked Wolf of the West used one of our packmates to steal another, leaving behind a taunting note for my mate.

You have my girl, Wolfson, and now I have yours.

Trish Danvers. Of all the females in the Mountainside Pack, my birth father snatched her to force me and Ryker to pay attention to him.

Of course it would be Trish. She was the one who told anyone who would listen that she would eventually end up Ryker's chosen mate; chosen because the Luna already whispered that I was his fated mate. Her crush on Ryker made her easy pickings when Shane Loup manipulated her—and, well, *me*—to believe she was the one Ryker wanted for his mate.

We're still trying to figure out the method to Walker's madness. Rumor said he never left the Wolf District, but I know that's not true. How did he find out so much about Accalia? Did Ryker's former Beta tell the Wicked Wolf all about her after he betrayed his

Alpha and traded Accalia for the Western Pack? Or did he have another spy in our midst?

We already discovered that one of the deltas who tended to the pack vehicles—a young wolf named Aidan Barrow—was working with Walker. He was the one who disappeared with Trish, leaving her spilled blood and the threatening note behind.

Was he the only one?

I don't know. And the fact that I *don't* has my wolf snapping at me to just go already.

I need to run. I need to break out into my fur and tear off down the mountain until my pads bleed and I've run past the worst of my guilt-fueled fury.

Now, I know all of the reasons why I'm not supposed to. As soon as Duke came to tell us about Trish, everything changed. My return to Muncie—to my job down at Charlie's, and the townhouse that Ryker bought for me as a mating gift—was put on hold. As part of the Alpha couple, I was needed here.

And if you believe that, I've got a bridge in Brooklyn I can sell you.

I'm an alpha. Only the second female alpha that our people have ever heard of. That means I'm worth something, and the bounty on my head is pretty freaking huge. But it also means that I can take care of myself.

Try telling that to Ryker.

He stops short of locking me in the cabin we share,

but only just. When he's not taking care of pack business, he's up my ass, hovering over my shoulder as if he expects that he'll blink and I'll disappear on him.

As if. The year I believed he rejected me aside, I spent more than a decade waiting for the moment when Ryker would finally be mine. Now that I have him, I'm not going anywhere.

Except, perhaps, for a much-needed run.

He's currently in the den of the Alpha's cabin. After dinner, he said he needed to take care of something. He invited me to join him, but I was already halfway out the door, making my own excuses as night fell and the Luna beckoned.

I don't ask for permission, mainly because I know that Ryker will refuse. Better to beg for forgiveness than waste my breath convincing my thick-headed, stubborn mate that the world won't come to an end if I cross out of our immediate territory.

There's a small grove in the trees that cover the mountains that I consider mine. It's where I keep my baby—my beloved Jeep—and it's so full of my scent that none of my packmates go near it. I've marked it as mine, and as I jog toward it, I'm already shucking off my shirt. Shoes are next, then my jeans. Underwear gets tugged off and folded, shoved in the back seat of my car until I need them later.

When all I'm wearing is Ryker's mark on my skin and his charmed golden canine fang hanging on a chain nestled between my boobs, I tap into my inner wolf and shift. I go from a tiny blonde chick to a majestic blonde wolf in the blink of an eye.

I give my new form a few experimental stretches, bounding back and forth on my paws as I breathe in deep. The mountain air smells of pine and earth and the early autumn chill. A few fallen leaves crackle beneath my energetic pounce. Out of the corner of my eye, my tail whips behind me. Shaggy and just as pale as the rest of my fur, it stands out against the greens and browns and blacks of the woods. With a yip, I chase it, then dash out of the grove.

I'm fast, but not as fast as I usually am. Weird. I spur my wolf, but she's as stubborn as the rest of me. After I've gone a few yards, I figure out what the issue is.

My wolf wants to run, but she also whimpers at the thought of leaving her mate behind. I should've expected that. So, promising her that we won't go *that* far, I get her to pick up the pace. We're just taking a quick run down the mountain and back. That's all.

At least, that was the plan...

Just once I'd like to be free to run on my own. For the first twenty-five years of my life, I pretended I was an omega wolf. In my old pack, omegas were treasured, and it was a miracle if I got to go anywhere without a freaking chaperone. Sure, my mom and dad knew the truth, but they agreed that that was even *more* of a reason to keep an eye on me. A female alpha is priceless, and my parents would do anything to keep me safe. In Lakeview, I couldn't be any more protected.

Same thing happened when I first arrived in Accalia the June before last. I was still Omega Gem, but I was also Ryker's intended mate. I had eyes on me all the time. You'd think it wouldn't be so bad now that my new pack knows the truth about me being an alpha.

Not even close. Especially since a forever mate wasn't the only thing I got when I came back to the mountains to perform the Luna Ceremony two weeks ago.

They're getting better at tailing me. I'll give them that. Usually, I can sense them almost as soon as I go from skin to fur. I must've been distracted or something, though, because I'm about a third of the way down the mountain when I finally realize that they're behind me.

Because of course they are. And if I don't confront them now, they'll follow me the whole rest of my run.

Sue me if that tends to put the edge back in my aggression. I'm twenty-six. I think I'm getting a little too old for a bunch of babysitters.

They call themselves my personal guard. Yeah. Right. They're babysitters, and I'm so not in the mood for them right now.

Just like I expected, when I wheel around on my

pursuers, I'm in time to see three wolves quickly closing the gap between me and them. *Three...* I take a deep breath, tasting the scents on the air, cataloging them instinctively. It's chilly, carrying the promise of a storm mingling with the musk coming from one, two, three, *four* distinctive male wolves.

Of course. It's the oldest wolf trick in the book. While these three idiots are trying to catch up to me, the fourth one is going around, ready to herd me back up the mountain.

Another sniff. Even if I didn't recognize the wolves by their size and their coats—a brindled wolf, a lean grey wolf, and a husky black wolf—I would've known from their scents alone that Duke drew the short end of the stick.

Of the four, Duke's the biggest both in his fur and his skin. I swivel my head, my ears twitching as I pinpoint where those massive paws of his are hitting the ground. I don't see him, not yet, but quiet Duke ain't. He's just behind me.

Good.

Digging my paws into the earth, I arch my back, snarling as I warn Jace, Dorian, and Bobby against continuing to chase after me.

Over the last two weeks, they've learned when I'm grateful for the distraction and when I'm seconds away from picking a throat and going for it. It's a snarl, but any shifter hearing it would be able to translate the wolfish command pretty easily.

Don't you fucking follow me.

Bobby and Dorian immediately fall back. Jace, the brindled wolf, takes a few pointed steps in my direction. I brace my front legs, baring my fangs. Another step and I snap. Throwing back my head, I howl.

The two younger wolves spin and run.

Though his legs lock for a few seconds, Jace lowers his muzzle to the dirt, visibly submitting before he slowly turns, then follows after the others. A deep breath assures me that Duke has heard the howl and, smartly, decided to go back the way he came without ever letting me see him.

I'm finally alone again, just me and my wolf.

It won't last long. Maybe for some of my other packmates, the howl would be enough to have them turning tail and heading all the way back to their cabins. With these four? The power in my howl is only second to their strange obsession to protect me. That seems to trump everything else, including me snapping my fangs at them.

I go another mile, pushing my wolf to her limits just to prove I can, but before I start on another one, I sense them for the second time. They're careful to keep some distance. They don't want to get too close in case I take it as a challenge.

Part of me wants to. The angry, reckless, *human*

side of me wants to tear them a new one—but I don't. After all, I'm the idiot who agreed that the four wolves could act as my personal guard. Can I really blame them for doing what they swore they would?

That's it. I give up. I have this urge to keep on running, but it loses some of its allure when I have four wolves tracking my every footfall. At this point, I might as well shift back, get dressed again, and return to the Alpha's cabin.

Our cabin.

Though we spent the first couple of days after our mating together in Ryker's personal cabin, after Trish was taken, he insisted that we make the Alpha's cabin our home base. We probably would have even if it wasn't for Walker; technically, the cabin is designed for the Alpha and his mate so once our honeymoon was over, it was inevitable we'd end up staying there together. It gives us more privacy than Ryker's, and its position is one that is essential to the safety of the pack. As Alpha, Ryker is the first line of defense. Though he's never come out and said it, I know he believes that he could've stopped Barrow from leaving Accalia with Trish if we'd been here instead of on the other side of the mountain.

This time of night, odds are fifty-fifty that Ryker will still be hard at work in the den. An office attached to the back of the oversized cabin, a shifter's den is an assigned room in the Alpha's cabin that is open to all packmates. When he's there, anyone that belongs to the Mountainside Pack can meet with him. Once he crosses into the next room, the Alpha's time is his own.

Mine, too, now. And as frustrated as I am that my run was cut short, my heart skips the tiniest of beats when I throw open the front door of the cabin and find him leaning forward on the couch, looking down at something spread out on the coffee table in front of him.

It's a map of the tri-state area. A clipboard is next to it, a marker and a pen tossed on top of the page. I know what the marker's about. Most of the map is covered with big X's as Ryker continues to send pairs of wolves out of Accalia, searching for some hint of the Wicked Wolf.

Even though the Western Pack is based in California, he's concerned that Walker has some kind of base of operations on the East Coast near where we live. It makes sense to me. Considering I saw my sperm donor in the flesh in Muncie a little more than two weeks ago, he very well could still be lurking nearby.

There hasn't been any sign of him yet. Ryker's nothing but determined, though. I mean, he searched for me for a year and never gave up. If Walker is within reach, my mate will find him.

The map means he's plotting the next patrol. It's necessary work, but I'm sure he knows I'm here. His wolf would have alerted him to my presence long before I walked up the walkway. If he's keeping his head down like that instead of greeting me with a kiss and a squeeze like he usually does since we've been mated, it's a good guess that he's hiding something from me.

Like, oh, a tiny smile?

Looking back on it, my howl should've been more than enough to give me a mile's head start. But if my guard was doing what their Alpha told them to? Not even my power over them is enough to shake the stranglehold Ryker has over his loyal pack council.

Dick. Luna, I love him, but he can be such a dick.

I slam the door behind me before snapping, "Really, Ryker. Really?"

He finally glances up from the map splayed out on the coffee table. His eyebrows lift, disappearing into the shaggy strands of his sandy brown hair, but there's no denying the hint of humor dancing in his golden shifter's eyes.

"Gemma. Sweetheart. Enjoy your run?"

I'm not even a little surprised that he knows where I've been and what I was doing. As the Alpha, he seems to instinctively know what each of his packmates is doing at any given moment. Add our mating bond to the mix, and I can't scratch my ass without him knowing it was itchy.

The moon affects him, too. It's part of who we are —*what* we are—but he's much better at concealing it than I am lately. Probably because he's always been free to be the alpha wolf he was born as while I've only allowed my wolf to have full rein in the last year or so. Or maybe it's because, compared to suffering from moon fever, the moon's pull on my mate is more of an insistent tug than a fucking yank.

I still feel kind of bad about that. Only kind of, though, because how was I supposed to know that Ryker would suffer the next twelve moons after I left him? He was the one who rejected me in front of his entire pack council. Sure, he had his reasons, and I've forgiven him, but he couldn't have expected me to stick around after that.

Especially since *my* reaction to his rejection left him with five silvery white scars circling his heart.

I jab a finger at him. "You had them chasing me again."

Ryker leans against the couch, stretching his arms along its back. He's reeled in the smile, giving me a deceivingly innocent expression that is such a firm contrast to his hard jaw and sculpted features.

Sometimes, when I look at Ryker, he's so ruggedly handsome that I can't believe that he's really mine. Especially when he's relaxed, when it's just the two of us, when he can let down his guard and show his teasing side... like right now.

His dark gold eyes lighten slightly as he says, "They

take your safety very seriously. I hope you don't expect me to blame them."

"You're the Alpha," I shoot back. "I expect you to stop them."

He drops one hand to a rock-hard thigh, slapping it invitingly. "You're my mate. So can you."

Ugh. I hate it when he's right.

I know I could. Just like how my howl paralyzed them long enough for me to take control, if I give them the express command, they'll obey me.

Which is exactly why I won't.

That's not what Ryker means, though. Regardless of rank, now that we're bonded, my word should be enough to get any other packmate to listen.

Except him, of course.

As his mate, I'm Ryker's equal; even if I wasn't a born alpha myself, I still would be. As soon as we performed the Luna Ceremony, then finalized our bond, he couldn't use his rank against me. Only a garbage mate would assert his dominance, and for all his faults, Ryker is exactly the right male for me. But while he's an alpha wolf, he's also *the* Alpha—and in a shifter pack, the little 'a' to big 'A' is a pretty huge distinction. Rather than be just one of the more dominant protectors, my mate is the most powerful wolf in Accalia. When he says "jump", the rest of the Mountainside Pack—the betas and the deltas and the omegas—all say "how high".

He used to expect me to do the same. Of course, that was when I was pretending to be an omega wolf, just like my mom. For as long as I could remember, I had acted the part of the omega princess. My dad is the Alpha of the Lakeview Pack, my mom his chosen mate, and ever since Paul Booker adopted me when I was a little more than one, I've been coddled and protected. When I came to live in Accalia more than a year ago, Ryker's intended mate, he treated me the same way.

Only, turns out that we both had a secret. Mine was that I'm not an omega. I'm only the second female alpha that our people know about, with the first being our revered goddess, the Luna.

And Ryker? His was that he's always known the truth about me—just like he's known since we were teens that we were fated to be together.

There's no point in arguing with him. And, honestly, I don't really want to. Maybe when I first walked in, I was kind of thinking about it—when both our wolves are riled up, the mating can be *wild*—but this is the first time in more than a week that Ryker's been in such a good mood.

So, rather than butt heads with my mate, I roll my eyes, stomp around the coffee table, and plop myself on his lap.

Ryker grabs me by the waist, yanking me closer. His hand is a brand on my hip, my wolf rumbling in contentment as I settle my chin against his shoulder.

"I didn't go far," I murmur. Ryker's ear twitches as my breath tickles his skin. I nuzzle closer. "I just had to run or I was getting ready to gut someone."

"As someone who's been on the receiving end of your claws, I'd much rather you take your aggression out with a good run. Still, it's dangerous, Gemma. You know that." He gives my hip a squeeze. "And I know it chafes you and your wolf, but if Walker was willing to take Trish, what do you think he'll do to get you?"

He has a point. Once again, Ryker is right.

Ugh.

Did I mention how much I hate that?

CHAPTER 2

Two weeks ago, back when I was young and stupid, I had hoped we could start our mating without any arguments.

After all, our mating dance had been full of them—probably because we're two alphas and neither of us is ever going to willingly admit defeat. He wanted me to say 'yes' to forever, I wanted him to say 'I love you' and mean it, and it's still a shock to me that we both ended up getting what we wanted.

Then Jack Walker had to come along and mess things up again for me.

For all of my twenty-six years, he's been a pain in my ass. When he had Barrow leave that note behind on his behalf, my first instinct was to rise to his challenge and confront him. It didn't matter that it was literally meant for Ryker, the same way Shane's ruby was meant for me. We both know that I'm Walker's true target.

My mate adamantly refused to let me go. Once I was thinking clearly, I knew he was right.

Still, it's no wonder I can't rein in my wolf.

I have to admit that Ryker's not *quite* pushing me, choosing instead to convince me in other ways that he knows what he's doing. If there's one thing he's learned, it's that if he pushes me, there's no knowing if I'll push back—or if he'll push me away. So what if we're fully bonded now? Old habits die hard. He puts his paw down when it comes to going after Wicked Wolf Walker without a plan—hence the map and the marker—but he'll let little things slide. Like my run.

Maybe it's my turn to try to do the same thing.

"Let's compromise," I tell him. "I'll do whatever I can to help you out when it comes to pack duties, and then you can come with me on my runs at night. We can make it a date. After dinner or something like that." A burst of inspiration hits me. "We can use it as an excuse to reinforce the territory borders. Then you won't have to worry about me, and I can get you out of the den before the Luna rises."

I know Ryker goes out every night with some of the council even after assigning wolves to search for Walker and patrol our borders. If I go with him, I can feel like I'm doing something while Ryker will be able to calm his overprotective instincts as he runs right next to me.

"Just me and you?" He makes a rumble of pleasure in the back of the throat. "Like an Alpha couple?"

I nip his earlobe. "That's what we are, isn't it?"

Turning his head, Ryker angles his chin, stealing a quick kiss that, as soon as he breaks it, has my tempered aggression quickly turning to lust.

I'm just about to shift so that I can straddle him when, all of a sudden, Ryker leans forward, gripping the clipboard.

Huh?

His eyes are sparkling. Right then, I figure I'm in trouble.

"All right, my mate. You want to know what will help me get out of the den earlier?"

My stomach sinks. I think I know where he's going with this, and I should've known better. How could I forget that Ryker is the most calculating male I've ever met?

Knowing I'll probably regret it, I nod. "Yeah. Sure."

He presses the clipboard into my hand. Reluctantly, I take it.

Glancing down, I see that it's a list of about twenty different packmates.

Yup. Totally regretting this.

"Okay. What's this?"

"An Alpha has to make himself available to the pack."

I'm not getting his point or what it has to do with this list of packmates. I mean, that's what a den is for, right? It's a place in the Alpha's cabin that's open to any and all packmates. There's an open invitation for the Mountainside Pack to sit down and meet with Ryker so long as he's in the den. No need for a list.

"I know that. Still doesn't answer my question."

"Alpha couple, right?" He nods at the clipboard. "Those are the ones that have requested to sit down with you, Gemma."

Wait—*what*?

"Me? Why me?"

Is it me or is Ryker biting back another grin? "Good question. Only way to find out is to meet with them. Unless you're avoiding them, that is."

He doesn't come out and accuse me of being a coward, but he doesn't have to. Both of us know that I have mixed feelings about the Mountainside Pack's den. To put it simply, the den is the place that I burst into the night I convinced me and my wolf that Ryker rejected us. I've gotten past that—and I really mean that—but ever since we became bonded mates, the den presented a new issue.

I'm part of the Alpha couple now. If I'm in the den, any packmate can meet with *me*.

And I... I'm not so sure I'm ready for that yet.

I've cost Accalia so much. One packmate dead, one a betrayer, one stolen away from pack territory. There's no denying that it's my fault, no matter how Ryker attempts to convince me otherwise.

Even now he's teasing me, trying to keep me from falling back into the same anger and aggression that's been plaguing me ever since we heard the news about Trish Danvers.

Because I know what he's doing, I resist the urge to break the clipboard over his head. Showing a great deal of restraint only because I love this idiot, I settle on sticking my tongue out at him—predictably earning a comment from my mate about what I could do with my tongue if I was willing—before I glance down at the list again.

At the top of it, I see a very familiar name.

Audrey Carter.

I swallow a sigh.

Yup. I played right into his claws, didn't I?

I SPEND THE NEXT FEW MINUTES TRYING TO THINK OF A million different ways to get out of this but it's obvious that none of them are going to work. Nothing short of using my alpha nature against them will keep the other shifters away from me, and even if I really don't want to do this, I tell Ryker that I'm ready to tackle the list.

My mom is an Alpha's mate. Growing up, I had a front row seat to what it was like to be part of the Alpha couple. If you asked anyone in Lakeview, they'd tell you that my dad is the Alpha so he's the wolf in charge, but my omega mother has the most power in the pack because she holds the Alpha's heart in her hands.

I've always envied their mating. It's not a fated one, but I always thought that made it more special. My dad chose my mom because he looked at her and knew she was the one; though, if you hear him tell it, he figured she was the she-wolf for him when she sank her fangs into his hind leg to protect her pup. Either way, it works. Twenty-five years later and they're as much in love today as they were the day they asked the Luna to bless their mating.

Watching them, I always knew what would be expected of an Alpha's mate, almost taking notes on what my future was going to be like. After all, ever since I was fifteen, I've always known that I was meant to be Ryker's—I just thought I might have a little more time.

Knowing that Ryker was not only an alpha wolf, but the next in line to be Alpha of the Mountainside Pack, I expected I would have to wait. Pack tradition says that the future Alpha doesn't get to bond with a mate until they take over a pack or build their own, and Henry Wolfson was still the leader of Accalia.

Turns out, it only took eleven years. Ten until the Luna confirmed what both Ryker and I sensed so long ago, and another year while I hid out in Muncie, nursing my wounded pride after Ryker "rejected" me in front of his pack council. Not as long as it might have been, since his father very easily could have been Alpha for years longer if he hadn't died in a freak car accident orchestrated by Shane Loup, but long enough for an impatient female who was head over heels for her male.

All I wanted was Ryker. All I've ever wanted was to be with him. He could've been a delta wolf instead of an alpha and I wouldn't have given a shit. When I looked in his dark gold gaze, my wolf recognized her mate in his.

I saw forever.

But he *is* an Alpha. Nothing changes that. Even when I first came to live in Accalia—when I was still playing the part of Omega Gem, the coddled princess from the Lakeview Pack—I knew that I was coming to mate the Alpha, to eventually be a part of the Alpha couple.

I guess I kind of just disregarded that when it seemed as if the Mountainside Pack didn't want me here. Back then, Trish made it clear that I wasn't good enough for *her* Alpha, and she wasn't the only one.

Shane did everything he could to land that message home, too.

Then I rejected Ryker because I felt like he rejected me and… yeah. I never thought we'd be mates.

For one of the only times in my life, I was pretty stoked to be wrong.

Reality set in a few days after the last full moon started to wane. So what if I'm an alpha in my own right? As Ryker's bonded mate, I have an important role in the pack that, honestly, I should've remembered before now.

Whoops.

Looks like I'm getting a crash course the next morning, shortly after breakfast. Ryker got into contact with Grant, letting the council member know that I'm free to talk to his mate starting at nine a.m.

At nine on the dot, there's a tentative knock.

"Come on in."

The door swings inward, followed by a pretty female shifter. She's at least a good decade older than me, though a non-shifter would never be able to tell thanks to our supernaturally slow aging. She has chin-length blonde hair, soft brown eyes, and a gentle nature about her that definitely fooled me once before.

"Audrey. Hi. Pull up a chair. Join me."

She hesitates.

It doesn't take a genius to figure out what it is that

has her stumped as she slowly approaches the desk I'm sitting behind.

"Gem," I remind her. "It's okay. Call me Gem."

A flash of relief crosses her face as she nods. "Thank you." A tiny pause. "Gem."

I'd tell her that there's no need to thank me but that would probably cause another moment where she looks at me like a deer caught in headlights.

I get it. I do. Ryker doesn't rule his pack ruthlessly without regard for the lower ranks, but a lot of the pack have no clue what to make of me. Unlike some other leaders, he doesn't insist that his packmates refer to him as 'Alpha', though many do as a sign of respect.

What about me?

As his mate, regardless of my rank before I bonded with him, pack tradition says that I could also be addressed as 'Alpha' just because we're a bonded pair now. Yeah... that's a hard no from me. It's bad enough that I've had to deal with my life-long secret getting out. No matter why they call me 'Alpha', it rubs my fur the wrong way to hear it.

I haven't been able to shake my personal guard of the habit just yet, but if I can get my preference across to Audrey, it's a start. Her mate, Grant, is a member of the pack council, and she's well-liked in Accalia.

She's also the sister of Shane Loup, which is the big, honking, elephant hanging out in the den with us.

This is the first time I've met with her since my

Luna Ceremony. If I close my eyes, I can see her collapsing in Grant's arms, sobbing. Loyal to a fault, she didn't show any emotion while her brother and her Alpha fought to the death, but once Ryker gave her permission to grieve, she did, and I still haven't been able to forget that.

Doesn't mean I've forgotten what happened during the time I met her before that, either. And though I made a point to forgive her, the catty side of me—firmly the human side—has me waiting for her to take a seat before I say innocently, "Thirsty? I've got refreshments. I know you drink Coke. Want one?"

She winces, but she keeps her back straight as she nods. "I'd love one. Thank you."

Ryker has a small fridge behind his desk. No alcohol, since the den is a family-friendly space, but I know he keeps bottles of water and cans of soda in there. I grab a Coke for Audrey, a water for me, then nudge the fridge closed with the tip of my shoe.

I slide her can across the desk to where she's sitting. "Here you go."

"Thanks," she says again. With a cracking sound, she opens the can and takes a sip.

My wolf approves. So does my human half.

That dig settled, I smile genuinely at her, hopefully putting her at ease. "Ryker said you wanted to see me."

She nods, blonde hair whispering into her face.

"Cool. But, just so you know, you don't have to

make an appointment to see me or anything. Ryker's Alpha. I'm just Gem. I can give you my number if you need it. I'm not so great at answering it, and I'm sure you know reception is shit on the mountain, but I owe you one."

Audrey's eyes widen. I guess she wasn't expecting that. "You do?"

Oh, yeah. "For the Luna Ceremony. If it wasn't for you and…"

I pause right there. Every packmate in Accalia knows what happened to Trish and they trust Ryker to handle the situation. He's an honest and open Alpha, and he refused to let his pack think that he banished her again so close on the heels of our mating. She might've earned getting kicked out the first time, but Trish apologized—and she meant it. She really wanted to start over in Mountainside.

And then my sperm donor decided she was a bargaining chip.

I bite back my scowl. Audrey doesn't deserve it, and from the way she lets out an involuntary yip, I know that her wolf is reacting to my wolf's dominance.

I gotta cool it.

With a harder jerk than I mean to use, I rip the cap off of my water. I take a couple of gulps, and when I swallow, I feel a little more settled.

"Anyway, you get my eternal gratitude for stepping in at the last minute and organizing my Luna Ceremony for me. Even before the Alpha challenge, it was an event to remember and— *oof*."

Jeez. Could I open my mouth wider and stick my shoe in any further?

Way to go, Gem. Gloss over Trish and jump right to the ceremony that was interrupted when Ryker was forced to rip her brother to shreds.

She drops her eyes to the floor. "That's part of the reason I asked to meet with you. I'm the only family my brother had left. It's on me to apologize for him. I—"

I hold up my hand, cutting her off. My claws unsheathe as I do.

Audrey glances up in time to notice.

She gulps.

I flex my fingers, forcing my claws to retract. Anger has a way of letting my wolf manifest while I'm still in my human form, but I don't want Audrey thinking that I'm angry at *her*.

Nope. There's only one wolf responsible for what Shane did and that's him.

When Audrey offered to help plan my mating and host the afterparty for the pack, that was her way of making amends for poisoning me with mercury. Even then I knew she was only doing what she thought was best for the pack so it was easy to let it go. But Shane... he only ever wanted what was best for Shane.

"Don't apologize."

"But—"

"Nope."

"Alpha—"

"Gem," I say firmly. "And I'm not accepting any apology about this from you because you have nothing to apologize for. You're a devoted packmate and you're loyal to my mate. Plus you helped set up my Luna Ceremony. I told you. I owe you, Audrey."

The worry on her face melts away as another expression replaces it. Her mouth hangs slightly open, almost in awe. "Do you really mean that?"

Why does she look so surprised?

"Of course I do."

A small, shaky smile spreads across her pretty face. "Ryker's not the only one who's lucky to have you. The rest of us... the pack... we couldn't have asked for a better mate for our Alpha."

It's my turn to be a bit taken aback. Because that? That was the last thing I expected to hear from anyone that wasn't Ryker or one of my guards.

"Thanks. I, uh, I'm glad I came back, too."

And isn't that the understatement of the year?

Later on, after I spend another half an hour chatting with Audrey about everything and anything, she leaves the den a lot more confident than she was when she first arrived. She only thanked me two more times, and I nipped one final apology in the bud before she jotted down my number. Then, before she leaves the den, she promised she'd invite me and Ryker to a meal with her and her mate. Considering how shifters say more with food than they do with words, it's obviously her way of welcoming me to the pack.

When I tell her I'm looking forward to it, I mean that.

You know what? This Alpha couple thing might not be so hard after all.

It takes two days to get through every name on that list.

On the third day, I join Ryker, sitting with my heels propped up on the edge of a desk he added to the den just for me, almost antsy since I don't have anything to do. Now that I've met with any packmate who wanted to congratulate me on my mating and welcome me to the pack—because, seriously, that was what most of my visitors wanted to tell me which, okay, is better than an apology—I'm back to feeling like my paws are tied.

As much as I tried putting off the meets, the last two days were a pretty good distraction. I couldn't really obsess over what my bio-dad was planning to pull next—at least, not *entirely*—while I was busy with my new mate-ly duty.

Every night, when I went home with Ryker, he told

me about any reports he received. To work off his own aggression, he ran patrols around our entire territory, even pushing it to River Run, the pack nearest to us. I haven't joined him yet, but I plan on it as soon as I can, especially now that the full moon is creeping closer.

It might be easier if there was some clue behind what the Wicked Wolf or any of his goons are up to, but there isn't. Ryker's map is completely X'ed out. Though I don't want to ask, since there's nothing anyone will let me *do* about it, having Bobby Danvers as one of my guards makes Trish updates unavoidable. Ten days after she disappeared, it's as if she vanished off the face of the earth.

Between my mate and me, we both realize what that means. With Walker and the Western Pack involved, the only way she could disappear so completely was if Barrow dragged her all the way across the country to Walker's headquarters: the Wolf District, a secluded yet militant shifter community hidden in California where Jack Walker rules over his pack with a silver fist.

He's gotta be back there. I know it. If Ryker wasn't so damn stubborn when it came to protecting me, he'd admit that he knows it, too. Just like how we both know that the note Barrow left behind, the note signed with twelve crisscrossing lines creating three bold W's, is as close to a challenge from one Alpha to the next without Walker approaching Ryker and demanding to fight.

It's an Alpha challenge which means that only Ryker can answer it. For now, he's refusing to acknowledge what Walker did outside of the pack.

And I get it. I do. After Shane's betrayal, the Mountainside Pack was left in a weaker position, and if there's one thing that a shifter will never admit to, it's weakness. Shane was Ryker's Beta, his second-in-command. When he joined the Western Pack instead, Ryker was forced to reinstate the Beta who served when Ryker's dad was Alpha. But Warren was already retired, and he made it clear he was filling the spot in name only until Ryker recruited a new Beta.

It's harder than it sounds, though. In Accalia, there aren't any fully-grown born betas. He'll need to lure on from another pack, but Ryker won't split his focus to do that while Walker is a much bigger problem for us.

Still, without a strong Beta, Ryker's almost as big a target as I am. Bigger, really. If anything happens to me, Ryker will lose it. But if anything happens to Ryker... well, that's the end of the Mountainside Pack as we know it.

Plus, I would burn down the world to get to the bastard who went after my mate.

So, yeah. I understand *why* we have to make a show of staying on our territory like nothing's wrong. Even Kendall, the River Run Alpha, has no clue why Ryker is suddenly so obsessed with knowing what the Wicked Wolf of the West is up to. Ryker's purposely closed ranks, trying to make sure that my bio-dad can't get to another packmate.

Me? I just can't get past the fact that he already *did*.

CHAPTER 3

That evening, we share dinner together in the kitchen before hanging out in the den for another hour or so. Then, around seven, I'm kicked out of it.

That's a snarky way of saying that Ryker scheduled a meeting for his inner council. When I accuse him of giving me the boot, I'm totally teasing. Trust me. I don't mind that he's busy, and I'm quick to refuse when he says I'm more than welcome to stick around.

No, thanks. Ryker's council business is strictly Alpha territory. If I wanted to know what the meet's about, I'm sure I could have asked, but—like my memories of the den—I'm still a bit bitter when it comes to the council. There are seven members aside from Ryker, and my mate personally vetted all of them after what happened with Shane. They're trustworthy and loyal. I just think most of them are dicks.

I mean, you gotta be a dick to pull a hood over a poisoned shifter's head, carry her like she's a sack of potatoes, then throw her to an alpha suffering from the moon fever, right?

Dicks, all seven of them—

Hey. Wait a second.

My four guards make up more than half of the seven members. And if Ryker called an emergency meeting in the den for the whole council...

From what he told me, he expects the meeting to go for a couple of hours at least. What are the odds that he excused all four of my guards from such a sudden council meeting so that they could be my babysitters again?

Not great. Not great at all.

Ha!

When I leave him in the den, I know Ryker is expecting me to head toward our side of the cabin—and I do. I make a quick pitstop inside to grab my keys before I pop back outside and start jogging toward where I keep my baby.

Taking a run along the outskirts of Mountainside territory was pushing it for my mate. If I told him that what I really wanted to do was stop by and visit my friends in Muncie, he'd have a freaking conniption.

So I'm just not going to tell him. And if I can make it back before the meeting is done, he'll never have to know.

Hey. Sounds like a plan to me.

I'M BARELY TO THE PATH THAT LEADS DOWN THE mountain when I sense a very familiar wolf on my tail.

I want to beat my head against my headrest.

I'm caught. And while my Jeep is fast, I've learned not to underestimate a determined shifter. If he's figured out I'm trying to leave, he's going to chase after me no matter what it takes.

Freaking wonderful.

The way I see it, I've got two choices: I can floor it and hope that I manage to outrace a wolf, leaving Jace to slink back to Accalia with his tail between his legs, or I can lead him into Muncie and risk another reenactment of the Claws and Fangs war.

Roman, the leader of the vampire-run Cadre, reluctantly accepts that I've made the Fang City my home. And, sure, my welcome might be strained considering how I left the state of my relationship with Aleks, but I live there. I have a life there.

Jace doesn't.

And if he goes without me...

Huffing out a breath, I slam on my brakes. I don't kill my lights, leaving myself a sitting target in the middle of the dirt trail instead.

I cross my arms in front of my chest, tapping my nails against my bicep. I give him to the count of five.

One.

Two.

Three.

Four—

A twig snaps. The air shifts, slamming me with the scent I've gotten to know so well. The brindled wolf is snuffling softly as Jace moves out of the shadows of the trees, hanging his head as he pads toward the side of my Jeep.

I'm caught, but so is the head of my guard.

Two and a half weeks. It's only been two and a half weeks since the last full moon and, somehow, this has become my life. As much as I'd hoped I could do what I wanted to all by myself, I should've known better.

And maybe I did. Rolling my eyes, I gesture at him to come closer before turning to reach behind me. There's a small bag stowed beneath my back seat. I snag it, pulling out the black sweats I keep tucked inside. This might actually be the first time that I've tried to drive out of Muncie since I've been mated, but I grew up with a pair of cousins who were convinced I was made of glass. An emergency pair of sweatpants is a necessity.

Us shifters are so used to nudity that I hardly bat an eye when Jace shifts from fur to skin. I just toss the pants at him.

"Put those on and get in."

He knows better than to argue with me when I get that tone in my voice. Shimmying into the black sweatpants, he hops into the passenger seat, gripping the bar with his human hand. "So, where are we going?"

Yeah. It's a 'we', now, isn't it?

"Just a quick drive down into Muncie. I've got to take care of something."

His shoulder-length pale hair is windblown from his sprint, even though he'd been in his fur as he chased after me. With his lips pursed, he shoves the silky strands out of his face as his eyes flash over to me. "Does the Alpha know that?"

"Nope," I say cheerily. "You still want to come with? You can always hop back out and pretend you didn't see me."

Jace swallows. "And let you go down there alone? That's worse than Ryker finding out that I couldn't stop you. At least he'd understand I had no choice about that. But staying behind while you drove out of pack territory? He'd have my head."

Good point.

"Then hang tight, Jace. We'll be back before he even knows we're gone."

He slants a look at me. "You don't honestly believe that, do you?"

With a wide grin, I throw the car into drive. "Not even a little."

I park my Jeep about three blocks away from the bar if only because it's the nearest spot I can find to Charlie's. The streets are packed, and when me and Jace take the quick walk downtown, I discover that Charlie's is, too.

This was a pitstop that I hadn't exactly planned on making. Since I didn't want to push my luck, I had intended on heading straight to see Aleks—and then I didn't. I guess I just needed a little more time before I faced my former roommate again because I came up with the brilliant idea to stop by Charlie's and see how my co-workers have been getting on without me.

Though service is spotty, I've been in contact with Hailey, Carmen, and Tony since I left. Charlie, too. I had to let my boss know that the week I scheduled off had been unexpectedly extended. Luckily, he was okay with it. My co-workers probably weren't too happy to have to pick up my shifts, but they were too kind to say anything about it. Even Hailey told me to enjoy spending time with my hunky shifter mate.

Still, it wouldn't hurt to say hi. And I had that thought all the way until I stood in front of the doorway that leads into Charlie's and, through the glass door, I watched the scene unfold.

I see Tony, bussing tables. Hailey's at one end of the bar, leaning over as she talks to a customer. Even from this distance, I can see the vamp marks she wears proudly on her throat as she angles her head just so. She's smiling, elbows on the countertop, her low-cut Charlie's tee pulled lower to show off her boobs.

I catch a sliver of the customer's profile. The alabaster perfection of his skin, plus the crimson shot in front of him, screams *vampire*. On a closer look, I recognize him as Dominic Le Croix, one of the higher-ranking vamps in the Cadre.

Huh. Looks like he took Hailey up on her invitation for a free drink down at Charlie's. And if he's responsible for the bites on her throat—which, considering that vamps are just as territorial as shifters, he's gotta be if he's still hanging around her—then Hailey's definitely working toward her goal of getting her own fang.

Good job, girl. If it'll make her happy, she deserves it.

My gaze skitters away from Hailey. Besides her being human and unaware of me lingering just outside, it feels a little intrusive to watch her when she's making those eyes at Dominic. Instead, I clock some of my regulars at the bar—Jimmy Fiorello is there, so is the perv vamp, Vincent, even Jane—before I notice something else.

No wonder Hailey can flirt with a Cadre vampire while Charlie's is hopping. Behind the bar, there are two other bartenders that I've never seen before. One's a brunet male, the other a blonde chick, and they're both wearing a black Charlie's tee.

I don't know how to feel about that: proud that it took two bartenders to replace me, or kind of stunned that Charlie actually *did* replace me.

I mean, I probably should've been expecting that. Still's a bit of a shock, though.

"Hey. You going inside?"

Only my wolf's amazingly perceptive senses and my stubborn pride keeps me from jumping when Jace sneaks up behind me. To be honest, I kind of forgot that he was with me until he sidled closer, peeking around me to see what I'm staring at.

I don't move away from him; I'm the alpha, and he's the one intruding on my space. Shooting Jace a quick look, he clears his throat and takes a few steps back.

Once he has, I shake my head. "Nah. This is supposed to be a quick trip. If I see some of my regulars, I'll end up in there way longer than I should."

That's true. Can you imagine if Vin or Jimmy want to chat? I can see it now. They'll tell me to pull up a stool and ask me all about where I've been. Vinnie for sure will have something to say about me mating Mountainside's Alpha, and Jane... oh, Jane will probably have a lecture for me. She really thought I should end up with Aleks.

Luna, I miss them. My regulars. My co-workers. My

friends... I miss everything about Charlie's, but it's different now. Everything's changed.

Including me.

I can't bring myself to go in there. Not yet. Not while I don't know when I'm coming back—or even if I am.

Technically, I didn't quit. Just like, *technically*, I haven't moved out of Muncie. When he was trying to convince me to mate him, Ryker bought a place on the edge of Muncie's downtown area; when I finally gave in, he gave me the deed as a mating gift. It's mine, so I have a home here. And if it wasn't for my bio-dad pulling his stunt, I probably would have been moved in by now.

All that's on hold. Ryker came down to Muncie himself with a couple of my guards shortly after Trish was taken, packing up everything I had left behind so that he could bring it to the Alpha's cabin. Since Aleks made good on his threat to have all of my stuff from the apartment packed up and moved to the townhouse, it was as easy as Duke, Dorian, and Ryker loading it into a pack truck and driving it back to Accalia.

When I headed to the mountains to get mated, I only brought enough clothes with me to last the week I planned to take off. Once it became obvious that I would be sticking around a little longer, Ryker made sure I had everything else so that I was comfortable living with him.

And if it's super obvious that he wants to keep me there for good, I pretend I don't notice. I knew what I was getting into when I decided to bond with an alpha wolf with a tendency to be overbearing and possessive. Until the threat hanging over my head is gone, I get that I'm going to have to stay on pack land.

This isn't me leaving. If I was going to leave, I would've done anything to stop Jace from coming with me, instead of letting him tag along. No. This is me realizing that I still have people I care about in the Fang City who probably need a head's up.

I don't have to worry about telling any of my human friends, my vamp boss, or my regulars at the bar. As soon as I get the message to the Cadre, word will spread. Especially if things are as serious between Dominic and Hailey as they seem, they'll be protected from another breach courtesy of the Wicked Wolf.

Roman Zakharov certainly needs to be told. I'm kind of surprised that Ryker hasn't already met with the vamp leader, but knowing how my mate feels about vampires—calling them bloodsuckers, for example—I guess it was the last thing on his mind.

Then again, he only played nice with Roman because it was the only way to earn a ticket into Muncie and I refused to leave the Fang City. Now that we're mated, maybe it doesn't matter.

To him, I correct. To him, it doesn't matter. His focus is on his pack—as it should be.

But me?

I still have some unfinished business here.

"Come on," I tell Jace. "We've got one more stop to make before we head back."

THE BACK DOOR TO ALEKS'S APARTMENT MIGHT'VE BEEN open like it always used to be, but it doesn't take long for me to realize that no one's been home for a while.

I take a deep breath. Over Jace's woodsy scent, I pick up traces of my own, Aleks's, and a whole lot of dust. If I was pressed to answer, I would say that Aleks hasn't been back to the apartment since, oh, maybe two weeks ago?

Gee. What a surprise. I've already learned that, when he's hurt, he bolts. He did it when I refused to take him as my mate over Ryker, and I'm beginning to think he had the same reaction after I told him I was making our mating final.

Just in case, I leave Jace in the living room. He'd insisted on joining me in the apartment when we hit the fire escape, and since I already suspected what I would find, I didn't argue.

I put my foot down when he starts to follow me

toward the hall, though. This is Aleks's territory and Jace can freaking stay put.

Knocking on Aleks's door is pointless; I can already sense his absence. My wolf leads me to my old room, and though I already knew he'd done exactly what he said he would, it's a little bittersweet to see it so empty. It's like he was desperate to erase every hint of me before he took off himself.

The rest of the apartment is unchanged. The tea is where Aleks left it in the kitchen, the row of mugs he kept specifically for me lined up as if he still believes that, one day, I'll return to drink out of them. The bathroom is the same, the same low fragrance body wash propped on the side. Even the living room is untouched.

On the newly repaired coffee table, I see a snapshot of Aleks. His glasses are folded neatly next to a book written in Polish. There's an empty notepad sitting crooked, a pencil tossed absently on top. And, there, sparkling in the lamplight Jace must've turned on, is a golden chain.

My heart sinks.

It's a golden chain with a pure white fang hanging off of it.

My fang—

No. Not mine.

My hand slips to the gold charm hanging off my throat. The enchanted canine that Ryker gave me to replace the loaded one that I'd worn for close to a year... this is my fang.

That one belongs to Aleks.

Looking past the fang and the book, my gaze lands on the empty pad again. Besides it being crooked, I notice that the top sheet is torn in half, the bottom part missing. Hmm. That's not like Aleks at all. He's usually too fastidious. The way his glasses are folded primly, the book centered just so... the pad and the pencil are more out of place than the fang is.

I wonder...

I pick up the pad. Maybe Aleks had to write something down so he grabbed a pad and a pencil, scribbled something, then tore the sheet before dropping the pad and pencil on the coffee table. That *is* an Aleks-type of reaction. He never would reach for his phone to make a note. He's more than two hundred years old. He'll always grab a pencil first.

Squinting, I look at the page underneath in the vague hope that I can make out an impression.

I scoff. What am I thinking? I'm not even close to figuring it out, and this Nancy Drew shit is for the birds.

Throwing the notepad back onto the coffee table, I pull out my phone.

I want an answer to where he is? Let me ask the damn question.

Oof. With a start, I notice that the last time I texted

Aleks is well before my mating. I can't help but cringe at that. It makes it so much worse that I really thought I could just show up here unannounced more than two weeks later and he'd be waiting for when I finally decided to stop by for a chat.

Why would he be? Not only did he stand by his promise to pack up everything I own and relocate it across Muncie, but he made it very clear where we stood when I called him out for reneging on his promise that we could stay friends.

He told me he lied. And, still, I decided to come see him instead of asking Ryker to get in touch with Roman.

Welp. I'm not going to make *that* mistake again.

Without even typing a message, I slip my phone back into my pocket. When I glance up at Jace, I discover he's watching me with a curious expression.

My wolf doesn't like that. Neither do I.

But it's Jace. So, biting back the urge to snarl at him, I make myself shrug. "I'm done here. Come on. Let's go."

CHAPTER 4

"So that's the place, huh?"

We haven't even made it the rest of the way down the fire escape before my shadow decides to comment.

I shoot Jace a look out of the side of my eye. "You say something?"

I've gotta learn how to be scarier. After spending most of my life pretending to be an omega wolf, most of my packmates—in Lakeview and in Mountainside—look at me and only see Shifter Barbie standing in front of them. Wide eyes, pretty face, long blonde hair... even though my old sundresses are a thing of the past, and I'm more likely to be wearing a scowl than a prim smile these days, I know what I look like when I'm in my skin, and scary I ain't.

"Just saying it's a nice place."

"You've been there before."

"Yeah, but not inside."

He's not wrong. The one time that he and Dorian stood guard outside of my apartment building while Ryker was chained up in his basement, they flanked the front and the back of the apartment building —*outside*. Even if I wasn't feeling the effects of moon fever myself, I wouldn't have let them in with Ryker indisposed and Aleks still gone.

He's a supe. Vamp or shifter, we respect territory. The apartment is Aleks's—or it was. If I couldn't bring myself to let Ryker inside, there's no way I'm going to let one of the lower-ranked shifters inside. It would be a slap in the face to my roommate, and Luna knows I've done enough of that.

Literally.

"Well, I'm glad you like it, but I don't think we'll be coming back here anytime soon."

He nods. "Yeah. I noticed that, too. Doesn't look like the bloodsucker's been back for a while, either."

Jace is matching me stride for stride as we step down from the last of the fire escape before heading down the street. He's not as big as Duke—he's more rangy and lean than big and bulky—but he still has a few inches on me. He could probably take the lead easily, but he'd never do that if it meant leaving me behind where I was out of his sight.

It's a weird quirk of me being a female alpha. Jace's wolf has this need to be both submissive to my more dominant wolf as well as protective of me because I'm smaller than he is and his Alpha's mate. If he moves ahead of me, he might miss any danger coming at me while also pissing off my inner wolf. If he falls behind, it's also a risk to my safety. So he stays right next to me as I resist the urge to roll my eyes.

With him next to me, my elbow finds a home in his gut. "Don't call him a bloodsucker. His name is Aleks."

"His name is Aleksander, not that you're worth getting to say his name, you mangy wolf." The accented voice is harsh and low, and it's punctuated by a spitting noise. "Brudny wilku."

I immediately went still the second I heard Aleks's full name mentioned by someone unfamiliar, but the Polish? That has my complete attention.

I don't know what the first word is, but the second? It's wilku. 'Wolf' in Polish.

Aleks used to call me mały wilku. Little wolf. It sounds a lot nicer than whatever the other male said because, even before I turn around, I know that—despite the accent and the language—the speaker definitely isn't my ex-roommate.

Later, I'll admit that I should've been better prepared. It's something about Muncie, I guess. After a year of growing used to being untouchable because I wore Aleks's fang, all it took was for me to come back for a few hours and I forgot all about how I gave it back to him. Returning the fang didn't just signal to Aleks that I was never going to be his mate. It also signaled to every vamp in the city that I was no longer under his protection. Add that to how my new charm doesn't cover up my shifter side anymore and, yeah, I should've realized that I might run into a vampire who wouldn't be pleased to stumble upon two shifters in a Fang City.

He has a menacing presence, and when I slowly turn to face him, his eyes are blood red. Vampires, a race, all have very pale eyes: soft blue, light green, a gentle hazel. It's like death has drained some of their color so that, when they rise again, their eyes mark them as different the same way their fangs do. The only time their irises go vivid and dark is when they're either on the edge of bloodlust or fully in its throes.

When a vamp's eyes go red, run or you're dead.

It's a silly little rhyme all shifters are taught from the time we're pups. Vampires are our ancient enemy, and though I never actually met one until I rode into Muncie, you never forget the warning.

The white-skinned, black-haired vampire has eyes as red as blood, with fangs that jut past his bottom lip. His long, black jacket flares behind him as he hunches forward, his body giving him away. If I give him any reason to, he's going to attack me.

Freaking *wonderful*.

I look him up and down, making it clear that I don't see him as a threat. And I don't. As a game, Aleks taught me how to tell the ages of the vamps I ran into in the Fang City. The older a vamp is, the more powerful it is. This guy is barely as old as I am. If pressed, I know I can take him.

Do I want to do that when I know it'll piss Roman off? Not really. I still plan on coming back to Muncie, one way or another. Having Roman decide to close the borders to all shifters because I can't control my temper will screw me over more than anyone else.

I give the vampire a tight-lipped smile. "A friend of Aleks's, I take it?"

"You could say that."

I highly doubt it. Considering Aleks is a high-ranking member of the Cadre with a great reputation, it's more like he's a sycophant.

"Okay. Since you're his friend, I'll give you the chance to turn around and walk away. I don't know what your problem with me is, but you can take it up with Roman. He gave me permission to be here, and you really don't want to try me. Trust me on that." I gesture to the wolf hovering just behind. "Let's go, Jace."

"But, Alpha—"

Nope.

"We're leaving. Now."

Hoping that I put enough of my alpha wolf into my voice to override his instincts to defend me or something equally as ridiculous, I give my back to the vampire and purposely stride forward.

Oh, the vamp doesn't like that one bit.

It's early autumn, but the night grows cold with the force of his vampiric fury. Jace catches it, too, and he begins to spin, his intent to go after the vampire obvious. Throwing my hand out, I stop him in time, but his wolf isn't too happy about it.

So, of course, the vampire has to keep testing us.

"Don't walk away from me," he orders. Then, after the tiniest of pauses, the vamp sneers in his accent, "Bitch."

As insults go, that's pretty weak. I mean, I *am* a female wolf. Calling me a 'bitch' is pretty on point. Still, ignoring him will only make this worse. The vamp is looking for a fight, but instead of giving him one, I just turn and offer him another tight-lipped smile as I shake my head.

Come on. Take a freaking hint already. You don't want to do this—

His red eyes gleam, like freshly spilled blood.

Oh, yeah. That's not a good sign.

Neither is the way Jace is snarling under his breath next to me.

He hasn't shifted. At least that's one thing in my favor. Another is that he has kept close to me so he had obviously listened when I told him we had to go. So far, Jace is in his skin, but something tells me that won't last if he feels like he has to protect me.

See? This is exactly why I didn't want to bring him with me. If it was just me, I could walk away from any kind of confrontation. My wolf would be annoyed, but the human half of me would realize that rising to a vampire's bait while in Muncie would be nothing but trouble. I've already received a visit from two members of the Cadre after the last time I had a run-in with a vamp. I don't need another one on my record for when I finally return to the Fang City.

With Jace here, the stakes are upped. Even worse, the only shifters who get a pass to walk around without a target are me and Ryker. As a show of respect from one leader to another, Roman had his patrollers look the other way when one of Ryker's pack council—including my new guards—came to watch over me while he was indisposed.

How much do you wanna bet he won't overlook Jace accepting a rogue vamp's taunting challenge?

"Like I said, if you have a problem with me being in Muncie, take it up with Roman."

The vampire's red eyes glitter viciously. "Not everyone follows Zakharov. When his head is on a spike, we'll keep plenty of space next to it for every one of you Mountainside dogs to join him."

I exhale roughly. Could he be any more of a dumb fuck?

The way he stood up for Aleks, I thought he was Cadre. Now I know better. This idiot has got to be part of the vamp rebellion that I learned about a couple of weeks ago. When Shane first found a vamp to give him a fang, then when my bio-dad was able to sneak into Muncie by promising he would back the rebellion going after Roman and the Cadre.

The small sect believes that the Cadre is holding them back. They wanted life in Muncie to go back to what it was like when Marcel Claret was the leader, humans were an unending buffet, and any wolf caught in their city was turned into a rug.

My guard understands the meaning of what the vampire just said a split second before I do. As seconds go, he makes it count. Before I can stop him, he lunges for the vampire.

I was able to keep Jace from attacking when it was just me the vampire was targeting. For this vamp to threaten the rest of the pack? Nothing short of a howl would've frozen him in place and, damn it, I'm too late. If I try controlling him now, I risk the vampire winning.

Luna *damn* it.

It all happens so quickly after that, mainly because the bloodsucker is fast, Jace is fast, and I never expected a challenge within a few feet of my old apartment. The vamp was prepared for the fight. Jace has no fear. They collide in a sound that rolls like thunder, and I hope that none of the vamps nearby decide to give Roman a head's up that two supes are brawling in his city.

Jace might have had the advantage if he shifted. Most vamps don't know a wolf's weakness the same way that they know a two-legged creature's. Jace could have ended the fight that way.

Unfortunately, he stayed in his human shape and that cost him. Though he gets in a few good strikes, he's dispatched within seconds. The vamp sunk his fangs in him, not even bothering to take a sip from his throat before he's ripping a chunk of it out and tossing Jace away from him.

Jace lands in a heap on the asphalt. I'm at his side immediately. It's not a fatal wound, though it isn't pretty. In the darkness, the hole on the side of his neck looks black, and I can smell the blood pouring out.

"Sorry," he says, almost choking on the word. "Sorry, Alpha."

Kicking him while he's down would just be wrong, wouldn't it? Besides, I'm part of the Alpha couple now. Taking care of my packmate is my responsibility even if he keeps insisting on calling me 'Alpha'.

"Stay down," I murmur. "I've got this."

Jace gurgles on his blood, but I already see that the wound is slowly beginning to heal. He'll be fine by the time we make it out of Muncie—so long as I can make sure we can get to the Jeep without any further injuries.

The vampire laughs. Despite his harsh voice, it's such a musical laugh, it sends shivers down my spine. "One wolf dead. One to go."

He thinks he killed Jace. If I didn't already guess this was his first attempt to challenge one of my kind, that proves it. With the rate that we heal, it takes a little more than a single bite to take us out.

But if he doesn't know that, I'm certainly not going to be the one to tell him.

Instead, shaking my head in disbelief, I look at the vampire as if he's an idiot. Seeing Jace's blood dribble down his chin only affirms what I'm about to do.

"I told you not to try me."

I'm goading him. Of course I am. As his Alpha's mate, I have the right to avenge my packmate; at least, that's how I'm going to spin this to Roman. But I want to be in the right. If I'm going to kill this bastard, I have to give him the chance to go after me first.

And he does.

My last thought is just how pissed Ryker's going to be when he hears about this before the vamp leaps at me.

CHAPTER 5

This time, he's the one who underestimates his opponent. Because I'm smaller than Jace—and, okay, I'm also female—he thinks I'll be easier to take down. The way he comes at me totally telegraphs his confidence. But that's the thing about a vamp targeting shifters. He got cocky because he beat a delta.

I'm going to have fun proving to him that an alpha is a little harder to defeat.

Watching him fight Jace, I figure he'll go for the same move: fangs meet throat. I'm willing to lose a little blood and deal with some pain to get in the proper position to retaliate. He deserves what's going to happen to him, too. I gave him the chance to walk away, and how did he repay me? By trying to kill Jace.

Welp, turnabout's fair play.

I've never actually slain a vampire before, though I

had a front row seat to the gruesome display when Ryker dispatched a killer vamp a couple of weeks ago. He managed to finish him off quickly by popping the guy's head off like it was a freaking dandelion.

I pretend to dodge his obvious attack. When he grabs me by the upper arm, swinging me around before hoisting me up by the waist, I can't believe what a fucking idiot he is. Like, seriously? Why not just hand me a sword while you're at it if you're going to leave my hands free.

Cocky idiot. He draws me up against him, striking like a rattlesnake as he sinks his fangs in my throat; it pinches, but I'm used to love bites from much bigger canines. Before he can do the inevitable jerk that would tear my flesh, I shoot my hands up, gripping the top of his head and the bottom of his chin in one quick motion.

Then, using all the strength my wolf has, I twist.

Pop goes the dandelion.

My own throat burns. He didn't have a chance to tear on his bite, but when I twisted his head, his fangs were still buried in my neck. A small price to pay to end this vampire who, for whatever reason, was prepared to kill Jace and me.

The blood spatters everywhere as I snap the neck and tear the cartilage keeping the head on its stump. Throwing it far away from me, I shove his still-standing headless body so that it slumps to the dirt.

I told him to back off. This wouldn't have had to happen if he listened.

My wolf yips in agreement. As an alpha, death isn't anything new to either of us, though I've never allowed myself to give in to my hunting urges unless I was chasing a rabbit or a deer. A vamp is much bigger prey than game, though, and I'm a little disappointed at how fast this hunt was over and done with.

Ah, well. Maybe next time.

Stepping over the corpse, I wipe the spatter of blood from my cheek with the back of my hand as I head to my packmate's side.

Jace is still on the ground. He's propped himself up, bracing his upper body on his elbows. His eyes are partially shifted, more burnt orange than gold, and his claws are currently carving grooves in the road where he hit. He looks like what he is—a supernatural monster—but the expression on his face tells me that if he's afraid of anyone, it sure ain't the bloodthirsty vamp that tried successfully to take a chunk out of my throat.

Nope. That expression—a combination of awe mingled with "oh, *shit*"—is just for me.

A stray lock of hair escaped my ponytail during the quick but brutal encounter. My claws are retracted, but that doesn't do a damn thing for the blood smeared all over my knuckles and palm. I use my wrist to knock it back, cheerfully bringing a smile to my face as I move closer to Jace.

He doesn't flinch. I'll give him credit for that. He doesn't flinch, but I can tell he almost wanted to.

Huh. Looks like I might just be scarier than I thought.

I hold out my hand. "Need some help?"

"I'm okay."

Right. Bloody hands.

As Jace pushes himself off the asphalt, jumping to his feet, I wipe my fingers against the side of my jeans before giving it up as a lost cause.

His wolf has a much better sense of self-preservation than that vamp did. He meets my gaze once, looking away before my wolf can take it as any kind of challenge. Instead of me, he turns his attention to something else, goggling at what he's staring at now.

I glance over my shoulder. Oh. Right. The currently headless vamp.

"Hey, Jace."

He swallows roughly. "Yes, Alpha?"

I let that one slide. "Do me a favor? Maybe we don't tell Ryker what happened here tonight."

I purposely turn it into a request. With the adrenaline thrumming through me, there's no way he could say no, but I want to at least give him the chance to refuse.

Jace's wolf eyes dart from me to the two halves of

the vampire and back. The delta gulps again, then nods. "You got it, Alpha."

Our ride back to Accalia is a quiet one.

Less than an hour later, I finally pull up in front of the Alpha's cabin. With a murmured "good night," Jace slips out of the side of my Jeep. The sound of his sweatpants tearing to shreds is the last thing I hear before he bounds away. It's obvious that, now that I'm home, he considers his duty done for the evening.

When I'm in Accalia, no one can touch me here. After what happened in the Fang City, maybe he'll finally realize that nothing and no one can touch me there, either.

Fat chance. After tonight's events, I wouldn't be surprised if he's more careful to keep watch over his Alpha's unpredictable mate—especially because, knowing Ryker, he'll put him up to it.

With a frustrated huff, I kill the engine of my Jeep. I'm not an idiot. Despite his agreement, I know that, as soon as he gets a chance, Jace will be reporting exactly what went down in Muncie to Ryker. The four guards might have sworn their loyalty to me in particular, but Ryker is *the* Alpha of our pack. How can we trust a packmate who keeps secrets from the Alpha?

We can't, and the both of us know that.

I shove my keys in my pocket, giving my hands a cursory glance. Though it was probably a fruitless gesture, I took a detour on the way up the mountain. Using my wolf's snout as a guide, I followed her to a river of running water. Then, leaving my Jeep in the care of Jace, I washed the blood off my hands, using the curve of a single claw to dig out the dried blood buried beneath my human nails.

It won't fool my mate, but I'd rather not walk into our shared cabin covered in blood if I can help it.

Peeking in my rearview mirror, I check my throat. I'd scrubbed the best I could at the riverside, but it was hard when I was still in the middle of healing. Now that the skin is fully knitted together, I see the splotches I missed.

Great. Just great.

Maybe I'll get lucky. Maybe Ryker will still be in the den with the other council members and I can sneak past him before he sees what kind of state I'm in. I mean, it could happen, right?

Yeah. It doesn't.

The second I let myself in through the front door, Ryker is standing there with his arms crossed over his muscular chest. I can tell that I'm in for one hell of a lecture. Something about, "where the hell did you go?," springs to mind.

I'm not looking forward to it.

Since I already know I'm in deep shit, I figure it

can't hurt to cut him off at the pass. "Okay. Don't get mad, but—"

Oof. Probably not the best way to start the conversation.

"Don't get mad?" His voice is deathly quiet. Uh-oh. "Barely an hour ago, my neck felt like it was on fire. I had to cut the pack meet short because I had a sudden feeling that you were in danger and I couldn't concentrate. Now, you walk in here, covered in blood—"

"Most of it's not mine," I pipe up. "It's mostly from the vampire who attacked me and Jace. But it's okay. I won the fight."

Hopefully that will help. I doubt it, though, especially since I'm kind of reeling at what Ryker just said. An hour ago his neck was on fire... right around the time I let the vampire sink his fangs in my throat to lure him close. Ryker must've felt the shock of pain through our bond, and without knowing what was causing it, had probably thought the worst.

I cringe. Oops.

It's obvious that my addition does *not* help him.

"You smell like vampire, Gemma." His eyes flash, nostrils flaring as he searches past the overwhelming stink of iron and rust and *meat* that belongs to the vampire who killed me. "You smell like Filan."

Uh-oh time two. With everything that happened after I left the apartment, I almost forgot about what we were doing in Muncie in the first place.

"Did you go see him?"

"Not exactly." When Ryker stares at me, I throw my hands up. "I went to see if Aleks was at the apartment. I thought maybe someone should finally tell him what the hell my stupid birth father is up to since, Luna knows, *you* weren't going to."

Of course that pisses him off more; though he's still silent, the way the muscle in his cheek tics tells me he's holding back what he really wants to say to me. Forget that I look like I've gone a round or two with Dracula. I have Aleks's scent on me. To my possessive mate, it's the end of the freaking world.

"Ryker—"

"You're my mate."

"I know that."

"The Luna gave you to me."

"I know," I say again. "She gave you to me, too."

Even though they're just words, the way I claim Ryker in return has him dropping his arms to his side. Before I can guess what he's going to do, he's crossed the room, heading right for me. Gripping me in a hold that's eerily like the one the vampire had me in earlier, Ryker lifts me easily, pressing me against the length of his body.

His chin dips. He doesn't bite me, though. Instead, he buries his face in the curve of my shoulder, his lips finding the four jagged scars that wrap around my throat, past my collarbone, before disappearing beneath my t-shirt.

"Don't leave me, Gemma," he whispers in a voice that just about breaks my fucking heart. "I sensed you leaving the mountain, then the pain... and I couldn't get to you."

That vamp was right. I *am* a bitch. Here I am, assuming Ryker's letting the old jealousy about Aleks rule him when it's so much more than that. If I thought the year I kept away from him was hell, it was nothing short of torture for my mate.

And what did I do? Sneak out and disappear into Muncie, just like I did that long ago May night.

"I won't." With his arms wrapped around me, it takes a little work to wiggle mine out of his tight embrace. When I do, I thread my fingers through his hair, keeping him against me. "If it means so much to you, I'll stay on the mountain."

For now. I'll stay on the mountain *for now*.

I don't have to say those last two words. Ryker knows. He'll never try to keep me locked up here, his captive mate on a silver chain, but if it makes his life easier not to worry about me while there's already so much weighing him down, easing his mind is the least I can do.

He's my mate. There isn't anything I wouldn't do for him.

THE NEXT MORNING, MY WOLF ROUSES BEFORE THE REST of me does.

I'm not ready to be awake. After Ryker's heartfelt confession, I took it upon myself to reassure my mate that he has nothing to worry about. There's only been one male I've ever loved like this, and no matter how jealous he is over my friendship with Aleks, I choose him. I'll always choose him. He's my fated mate, the other half of my soul, and if he really asked me to, I'd give up everything for him.

It's hard for me to reconcile the strong, powerful, calculating Alpha with the male who broke down in my arms last night. From the moment he found me in Muncie, claiming me in front of the crowd in Charlie's back in June, he's been cocky and sure that we'd end up together. After all, we're fated. In theory, that's how it's supposed to work.

But, as my mom and Jack Walker proved, the Luna doesn't always get it right. That's why a mate has to choose. He could never force me, just like how Walker could never force my mom. We get to choose, and I think that's what part of Ryker's problem is. He's convinced that I only chose him to get back at my bio-dad.

Hopefully, after the night we shared, he believes me when I swear that Walker has nothing to do with how much I wanted to be Ryker's bonded mate. Sure, I might've moved a little faster than I planned because I felt Walker and Shane breathing down my neck, but it doesn't change anything. I've *always* wanted Ryker, and I finally just let myself have him.

It's only been a couple of weeks since our Luna Ceremony. The time we were supposed to have to get used to this new stage in our relationship was cut short when Trish went missing. I guess it's affecting us both in different ways. I'm eager to face Walker and demand he give us our packmate back, while Ryker is trying everything he can to run his pack and keep his alpha mate from running off half-cocked.

'Cause, you know, it's not like I don't have a history of doing that or anything...

We're in this together. I have to remember that Ryker is my mate. My partner. I have to trust him, just like he has to give me some more freedom. If we can learn to respect each other, we'll learn to live this new life together.

I mean, I already love him. I claimed him, and he claimed me. The hard part is out of the way. Sure, we'll have some growing pains as we figure out how two alphas can exist without one trying to dominate the other, but if anyone can do it, me and Ryker can.

Last night, I told him all of that before doing something an alpha rarely does: I apologized to him. I was so intent on sneaking away, I never thought about how it would make Ryker feel if he realized that I was gone. With a promise that I would try not to do that again, I invited him to join me in the shower to help me rinse off the lingering scent of Aleks's apartment and the vampire blood from my skin.

He did, and once I was clean, he spent the next couple of hours making sure that I was completely coated in his scent. Ryker probably went a little overboard, but considering he was single-mindedly devoted to my pleasure, I really can't complain about his methods.

Still, when I say hours, I mean *hours*. A shifter's stamina is something amazing, and though we stopped halfway through for a late dinner, my mate decided going down on me was the only dessert he was hungry for. I think I passed out after the second time he made me come with his gorgeous mouth, only to wake up when he pulled me on top of his chest, nuzzling his marks gently.

He does that a lot. Almost as if he can't believe that I'm wearing his marks, whenever we're alone and he lets down his guard, he inevitably ends up paying them close attention. I always end up melting in his arms when he does which is probably another reason why does it, but I don't care. In some ways, even I can't believe that I've finally bonded this amazing male to me for life.

My body is well-used. A human would probably be

achy from how fierce the two of us mated at one point, but I'm a wolf. As soon as I accept that I'm getting up, I'm feeling the need rushing through me. I'm totally ready to jump my mate again.

Before I reach for him, though, my wolf yips to get my attention. All thoughts of a little morning mating flee from my head as I realize what my wolf has been trying to tell me: an unfamiliar wolf is approaching the Alpha's cabin.

Another breach? Oh, *hell* no.

CHAPTER 6

Rolling over, I find Ryker's already up and out of bed. Rooting around the floor, he's searching for his jeans from last night. His head turns when he feels my stare on his bare back, eyes blazing.

Yeah. He senses it, too.

Following Ryker's lead, I get up, looking around for where my clothes disappeared to. You'd think that, for once, I could strip down and toss them in the hamper where they belonged so that I wouldn't waste time searching for something to cover up with. Nope. I blame it on us still being in the honeymoon of our mating period, plus how revved up he was after I came back from Muncie. Give me and Ryker an empty room, a few minutes to ourselves, and it's a race to get undressed. Who the hell knows where our clothes end up half the time?

When all I recover is my half-torn shirt and a single sock, I give up. As Ryker yanks on his shirt, I dart past him, aiming for the dresser. Once it became clear that I would be staying in Accalia for longer than I initially planned, he made room in here for me after he went down to Muncie and gathered all of my stuff up.

As if I needed another sign he didn't want me leaving...

I grab the first fresh shirt I find, tugging it over my head. I think about running out without panties before remembering just how jealous Ryker was yesterday. Probably not a good idea to skimp on them, even if I'm wearing his scent in my skin. Panties first, then jeans.

No time for shoes. Ryker's already storming toward the hall. I'm not about to let him leave me behind, so I fasten my jeans and pad after him in my bare feet.

He doesn't wait for me. I wish I could say I was surprised, but I'm pretty sure that if Ryker thought he could get away with shutting me in the cabin, he would've. Since he knows that he'd be a fool to even try, he settles on speeding ahead of me.

By the time I catch up to him, he has the front door open, and he's moved out past the edge of our walkway. His hands are perched on his hips, his legs braced as he positions himself firmly between the male walking out of the forest and our cabin.

It's a wolf shifter, and not any I recognize. A couple of inches taller than Ryker, with a thick build and paws that remind me of a catcher's mitt, I might be wary of this dark-haired idiot if his rank wasn't only a blip on my radar.

That still doesn't make me any less guarded. Lower-ranked or not, to get this far into Accalia without one of Ryker's patrols picking up on his approach is impressive. Making it so close to the Alpha's cabin before me and Ryker were aware is even more so.

Who the hell is this guy?

Ryker asks the question before I get the chance. "Who are you and what the fuck are you doing on my territory without my permission?"

I'll give the shifter credit. Before we were mated, even I would've quailed if Ryker took that tone of voice with me. Though he looks like he wants to, he stays right where he is.

"My name is Patrick. I'm here on behalf of the Alpha of the Western Pack."

I figured that would be the case, but *damn*. My bio-dad is really fucking ballsy if he thinks it's a good idea to send a single wolf into our territory.

"Yeah?" Ryker makes a display of looking behind the wolf. "You alone, Patrick?"

"I am."

"Funny, 'cause I thought I sent a message to your Alpha that, unless he returned my packmate to me —*unharmed*—that I would take any other action as his declaring war on my pack. Is that what you're doing? Telling me he wants war?"

Patrick swallows roughly. "No. I came with this." Reaching behind him, he pulls out a white envelope.

I move so that Ryker isn't acting like a barrier between me and this wolf. I just wanted to get a better look at what he has, but I realize almost immediately that I goofed.

Patrick's eyes land on me. He's not looking at my face, though, and not because he's trying not to challenge an alpha wolf by staring directly at me. Oh, no. His gaze is perfectly angled so that he's looking at my boobs.

Males. Wolves, vamps, or humans, they're all the same. I've barely got anything there to begin with, and he's staring like I'm freaking Dolly Parton. Scowling, I glance down to see if maybe my A-cups turned into C's overnight or something.

Oh. *Oh.* Yeah... I see what's going on here. In my haste, I pulled on a plain white tee to cover up—and no bra. Doesn't matter that I'm basically flat. In the early morning sunlight, you can see *everything* I have.

Whoops.

A second later, Ryker catches on to what the other wolf is staring at. His expression immediately goes flat, almost as if it doesn't bother him at all that the wolf is staring openly at my tits.

Yeah. That's not a good thing.

I've known Ryker since I was fifteen, but I've only really gotten to know the man behind the roguish smile, the hard eyes, and the mantle of being a young Alpha in the last couple of months. I'd had my own ideas of what kind of male he was, and now that he's let down his guard enough to let me in, I'm more than willing to admit that I used to be wrong about him.

Still, if there's one thing I picked up on in the beginning, it's that the more disinterested and careless Ryker sounds, the more dangerous he really is. If this wolf doesn't watch himself, this could end with Ryker plucking out his eyeballs for watching me like that.

Now, I can take care of it myself. As strong as this other wolf appears, his rank is nothing compared to mine. He tops out as a beta wolf. The Wicked Wolf's new Beta maybe? After the way Ryker won his challenge, my bio-dad was out his last one on account of my mate being forced to put Shane Loup down the way he had. Even so, I'd be lying if I said it didn't turn me on, knowing that I have a mate who will do anything to stake his claim.

It's a shifter thing.

As if he's asking to be polite, he nods at the card clasped in the other wolf's hand.

"What's this?"

He holds it out to me. "My Alpha thought you might need it spelled out for you. You've ignored all his other summons home."

Oh, you poor moron. It's almost like you want Ryker to send you back home to the Wolf District in a box.

Again, Ryker moves so that he's blocking me from Patrick. "This is Gemma's home."

"Gemma." Patrick looks past Ryker's shoulder, directly at me. "Nice name."

"Thanks," I say, giving him a dazzling grin. "My mom always liked it."

When I was still pretending to be an omega, a smile like that had dominant wolves tripping over themselves to do anything I asked. So enchanted by the act, they never noticed the sharp edge to the curve of my lips—and neither does this idiot.

He lifts the envelope again. "This says 'Ruby' on it."

Of course it freaking does.

"There's no Ruby here," drawls Ryker. "And, if you know better, you'll bring that back to your Alpha and tell him not to try this bullshit again until he's ready to give me my packmate back."

With an almost apologetic look shot my way, Patrick shrugs his massive shoulders. "If you really want your other girl, then take this."

For a second, I'm sure Ryker's going to refuse. But he doesn't. Though the envelope is clearly meant for me, he rips it out of Patrick's loose grip.

He doesn't open it. Not yet. Instead, with his eyes

lighting up like they're on fire, he says, "You have five minutes to get off my territory. If you're still here, I'll assume you're just like Loup. That you want to challenge me. I assure you that the outcome will be the same."

Patrick nods. With the envelope in Ryker's possession, he's done his job. And maybe he isn't such an idiot, after all, because he doesn't need a second warning. With only one backward look at me, he slinks away into the trees.

The two of us wait outside our cabin until Ryker's wolf announces that the outsider is gone. Since my wolf assures me the same thing, I immediately forget all about the Wicked Wolf's errand boy.

He's not important, but the envelope he left behind with Ryker sure is.

I move into Ryker, reaching up on my tiptoes to look over his shoulder. Patrick wasn't kidding when he said that the envelope is addressed to 'Ruby'. In the same sharp lines as his signature at the bottom of his last note, Walker's drawn my name so deep, the ink bleeds through to the other side.

Ryker offers me the envelope. I wave at him to open it instead.

He does.

The first thing I look at is the bottom of the page. And there they are: the same twelve crisscrossing lines forming three Ws. Wicked Wolf Walker. He's such an arrogant bastard, he actually signs his missives with his cruel nickname.

As I'm looking at the bottom, Ryker's reading the words centered on the page. Halfway through, he grips it so tightly, he crinkles the thick paper.

I nudge him in the side. "What's it say?"

"You are cordially invited—"

With a scoffing laugh, I say, "You've got to be shitting me. It doesn't say that."

"Read it."

This time, when Ryker offers me the page, I take it. Within seconds, I realize that he was dead serious. It's an invitation—and, yet, it's infinitely more threatening than Walker's last note:

> YOU VE BEEN CORDIALLY INVITED TO VISIT THE WESTERN PACK, LOCATED IN THE WOLF DISTRICT OF CALIFORNIA. AS ALPHA, I GIVE MY SOLEMN WORD THAT THIS INVITATION SERVES AS YOUR PASS TO ENTER AND LEAVE THE TERRITORY WITHOUT PENALTY. SHOULD YOU DO SO, AT THE CONCLUSION OF YOUR VISIT, YOU CAN LEAVE WITH ANY PACKMATE OF MINE WHO WANTS TO LEAVE WITH YOU, INCLUDING RYKER WOLFSON S CHOSEN MATE, TRISH DANVERS, WHO IS CURRENTLY MY HONORED GUEST.
> SHE ACCEPTED MY INVITATION, RUBY.
> NOW IT S YOUR TURN.
>
> XXX
>
> P.S. TELL YOUR MOTHER I SAID HI.

My jaw drops.

Oh, you've gotta be *kidding* me.

"No."

Ryker doesn't even make it past the threshold before he's trying to use his dominance against me. I feel it in the way the air goes heavy around him. I hear it in the guttural sound of the single syllable. *No.*

"Ryker, can we talk about this?"

"No."

"Come on—"

"I said no, Gemma. Now drop it."

I can't.

Maybe if Walker hadn't explicitly mentioned that, if I accept his invitation, I'll get to come home with Trish, I could've. She accepted my invitation... yeah. Considering the amount of her blood we found in the pack garage where Barrow ambushed her, I don't think she did so willingly.

For the last two weeks, I tried my hardest to pretend that this wasn't my fault. That what happened to Trish was an unfortunate coincidence. Did I pull it off? Yeah... no. Not quite. I knew it, and my wolf knew it, too. She was nothing more than a pawn in a dangerous game where only the Wicked Wolf knew the rules—and the bastard cheated anyway.

I crumple the invitation in my fist.

There's no denying it now. First, he sent one of his sycophants into Muncie with the ruby. When that didn't work, he sicced Shane on me, but I refused to rise to the bait. Not even when he tracked me downtown, allowing me to see him. My bio-dad was showing off, letting me know that he could find me. He made it obvious that he wouldn't be satisfied until I showed up at the Wolf District, willfully heading to his territory, serving myself up on a silver platter for him.

Now, I'm stubborn. I'm the first to admit I can be reckless and impulsive, too. Hot-headed? Yup. But I'm not a moron. I refused to answer his summons, to play his stupid game, so he intruded on *my* territory, testing *my* mate, and messing with *my* pack.

That arrogant prick is behind Trish's disappearance, just like we figured. No wonder he gave us the last two weeks to stew over what his next move could be. With Trish trapped across the country, a "guest" of the Western Pack, he doesn't need one. Sending Patrick with this ridiculous invitation proves it.

Not to mention his lovely little postscript there.

Tell your mom I said hi...

He thinks snatching Trish was some kind of checkmate. And, Luna damn it, it kind of is.

"I have to go."

"No."

Does he think, if he keeps repeating it, I'm going to listen?

Silly Ryker.

I harden my jaw, utterly determined as I tell him, "We have to get her back."

"Gemma—"

I ignore him. He'll try to tell me that it isn't worth risking me to save Trish. I've already heard it all before. Only, before, we didn't have confirmation where Trish was, or even if she survived Barrow's attack on her. Though a few scents are clinging to the invitation, my wolf knows Trish's all too well. At least she was alive when the note was written. I hold onto that.

The invitation is a promise. To a shifter, that means something. A pass in and out of the Wolf District, plus the chance to bring her home? I know Ryker is totally against it, but I don't see how I have any other choice.

I have to *try*.

"She's part of our pack. And, even if she wasn't, I wouldn't leave my worst enemy with my psycho sperm donor. We have to get her back."

He searches my face. It's not another no, and I take heart in that.

"He'll kill her if I don't," I tell him needlessly.

"And we'll mourn the death of a packmate if he goes through with his threat."

"Ryker—"

"I won't lose you, Gemma."

"Oh, come on."

His big hands are hot and heavy as he lays them on my upper arms. They're a brand on my skin, his fingertips digging in just enough to show me that he's still super serious. This isn't the Alpha trying to pull rank on me. This is Ryker—my *mate*—being vulnerable with me again. Open with me.

Honest.

"I went too long without you. I finally got you back." His voice goes low and throaty as he bends his knees, putting us on the same level. I'm lost in his gaze, his unblinking stare locked on my face. "I won't let anyone get between us, sweetheart. Especially not Trish. Not again."

Oof.

That one? That one *hurt*.

And I know perfectly well that that's not what Ryker meant to happen. Maybe last night, after I went to see Aleks without telling him, he might've wanted to land his punches. But now? He's just trying his damndest to make me understand why he's so adamant that I give up on her.

But I can't.

I *can't*.

I lift the invitation. "It doesn't say I can't bring anyone with me. How's that for a compromise? You come with me, we both stick our middle fingers up at Walker, and we leave with Trish. Then you won't have to worry about me getting into trouble, and I'll have you watching my back."

For a moment, I think I might've convinced him. Either that, or he's regretting the hurt that escaped down our bond before I could stop it.

And then he sighs. "That's a really great idea, and I wish it would work. But it can't. I'm the Alpha, Gemma. If I leave, who will protect the rest of Mountainside?"

Is that all he's worried about? "Warren can do it. He's your Beta."

Ryker gives his head a quick jerk. Another no, but something about this one has my stomach tightening.

Uh-oh. What don't I know?

"Why not?"

"I didn't get the chance to tell you last night, but that was what I had to deal with when you went down to Muncie. The emergency pack meet? Warren came to me and told me that he's stepping down as Beta effective immediately. There is no Beta right now."

Great. Our temporary Beta wants out and there's no one in line to take his place. Ryker's right. He couldn't come with me to California even if I wanted him to. A pack without an Alpha or a Beta is just begging to be attacked.

And how much do I want to bet that Walker is waiting for a situation just like that?

I'm not giving up, though. Not yet.

"What if..." I wait for a spark of brilliance, grinning

up at him when it hits me. "What if I bring a couple of my guards with me? You already trust them to watch over me. You stay here and keep the rest of the pack safe while me and a few of the guys fly out west, grab Trish, and bring her home. We'll be gone one, two days tops. Then we can put this behind us. What do you think?"

"You would do that? Willingly bring Jace or Dorian or any of the others with you?"

Moving into him, I grab his shirt, clutching the material as I tilt my head back to look up at him. I have to make him understand. "He won't stop. You know that. I know that. He won't stop until he gets what he wants. But the thing is... I don't know what he wants. Going there could change that. We need to be prepared."

What I *don't* say is that, if we'd been prepared, this never would've happened. Trish would still be in Accalia, and we wouldn't be having this argument.

Ryker exhales softly. I know then that the 'no' has become a pretty shaky 'maybe'.

"Let's bring this to the pack council," he says at last. "You're right. This isn't just about me and you. We're the Alpha couple. This is a pack issue. Let's see what the council says about your idea. Deal?"

Lifting up on my tippy-toes, I press a kiss to the underside of his jaw. "Deal."

CHAPTER 7

It's a bit of an understatement to say that I'm not the biggest fan of Ryker's pack council.

I can't really blame them for standing by and watching as their Alpha rejected me in front of them. Actually, I should give them credit for not interfering when I went a teensy bit feral and jabbed my claws into his chest. It was a tussle between the future Alpha couple, and until Ryker made that final declaration that I was nothing—all because he was still trying desperately to protect my secret for me after I recklessly showed off that I was a female alpha—they stayed back. Of course, after that, a couple of them tried to stop me anyway, but I made it out in time to disappear into Muncie.

Know what I can blame them for? Their ridiculous idea that, if I was going to refuse to give their Alpha another chance, they were going to *force* me to. Like, really? Those dumbasses went so far as to poison me, then toss me at a near-feral Ryker. The seven remaining pack members all made their apologies to me in some way or another since the Luna Ceremony, but... yeah. Still not a fan.

The same afternoon Patrick delivers Walker's invitation, Ryker tells the council he's hosting another meet. I don't miss this one. I get a few curious looks as the council members arrive to discover me sitting behind my desk the same way that Ryker's behind his, but they're smarter now. They greet me with as much reverence as they do my mate—something that mollifies my bristling wolf—before filing into the den.

Because this is my show, Ryker lets me take the lead in addressing the pack council.

He's not happy, a fact that the rest of the council picks up on, but he stays silent as I tell them about our visitor from earlier that morning. Jace curses under his breath, Duke's body seems even bigger as anger pulses off of him, and Benjamin mutters to Grant that we need to think about pulling in some other packmates to increase the patrols.

With barely a quick silencing look over the group, they go quiet again.

I continue. "Without an installed Beta... and I thank Warren for stepping up before, and wish him well on returning to his well-earned retirement as a gamma... but without a Beta, Ryker can't go with me.

I'm okay going alone, but my mate is right. This could be a trap." Could be? It most likely is. "So, if you agree that it's worth taking a quick trip to California to get our packmate back, I'll go. I'll even take a couple of wolves with me if there are any volunteers—"

The second the word is out of my mouth, Duke's hand is up. "Tell me when you're ready to leave, and I'll be there."

"Me, too," chimes in Jace. "We won't let any harm come to your mate, Alpha."

Ryker nods.

Okay. Looks like I have my volunteers.

Bobby, Dorian, and two other wolves drop their paws.

I resist the urge to roll my eyes. I figured my personal guards would be the wolves quickest to offer—the only reason I was willing to accept taking a couple of packmates with me in the first place—but it's still a little annoying how nearly the whole council are ready to treat me like I still need to be protected. Weren't they there when I nearly ripped Ryker's heart from his chest?

Whatever.

In a way, I see their point. To them, I'm not just a female alpha—I'm their Alpha's mate. Taking care of me is another way to show respect to Ryker.

Eh. Pack life. It's not for everyone.

Ryker clears his throat. "Let's not get ahead of

ourselves, Gemma. We called this meeting to ask the pack council to give us their perspective on this." Shifting in his seat, he leans forward to address the seven wolves giving their Alpha their undivided attention. "I'm willing to find another way to bring Trish home. Gemma says she'd rather make a move now while we can. She'll walk into the Wolf District with a few volunteers, and she'll walk out with Trish." He pauses. "At least, that's her plan."

"It's a good plan," I pipe up. "What's the worst that can happen? He can't keep me there."

He could try again later, but that's another reason why I should go. All the intel we have on Walker is pretty outdated. Wouldn't it help to let him think he's gotten what he wants all while I get what *I* want?

I already explained that point to the pack when I first proposed my idea to them. The fact that Ryker didn't argue against it tells me that, logically, he agrees with me. The pack Alpha understands that this is our best chance to nip this issue with an enemy pack in the bud. My mate, though? He's probably wondering how pissed I could really get if he locked me in his basement to keep me out of harm's way.

Hey. Good chance he still has that set of chains down there...

And I get it. I do. If our roles were reversed, I don't know if my wolf would be happy to stay behind while he walked into such an unknown situation. It was bad enough when I had to watch him fight the Alpha challenge with Shane. At least, then, I knew the rules. I knew the traditions.

Now? All I have to go on is a written promise by a male who threatened to drown me when I was barely a year old.

That's not going to stop me.

Poor Ryker. As his mate, I'm his priority. But this is a pack issue. If I'm willing to stand between Accalia and the Wicked Wolf, how can he really justify putting his paw down and telling me I can't go?

He knows I'm right. I know he does. And if we weren't still in the honeymoon stage of our mating, where his possessive urges overrule his duty to Accalia, he'd realize what he's doing. The way I see it, I have no choice. The invitation with my birth name was just the last straw.

When he mated me, I became a member of the Mountainside Pack. I became the Alpha's mate. I can't just stay inside of our cabin, waiting for my deranged sperm donor to attack because he suddenly decided after all these years that he wants to play daddy.

I don't really have any clue what Wicked Wolf Walker wants with me. Not really. I mean, I know it has everything to do with being a female alpha, but I figured he would take a hint once I chose Ryker. He can't force me to bond with another wolf just so he can control me, so why is he playing this game? Giving me an open invitation to visit his territory, knowing that an Alpha's word is their bond. Even for a bastard with Walker's reputation, if he broke his word, the whole Alpha collective could make him pay. He'd never risk losing his stranglehold on the Wolf District.

Of course, all that tells me is that he *has* a plan, but I won't know what it is until I go.

At this point, we've already been discussing the matter for almost an hour. I've said my piece, Ryker's said even more with his stony silence, and the council members are obviously reacting to the rising levels of dominance in the small den.

It's time to end this.

"Ryker?"

"Yes, sweetheart?"

Ah. So he feels the crackle of our auras bumping up against each other, too. "You said we can put it to a vote. Talking this to death isn't going to change either of our minds. If the council says yes, I go. If they say no, then we figure something else out. Okay?"

He nods. "Okay. All in favor of Gemma going to the Wolf District to rescue Trish?"

Four hands shoot up. Bobby. Dorian. Jace. Duke.

I bite back my smile.

Ryker's face is expressionless. "All opposed?"

The other three members hesitate before raising theirs.

"Four to three," I point out.

Back when we were first starting the mating dance, I noticed one vein on Ryker that had a tendency to throb when he was fuming. I nicknamed it Duke, and when I started calling the big shifter in Ryker's inner circle the same name, it's totally because of that bulging vein.

It's been a while, but ol' Duke's made a sudden reappearance. Though I can easily sense his frustration, the pulsing vein in the side of his thick neck is the only outward sign that this meeting didn't go the way he hoped it would. "Then I guess we have an answer."

As a majority of the members quickly flee from the den and their ticked-off Alpha, I admit that I do kind of feel bad for the whole pack council. I know there isn't a single one of them that *wants* to go against their Alpha. Whether they agree that I'm right or not, Ryker's still the wolf they owe their loyalty to. I'm not even a little mad that three of the wolves—Grant, Benjamin, and Forrest—voted with him. I expected it.

Just like I expected that the four wolves that make up my guard would feel the urge to side with me.

Whoops.

Compromise. It's all about compromise.

Me going through with this is the last thing Ryker wants, but once the pack council backs me, he's all in on helping me figure out what's next. It's his way of maintaining some control so, even though he takes over the planning, I let him.

Shit. I'm still kind of in shock that he's not secretly planning on following behind me or something.

If it wasn't for Warren, I really think he would be thinking it; not because he doesn't believe I can do this, but because his wolf would be nudging him to keep me within arm's reach. After the pack council meeting, Ryker had a one-on-one with Warren, but the outcome was the same. The older wolf had meant it when he said that he was stepping down again. He'd already made arrangements to visit a cousin in the Northern Pack, so even if he was willing to take control of Accalia for a few days, he was leaving the next morning for a month-long leave that Ryker had already approved.

My mate is a good male, and a better Alpha. Though it frustrates the hell out of him, he would never take back the permission he gave to one of his packmates. Warren would be gone the next morning, and once he reluctantly agrees that I can answer my bio-dad's invitation, I'm heading out the day after.

Well, me, Jace, and Duke are.

That's another compromise. Me? I was all ready to head back to the cabin and pack my bags the second the council meeting was over with. Not Ryker.

When the den cleared out, Jace and Duke lingered behind so that we could come up with the best way to do this. It's a quick discussion, mainly because I want to get started, but as soon as Jace and Duke follow the rest of the council out, my mate turns to me.

"You know, I think you should wait until after the full moon."

What? I thought we just decided that we'd leave ASAP.

"But that's days away," I argue. "I get not wanting to jump right away when Walker beckons, but I don't think we should wait *that* long. What if he figures I'm not coming and something happens to Trish?"

Because that? That right there's my biggest worry. That he'll snap and, instead of pretending to play nice, he'll use his bargaining chip against me. For a male who's gone through more than a hundred Betas, and won just as many Alpha challenges, what's another death on his hands? He wouldn't lose any sleep at night, but I sure fucking would.

"It's been almost two weeks since she went missing—"

"Exactly. A few more days won't matter."

I'm not so sure he's right—but I do understand what's bothering him.

The Luna.

We're already passed the new moon phase, closing in on the third quarter. In less than ten days, it'll be the full moon again.

"I'll be back way before then," I promise. After all,

I'm not planning on being there for more than a day or two. With over a week left, I'll be back in time to spend the next Luna with my mate.

Ryker's dark gold eyes gleam down at me. "You better."

I reach out, taking his hand in mine. Rubbing the side of my finger against his knuckle, I purposely meet his gaze, letting my love for him shine through. "I will."

With his other hand, Ryker cups the back of my head. I part my lips for him, accepting his kiss, and returning it with as much feeling as I can. I may not be the best with words—as stubborn as I am, it took me way too long to confess that I loved him—but I put my devotion to him in that kiss.

When we finally break apart, my mate seems a lot more settled. His wolf has calmed down, his possessive side finally taking a backseat to his alpha nature. Being an Alpha isn't just about barking at packmates and giving them orders. It's about keeping them safe and protected.

In our own ways, that's exactly what we'll both be doing. Just... Ryker will be doing that in Accalia while I deal with the situation in California.

We got this. Wicked Wolf Walker doesn't know what kind of box he opened when he started this over the summer, but between Ryker and me, we got this.

The kiss does something to my mate; the kiss, or maybe my promise. Either way, the matter is settled.

I'm heading to the Wolf District with Jace and Duke, and we're leaving in two days.

To save some time, Ryker figures that flying is our best shot. As much as I want to hop in my Jeep, slam my boot on the gas, and speed all the way across the country, I know better. It's a three thousand-mile trip from coast to coast, and if I could drive non-stop—no sleeping, no eating, no bathroom breaks—it would take me at least forty-eight hours. Since I'm a supe, but not one of the undead, I need those things. Two days will easily become five or six, and Trish has already been gone for long enough. A flight that's over and done with in half of a day… yeah. The sooner we arrive at the Wolf District, the faster I can snag Trish and bring her back to Accalia with me.

Ryker makes all the arrangements, from the airplane tickets to the car I'll rent when we arrive in California. It's another way for him to be involved, and if he knows when I'm leaving and when I'm scheduled to come back, I'm sure he'll feel better.

Besides, I have something I have to take care of that I have to do by myself. And I really, really wish that Ryker could do this for me, but he can't. This responsibility is all on me.

So, while my mate deals with the humans at the airport, I pick up my phone.

It's time to call my mom.

It takes a lot of explaining, and my stomach aches to hear the fear in my mom's voice when she realizes that I'm willingly going to face Jack Walker, but eventually she agrees to help me. Honestly, I have my real dad to thank for that. If he hadn't jumped in on my side, I don't know if I could've convinced her on my own.

Thank goodness for my mom's habit of using speakerphone. My dad heard everything, and though it's not like he's happy about me going to the Wolf District, he's another alpha. He had to figure this would happen sooner or later once I was grown, and he's spent my whole life training me for this exact scenario.

With Paul on my side, my mom reluctantly understands that this is something that I have to do. Besides, if the male who taught me to go for an enemy's heart thinks I'm prepared to face my bio-dad—not like I plan on fighting him or anything—then what excuse does my mom have for trying to ground me?

Which, yeah, she totally did. I chalk it up to her omega nature, trying desperately to do anything to keep me safe. It's still a bit ridiculous that she tried. I'm twenty-six, mated, and haven't lived at Lakeview in almost a year and a half. Even my dad muffled his laugh when she tried.

It took a while to get her to come around. When I

finally do, she realizes that it would be better to help me than to hinder me, and with utmost reluctance, she tells me all about the Wolf District—including its location. Thanks to my mom's directions, I know exactly where to go as soon as our plane lands in California.

I'm glad she gave them to me. From some of Ryker's allies, we had a pretty good idea where the Wicked Wolf's territory was located, but my mom is one of the only shifters to make it out of the Wolf District alive. The Western Pack is the type that demands loyalty; its psychotic Alpha has no problem eliminating anyone who rises up against him. The only thing that saved my mother was her omega nature. Jack Walker never believed she'd risk her life for her freedom, or that she loved her pup enough to risk escaping when us both being put down was a pretty likely outcome.

But she survived. Because of her, so did I. She sacrificed so much to escape her ex-mate, so I expected her to put up a fight when I told her that I was heading out West to face him.

I'm an alpha. Like my mom, I'm an Alpha's mate now, too. I can take care of myself. If Ryker could be convinced to let me go with only two other shifters watching my back, I hoped that my mom would understand.

Yeah, that would be a *nope*.

It took my dad jumping in, gently reminding my mom that the decision was mine. Since I made it clear that nothing was going to stop me from finally going to see the male who sired me, it was their duty as my parents to help get me ready for the trip. Trying to convince me that I shouldn't go wasn't going to work. He knew that, and after my mom got past the worst of her protective instincts, my mom admitted that so did she.

She couldn't stop me, but she could prepare me. My dad, too. Warnings about Jack Walker, the kind of wolf he was, the way he ran the Wolf District... and where precisely it was located.

Most shifter packs are insular. We keep to ourselves. But that doesn't mean that we don't interact with the outside world. Like how Ryker had to buy tickets from a human airport or how most of the goods we have in Accalia come from the human city set on the other side of the mountain.

The Wolf District doesn't do that.

From what my mom can tell me about living there when I was still a pup, it was a community built on the shifters relying on each other. Walker liked to think of himself as the untouchable leader, like a feudal lord who had his serfs do his bidding. They grew their own food for him, hunted meat, made their clothes, bartered, and shared. There was a square in the center of the district that was a community spread of food for those who didn't want to eat by themselves, and each wolf did precisely what they were told in fear of being the next victim of their Alpha.

Because of that, it's a massive patch of land, but it's also hidden away. Before my mom left the Western Pack, Walker's territory butted up against the Lakeview Pack. From the rumors that spread in the decades since, once my dad relocated the Lakeview Pack from the West Coast to the East Coast, Walker claimed that territory, too.

We know where it's supposed to be, but it's still a good thirty miles from the airport we landed at.

When we first planned this trip, I was all for going on foot once we touched down. Jace, too. Surprisingly, it was Duke who had put his big paw down. Driving would be safer, especially since none of us know the terrain. If we approach as wolves, Walker might take that as an aggressive move. He sent his wolf in his skin, so that's how we would arrive.

Plus, if we find that we have to make a quick getaway, a car works in our favor. Trapped in the enclosed vehicle, it's much harder for us to leave a scent trail for any shifters to follow. I learned *that* one the hard way when Shane hopped in a car and drove away from Muncie when I was chasing him in my fur.

I agreed, but only if I could drive. No arguments from the others, so Ryker included a rental when he planned our flight.

The four-door sedan is rough. There's a reason why

I've always driven a Jeep. I need my freedom, and being enclosed with two male wolves just makes me realize I miss my mate desperately.

We've only been separated for eight hours and I'm already wishing I could turn back. It's not night yet—thank you, three-hour time zone difference—but the pull of the Luna on my wolf is a bitch.

Damn it. I hate when Ryker is right.

CHAPTER 8

The prickle of the territorial lines has the hair on the back of my neck standing straight. That's even more impressive when I note that my windows are tightly rolled up. I snuck some fresh air when we were still a few miles out of Western Pack territory, but as soon as we got closer, I shut them all.

It doesn't matter. I still feel the warning exuding from the trees the further we drive. Glancing in the rearview mirror, the dark look on Duke's face, plus the way Jace is leaning in his seat, lips raised just enough to show a hint of his canines, reveals that they're feeling it, too.

There's a point where my wolf warns me that, if I keep going, I'm crossing into enemy territory. Smart girl. I pull the rental car over to the side, parking it just past the first break in the trees I find. The plan is to leave it here and hope that none of the Western Pack waste their time trying to figure out why someone abandoned a car at the edge of their land.

Claws crossed.

We have a quick, muttered argument when we surround the trunk. It's the same one we had on the way to the airport, and when we disembarked. I tell the two shifters that I'm more than capable of carrying my own suitcases. Duke points out that he's a big guy, that it's easier for him to carry them along with his own. Jace just tries to grab one to help me.

I snap my teeth and, of the three bags I brought, I end up with one of them.

Again.

Ugh. At least they let me hold onto the invitation.

I look at my two guards. "Ready?"

Duke nods, his lips thinned into a line. Jace's golden eyes gleam, almost as if he's looking forward to this.

At least one of us is.

"Come on."

This was another argument we had in the car. Duke thought it would be smarter to keep me between him and Jace. One wolf would be at my front, the other at my back, with me completely protected. I thought it would make me look weak. I have no idea if Walker's pack knows my open secret, but he definitely does. An alpha wolf flanked by two deltas? If I want him to take me seriously, I have to lead the charge, not be tucked between Duke and Jace.

I won this round. So, with my bag slung over my shoulder, and the invitation in my hand, I start moving toward the forest. They're right on my ass, but there's enough distance that I don't feel stifled by them.

I don't know what I expected. I didn't RSVP or anything, so it's not like Walker has any clue I decided to take him up on his invite. Still, when we move almost a mile into the outskirts of Western Pack territory, I start to wonder if this is the wrong place. Someone should've found us by now, right?

Either that, or security's really shit around here. Which, I guess, makes sense. With Walker's reputation, he probably doesn't *need* security.

Just as I have that thought, I hear footsteps in the distance. From the way they fall—plus the new scent wafting toward us—I can tell that it's a pair, and at least one of them is in their fur.

Without a word, Jace taps me on the shoulder. He gestures with his fingers, pointing toward the gloomy trees. The sun hasn't set yet, but we've gone deep enough in the thick forest that the branches provide cover to turn this part of the territory dark.

He's asking me if I think he should scout ahead. I nod, and he lopes off quickly.

Duke shifts a little closer to me.

We wait.

It's only been a minute or so when a warning howl rolls around us like a crack of thunder. Without hesitation, Duke moves his big bulk in front of me.

What the—

Stalking out of the woods, I see a grey wolf with gleaming golden eyes. His head is angled down, shoulders hunched. In a shifter's body language, that's a clear warning: I'm coming for you.

How lovely. He's looking right at me.

His slow padding suddenly becomes a full-out sprint.

Shit!

Before I can even think to react, Jace comes barreling in from the east side of me. He's shifted, a sleek shadow with his ears arrowed back, lips curled to bare his fangs as he leaps, going for the throat of the big grey wolf.

The wolf dislodges him easily before turning his attention on the brindled wolf attacking him. Fur flies, angry snarls and short howls splitting the air as the two wolves fight.

No. *No.* This isn't supposed to happen. I was promised that I could come and go in the Western Pack without any threat to me. Damn it, I have an invitation!

Tell *that* to the grey wolf that came at us.

So consumed with watching the fight, I don't notice that another male has joined us right away. That's my fault, and I want to kick myself that he was able to get as close as he did before Duke's warning growl pulls my attention away from the battling wolves to the shifter standing in his skin.

First thing I notice is that he reminds me of a funeral director. His brown hair is cut short, his face long and unnaturally thin. Gaunt, I guess. He has a solemn expression, and his shifter's eyes are so dark, they appear black. He's even wearing a freaking suit! Black jacket, black slacks, black tie over a white shirt, he's unlike any shifter I've ever seen before.

He's a beta, too, which definitely doesn't bode well. Is he Walker's Beta? Is my luck really that shitty that the Wicked Wolf's right-hand wolf just so happens to show up when my packmate is fighting one of his?

Or is this some kind of set-up?

His voice is deep, yet almost unfeeling as he says in a bored voice, "Stop them."

Two brawling wolves are almost impossible to separate. In fact, I'm not even sure it can be done without some kind of magic.

Like, oh, the power of the Luna.

Does he know what I am? I'm beginning to think he does, otherwise he'd never think I could stop them.

Am I going to come out and tell him that I'm a female alpha, though?

Not a chance.

"Get in between two snarling wolves? I know you're kidding."

"Call off your mutt or I'll tell mine to finish this."

"I can't," I try to lie.

He's not having it.

His face as hard as ever, he says gruffly, "Oh, but you will."

Shit.

Giving him a well-practiced frightened look—a hallmark of an easily spooked, gentle omega—I move past the beta and let out a soft cry.

"Please, stop this!"

Yeah. That doesn't make an impact. Like, at *all*.

Omega Gem isn't enough to stop a vicious Western Pack wolf; too late, I decide I probably should've traded my t-shirt and jeans for one of my old sundresses if I really wanted to sell the act. Oh, no. This is going to take Alpha Gem—and I'm beginning to understand that: Yes. This had definitely been a set-up.

What else can I do? I can't watch the scrappy Jace try to defend me again without doing something to help him. My hesitation in Muncie led to a disaster, and one that Ryker had to add to his plate by having a long conversation with Roman to keep me from being banished from the Fang City.

I won't let something like that happen again.

So, tapping into the power of my wolf, I snap, "Stop. *Now.*"

The grey wolf heels immediately. So does Jace.

And I realize that if the beta wolf has any doubts as to who I am—to *what* I am—I just settled them for him then and there.

With a jerk of his chin at the grey wolf, he gives him a wordless command.

At once, the grey wolf gets up, sprinting for the trees before disappearing into the forest.

As he does, another shifter steps into the clearing. It's a third male, since I saw the tail of the attacking wolf brush against the newcomer as they switched spots, and when I focus on him, I find myself frowning.

He's a good-looking male, with a lean build, styled black hair, light gold eyes, and a freaking cleft in his strong chin. Something about him says he should be as intimidating as the other wolf, only he's smiling, in a much better mood, so his dangerous air seems tempered. But none of that is what makes me frown.

I suddenly understand his dangerous vibes. Based on his aura, he's an alpha wolf. Not *the* Alpha, of course, but the same rank as me.

Huh.

If this is the Wolf District, the three shifters we've met so far must be part of the Western Pack. I never would've thought that the Wicked Wolf would let another alpha run in his territory.

But there he is.

Weird.

He nods at the beta wolf, casts an interested look

over Jace in his shifted form, then Duke looming over me, before his pale gold eyes land on me. "Hello. Sorry about the welcome. As you see, we don't like trespassers in the district."

I hold up the invitation that I managed to hang onto. "We're not trespassing. We were invited."

"Ah." His eyes brighten, a bit of a tease as he says, "The prodigal daughter returns."

The way he says that has my wolf's fur ruffling. "It's Gemma, thanks."

"Then let's try our hand at another welcome for such a special guest. Welcome, Gemma. Hi. I'm Theodore Michaels. But, please, call me Theo."

On the plus side, at least he's not going to insist on calling me 'Ruby'.

"Theo," barks the dark-haired beta. "The Alpha waits."

His slight smile dips. Interesting. He might be an alpha, but it's easy to see that he's submissive to the lower-ranked wolf. The only way that could be is if the beta has a higher place in the pack's hierarchy.

So I was right. He's not just a beta wolf. He's Walker's Beta.

Looks like he was quicker to replace Shane than we were. Lucky bastard.

"Yes, Christian. Of course." Theo nods, the playfulness already gone. "Come on. Our Alpha is simply dying to meet you."

I'm absolutely sure he is.

Remind me again why I was so determined to do this?

I KNOW THIS RIVER.

As Theo and Christian lead us out of the depths of the trees, toward a raging river with a hand-made bridge built over it, I can't help but recognize it. Not because it's something I remember myself, but because I've heard about this river my whole life.

If there was a bridge here when I was a pup, I never knew about it. I don't think my mom did, either. On the night she fled the Wolf District with me, we swam across the river until we ended up on the Lakeview side. Considering we almost drowned—and my mom went on to convince the Wicked Wolf that I *had*—a bridge would've come in handy.

I wonder if that's why my bio-dad had it built. Based on the stories I've been told, that wouldn't surprise me one bit. Just like how he conquered the old Lakeview territory once he didn't have to face my dad again, I could totally see him building a bridge so that he would never have to swim the river himself.

And if that doesn't tell me everything I need to know about Wicked Wolf Walker, then I don't know what will.

Theo and Christian walk ahead of us. This time, when Jace and Duke take up position on either side of me, I let it go. They might pretend we're guests now, but I haven't forgotten how that growling grey wolf went after Jace when they thought we were intruders—and, honestly, I'm pretty sure the Beta knew who we were all along.

About fifty feet away from the far edge of the river, I notice a fourth male waiting for us. The alpha aura slaps out at me first, a sharp contrast to the much weaker one that belongs to Theo.

Even if I didn't recognize him by sight, the way his wolf has mine up and prowling around inside of me is a pretty big clue to his identity.

Three weeks ago, I caught a glimpse of my bio-dad in downtown Muncie, beneath the nearly full moon. At least four blocks had separated us, but I hadn't been able to ignore how much I look like him, even from the distance. I didn't get close enough to check out his features, but the blond hair, bright golden eyes, and alpha aura were just like mine.

The last time, he was also nothing but a distraction in a tailored suit. He came all the way from the Wolf District to Muncie, paying off a vampire to attack me with a silver knife. He didn't want me dead, but controlled, and he used a mutual partnership with an anti-Cadre vamp to get at me.

Of course, he underestimated me and my mate. He

thought I was alone, that I would cower in the face of the psychotic vamp.

Wrong on both counts.

But that was a few weeks ago. One glance at Jack Walker and I realize that he's trying a totally different tactic with me today.

The suit is gone. So is the overly menacing aura. He's wearing a t-shirt that shows off his powerful form, denim jeans, and a good pair of hiking boots that are a sure sign he doesn't plan on shifting right now. He looks closer to thirty than his true age of fifty-two, and his aura exudes pure alpha strength.

I can also smell him. That's new. While he and Shane skulked around my territory, they did something to cover up their scents. Honestly, once I get a snout full of his innate scent, I wish he was *now*.

He smells dark, almost like burned molasses. Something sickly sweet that stayed over the flames for far too long until it turned.

Though I've never caught a whiff like this before, I instinctively recognize it.

It's the scent of pure evil.

Ugh. I want to gag for so many reasons. Probably not the best idea if I don't want to offend him right off the bat.

I swallow my distaste as I purposely meet his stare. While Theo and Christian fall back in an act of deference to their Alpha, I keep going until only five feet stand between us.

He looks at me for a moment, drinking me in, before he gestures to his packmates. "Meet me at my cabin," he tells them, the words echoing with his command. "Bring the other wolves with you. I'd like to speak to my daughter alone."

From behind me, I hear Jace murmur my name. I wave my hand at my side.

It's okay, guys. I got this.

Though it's obvious that Duke and Jace would much rather stay with me, if we want to get this over with sooner than later, we have to pick our battles. I'm not too happy to be left behind with Walker, but my mom made sure I understood that he's another stubborn bastard. If he wants to talk to me alone, he won't say another freaking word until the other four wolves are gone.

Once they are, his honey eyes—so like mine, ugh—track down my face, landing on the hollow of my throat. His lips curl when he spies the marks that curve around the side of it, slashing past my collarbone.

My mating marks. As soon as I made the conscious decision to keep them, the wounds from Ryker's claws went from blood-red to silver to a shocking white by the next morning.

On Ryker's tanned skin, the five claw marks forming a circle over his heart are noticeable, even if

I'm the only one honored enough to see them. Me? I'm much paler than he is. The marks—while in a pretty freaking visible spot—don't stand out as much, especially from a distance. But from the way Walker doesn't even try to hide his disgust at my marks, it doesn't matter if he can see them. He can definitely sense them, and he doesn't like what they mean at all.

Ah. Poor guy. It must really suck to realize that all the plans he has for me are useless now that I've taken a bonded mate. Nothing can separate me and Ryker, not even this psycho Alpha.

I can tell the exact moment he realizes that. The dark edge of his scent turns bitter, his eyes deepening to the color of molasses.

Point, Gem.

I reach into my back pocket, using two fingers to pull out the envelope I jammed in there earlier before showing it to him. "Got your invite."

"Where's Wolfson?"

Walker has a voice much richer than it has any rights to be. Of course. If he looked and sounded as ugly as he truly was, he never would've been able to trick an entire pack into following him. Like his claws and his fangs, he wields his handsome face like another weapon.

My mom warned me about that. She wasn't even a little wrong.

Looking at him, I could totally see why he had no

problem luring half the Wolf District to his bed while he was my mother's mate. If I wasn't able to sense the evil clinging to him—or didn't know the stores of all the bad shit he's done—I might've been fooled once upon a time, too.

His question? On the surface, it seems like nothing more than a casual way of asking after my mate.

Good thing I know better.

Following his lead, I keep my voice pleasant. "He couldn't make it."

"No, but he sent guards to watch over you in his place."

"The invitation didn't say I couldn't bring guests with me."

His eyes sparkle in a dare. "An alpha doesn't need guards."

If he thinks I'm going to bow to him because he's an Alpha and this is his land, I need to set him straight right away otherwise he'll get the wrong idea that I'm some kind of submissive wolf.

Nope. I just played one for twenty-five years.

"An alpha doesn't sneak into another pack's territory and make off with one of their wolves, either," I point out lightly.

"But I didn't."

True. Though it's hard to look past his darkness, he's telling the truth.

Okay. Not surprising. I didn't think he was the

one skulking around Accalia, looking for some way to get at me, especially since we already know that another one of our packmates betrayed us by serving Walker.

"That reminds me, how is Barrow?"

"Barrow?"

"Aidan Barrow."

Walker repeats the name to himself, lifting his hand to scratch at the underside of his chin. "Nope. Can't say I know who you're talking about."

Of course not.

I asked Ryker about Barrow before I left. If I saw the wolf who attacked Trish and dragged her out of Accalia, what did he want me to do? He thought about it long and hard and decided that the betrayal was too deep. He was already a dead wolf, only now I'm sure Walker was his executioner.

As if I needed another reason to know he's nothing but a terror.

You know what? We could do this all day. The faux pleasantries, the tension crackling between us, the promise of everything he's holding over me swinging above my head. He dismissed his goons right as he insisted on Jace and Duke going into the district ahead of me, but I'd be a moron if I believed that he didn't have countless others watching us as we talked. Not because he's afraid of me—I have no doubt in my mind that he'd snap my neck without a second thought if he got the urge to—but because he wants to flex his power.

Dick.

"Okay. You wanted me here. I'm here. Let's get right to it. What the hell do you want from me?"

"Can't a father want to get to know his daughter?"

I so want to tell him pointedly that he's not my father. He's my sperm donor, the male who impregnated my poor mom, and he never cared that I was his pup until he decided I could be of use to him.

Instead of answering his question, I ask one of my own. "Where's Trish?"

I swear to the Luna, if he tries to play it off like he doesn't know where she is, either, I'll walk right out of this dark territory and there isn't a wolf around who could stop me.

"I put her somewhere safe for now. Once I get you settled in here, you can see her, if you'd like."

"She's alive?"

"Of course." Walker's eyes darken, going molten. "I don't know what you've heard about me, my daughter, but I'm not a monster."

He reeeeally needs to stop calling me his daughter. My skin crawls every time he does. "We'll have to agree to disagree about that."

He smiles. I lost my temper and openly insulted him, and he smiles.

"Twenty-five days."

Huh? "Excuse me?"

"Going back to what you said. You asked me what I wanted. I want you to stay in the district for twenty-five days. Let me get to know you. Show you what it's like to live under a true Alpha, not a little boy who's playing pretend. Then, if you decide at the end of those twenty-five days that you'd rather return to Wolfson, I won't stop you."

Yeah, right.

"Why should I believe you?"

"Why shouldn't you?"

Oh. He really doesn't want me to answer that.

Twenty-five days? He's gotta be kidding. I would never agree to that, and I know precisely how to get out of his crazy proposition without offending him to the point that he drops this facade.

"If you mean what you say, swear it. Swear to the Luna."

The Luna is our revered goddess. If he pledges something in her name, even a brutal shifter like Walker would be held to it.

"If that's what you want..." A hint of a smirk curves his lips before he says, "I swear to the Luna that, after those twenty-five days, you can leave with your pack-mate if you want to."

"All of them?"

"Yes. Anyone from the Mountainside Pack who

wants to leave with you, I won't stop them. Is that good enough for you?"

Not quite.

"And they can leave alive, right? You swear that, too?"

"Of course." He agrees so readily, I can't help but wonder what I'm missing. There has to be some catch. After everything I heard about my bio-dad, he's not supposed to be this rational. This agreeable. Something's not right, but I forget all about that when he gives his head a mocking bow and says, "Your turn, daughter."

He's pushing me. My acting days—back when I had to pretend to be Omega Gem—are long behind me. I don't even know if I could fool the Wicked Wolf of the West if I tried, and I'm definitely *not* trying. Anger has my cheeks going hot, my fingers flexing and curling into loose fists, my back stiffening every freaking time he calls me daughter.

So, of course, the big bastard keeps on doing it.

I refuse to give him the satisfaction of snapping my jaws at him.

"It's only for twenty-five days?"

You think I would've understood what he was getting at by such a specific number of days.

"That's right. One for every year you've been gone. If, at the end of the twenty-five days I haven't convinced you to choose the Western Pack, then you and your...

guests can walk away from me. And, I vow to the Luna, I'll never bother you again."

It's the last vow to the Luna that seals it for me. Not even he can break *that* vow.

Ryker's going to hate this. I'm going to have to grovel a ton when I get back to Accalia. I promised him I would only be gone for a couple of days, and now I'm about to agree to *twenty-five* of them. But, hey... if I can accept his groveling for making me spend a whole year believing that he chose Trish Danvers over me, he can understand why I have to say yes to this.

I'll never bother you again.

"Swear to the Luna that the same goes for Ryker. You won't bother my mate or the Mountainside Pack again, either, no matter what happens."

A small smile plays at the corner of his mouth. He's enjoying this.

Asshole.

"I swear that, too."

"Fine." What else can I say? We've come this far, and if this is what I have to agree to to rescue Trish and keep both Jace and Duke safe, I will. "I'll stay."

I don't swear, though. And if he notices that I refuse to even after I pinned him down and made him do it, he doesn't mention it.

Arrogant bastard.

CHAPTER 9

Show no fear.

That's what I tell myself as I walk through the Wolf District alongside Walker. Show no fear because I know damn well that the wolves here are just waiting for me to portray some sign of weakness so that they can pounce.

I have no illusion that they're giving me a wide berth because of anything that I've done. The Wicked Wolf wanted me in California and now he's got me. For twenty-five days—or until I can gather my packmates together and get out of here—I'm a visitor to the Wolf District.

And, as his "honored guest", he tells me that I'm going to stay in one of the more secluded cabins where I'll at least have some semblance of privacy.

I'm going to need it, too.

Now, I'm used to having eyes on me. This... this is

different. I can't tell if they're in awe or afraid or trying to figure out who I am, but no matter where Walker leads me, we're the center of attention.

Thanks. I hate it.

It makes it so much worse that I don't know where the guys are. Walker tells me not to worry about them, that they've gone ahead, but there's a barely-there smirk on his face that has my hackles rising. It's bad enough that my bio-dad made a point to notice that I came with a pair of bodyguards instead of my mate. Keeping us separated is a smart move. It's also bothering me more than I want to admit, since they're pack and my alpha side is pushing to make sure they're okay, but it's exactly what I would've done in Walker's shoes.

I actually expected him to pawn me off on another wolf as soon as he possibly could. When he doesn't, I'm even more on my guard. He didn't strike me as the type of Alpha who would actually tend to any "guest", but he shows me around without purposely drawing attention to us.

Then again, he doesn't really have to. Wherever he goes, his packmates are drawn to him the same way I'm drawn to the Luna. If she's the moon, Walker is their sun. Whether it's out of fear, respect, or mutual affection, I don't know, but the way the Western Pack treats him, it's like he's their god.

Murmurs follow in our wake as he leads me

around the district square. Most of the pack lives in the small houses that border this part of the territory. Like Accalia, there's a need for community, and the square provides it. Walker points out the open dining area, with filled tables, and a spread of food that has my nervous stomach feeling a little hopeful.

Hey. Just because I signed a deal with the devil, it doesn't mean I'm not going to want to eat eventually. It's been hours since I last ate, and the food smells amazing. Too bad that I still don't know the rules of this place. What if, by asking for some food, I'm signaling something I don't mean?

Nah... better not risk it. So even though he'd have to be oblivious not to notice my hunger, I refuse when he asks if I'd like to stop for a snack. He just shakes his head—yeah, I figured he knew—and continues to lead me toward a more open, private tract of land.

He eventually leads me up to a cozy cabin that reminds me of the ones that we have in Accalia. It's one floor, quite quaint, but... I don't know. Something about this particular cabin is familiar.

Weird, right? I might've been born on this land, but my mother escaped with me when I was barely a year old. Just a pup. Not surprisingly, I have no memories of my life before I was adopted by my dad and his pack in Lakeview, only the stories that she told me to prepare me when I was older.

And, yet, as I approach the cabin on the outskirts of

the Western Pack territory, I can't shake the feeling that I know it.

Super weird.

As I move down the walkway, I see that something is placed on the front porch.

Following my stare, Walker says, "I had Theo drop off your suitcases for you so that you have everything you need."

That's right. Duke was carrying one of my suitcases, Jace the other. He handed his to Duke before he went to scout the area ahead of us, so the big shifter ended up with both of them. Once Christian and Theo ordered us further into the district, he insisted on taking the third from me. By then, I was done arguing and I let him.

The suitcases are here. But what about Jace and Duke?

"And my friends? Where are they?"

His eyes brighten. "They're in a cabin of their own, of course. I'm sure you'll see them soon."

And I'm sure he's full of shit.

Something really strange is going on. Most of our limited conversation has been very shallow, neither one of us giving anything away as we crossed the Western Pack territory, but I kept waiting for the sour tinge that he was lying to me. With the Wicked Wolf's reputation, I figured it was inevitable. Only it never happened, so then I decided it was because he was hedging his bets until he got to know me a little better.

But that last answer? It's... it's odd. I don't get the vibe that he's lying to me, but neither do his words ring with truth. Huh. That's never happened to me before.

Maybe I'm looking too much into it. I got his promise, after all. He swore. Jace and Duke will be fine.

At least, they *better* be.

Moving ahead of him, I pick up the first suitcase, then the second. I wait a moment to see if Walker will offer to grab the third, and when he doesn't, I exhale softly. Okay. That's more like what I expected from him.

"Settle in. Get comfortable," he tells me as I shift the other two before reaching for my last suitcase. "I *will* see you soon."

No *sure* in that pointed statement. Pity. I guess it was too much to hope that I could spend the next twenty-five days in the cabin avoiding him.

With a tight-lipped grin I don't mean shot behind me, I turn the knob, shove my shoulder into the door, and let myself inside. Dropping my suitcases to the floor, I use the heel of my shoe to slam the door shut behind me.

Hit the road, Jack, I think with a small smirk of my own. Then, feeling pleased with myself, I look around the front room of the cabin—just in time to notice a pretty female she-wolf standing up from her place at the corner of the couch across from me. She's a few inches taller than me, with a finely-boned, delicate body, and a face that's quietly beautiful. Her mahogany-colored wavy hair spills down her slender back, swaying gently as she takes a few hesitant steps toward me.

My wolf barks a warning at me about two seconds too late. Thanks, girl. A little head's up that we weren't alone would've been nice *before* I shut the door. Too late, and now my wolf has reared up, rumbling as she watches the strange female in alarm.

What the—

Since 'who the hell are you?' seems pretty damn rude, I press my lips together so I don't just blurt it out. Because something about her is... it's not right.

Great.

The first thing I notice beyond the obvious is that she has no discernible scent of her own. The second? Her aura is... different. It's unlike anything I've ever sensed before. In its own way, it's as powerful as an alpha, with the gentleness of an omega, plus the devotion of a beta wolf all mixed into one.

The third thing?

Her eyes.

They're silver. Seriously. And I mean "gleaming like a freshly polished quarter" silver. They're kind of spooky, too. I've seen shifters with dark gold eyes, bright gold eyes, honey gold eyes, hazel eyes, brown eyes, even a few rare ones who have a striking blue color... but silver? Never.

Okay, then.

She smiles. It's a friendly smile, but that doesn't make me feel any better about how she affects my wolf.

"Hi there. I'm Elizabeth Howell. Welcome to my cabin."

Wait—*what*?

"Your cabin? I thought—" I suddenly remember the smirk on Walker's face before I slammed the door in it. And I had been so proud of myself, too. "Shit. Am I in the wrong place?"

"No, no. You're in the right spot. I have a spare bedroom I don't use, and the Alpha decided it would be yours." She hesitates for a moment. "You are Ruby, aren't you?"

"It's Gemma, actually."

Her brow furrows. "But aren't you the Alpha's—"

Oh, *fuck* no. If I had it my way, I wouldn't be the Alpha's anything; at least, not *her* Alpha's. And Ruby? Nope. Nope. Nope.

"My name is Gemma Swann," I say firmly. See? Gemma Swann, not Ruby Walker. "I guess you can say I'm just visiting the Wolf District for a bit."

From the way her smile dips, I can tell that she's still struggling with my name. Oh, well. Just like how I haven't been back here in twenty-five years, the name I was born with has nothing to do with who I am now.

My mom shucked it, choosing to call me Gemma Swann, and that's who I'll always be.

Except, as I have that thought, I think of something that I probably should've realized a couple of weeks ago.

I'm not just Gemma Swann anymore. I'm Gemma Wolfson. Supes don't make it legal the same way that humans do for the simple reason that, once we're bonded mates, there is no such thing as divorce. Who needs a priest or a Justice of the Peace when the Luna's blessing ties two shifters closer than any piece of paper?

"Sorry. I'm newly mated. It's Wolfson now. Gemma Wolfson."

Her pale eyes go impossibly lighter. It's more than a little eerie as she meets my gaze, forcing me to lock eyes with her if only because a dominant wolf will never act submissive if they can help it. Usually, a lower-ranked wolf daring to stare right at an alpha is a challenge, but I can sense that that's not what she's doing, especially since she looks away almost as soon as she notices she's snagged my attention.

I don't know what she is. She's not an alpha, and as delicate as she appears, she's no omega, either. She's... different.

My inner wolf rears back, ears flat against her skull as she continues to gauge this Elizabeth. A pack animal who lives and dies by the hierarchy of rank, she doesn't like *different*.

She's not the only one, either.

"Wolfson?" Elizabeth cocks her head slightly, her long waves falling over her shoulder. "Of the East Coast Wolfsons?"

My eyebrows wing up. "You know them?"

"I didn't always live in the Wolf District," is all she says about that before she shocks me by adding, "Henry Wolfson was the Alpha in Accalia."

Was is the key word there.

I know what she's asking me. If she knew who I was when I walked into her cabin, then I'm betting she knows who my mate is; if not Ryker's name, then that he's another Alpha. Me? I'm the genius who went and confirmed it because it just dawned on me that there's more to a formal mating than just moving into Ryker's cabin, banging him whenever I want, and actually listening when he talks to me instead of refusing because I know best.

"Henry was killed by the former Beta of this Pack," I tell her, my hands folded at my side so that she doesn't notice that my claws are out, curling against my palm. I don't want to threaten her, but I also don't want her thinking we're friends just because the Wicked Wolf is insisting that I stay in this cabin for some reason. "About a year and a half ago."

"Davis killed him? Or... wait. You said a year and a

half ago." Elizabeth nibbles on her bottom lip. "That could've been Rob. Maybe Martin."

Oh. That's right. My bio-dad has a nasty habit of going through Betas the same way I go through hair ties: I'll use the same one for a couple of weeks to pull my blonde hair out of my face before it snaps, or it's stretched out of shape, or I set it down on the bathroom counter and it just—*poofs*—disappears. Something that should last a while is replaced in an instant, as Gem grabs another one from the pack of fifty in her dresser drawer. Jack Walker treats his second-in-commands the same way. I wasn't exaggerating when I threw the number in Shane's face when he confronted me back in Muncie. He was lucky number one hundred and fourteen, and I can only imagine how many were between him and Christian.

"It was Shane," I correct. "Shane Loup. And he wasn't the Wicked Wolf's Beta at the time—he got the promotion to the Mountainside Pack's position after he betrayed their Alpha before trading his loyalty to the Western Pack instead."

And that wasn't the only time Shane betrayed a Wolfson or our pack, either.

"Henry was a good man." For a heartbeat, she dares to meet my gaze again. I swallow my gasp as she says, "He didn't deserve that."

Holy shit. Black eyes. All of a sudden, her irises have gone the color of ink.

Now, that's a bit unusual, isn't it?

Elizabeth lowers her gaze almost immediately, her eyelids gone hooded. I have no doubt in my mind that I saw what I did, and that she's aware of that, too. Now she's hiding, and I don't blame her one bit. Black eyes? I've seen Ryker's go the color of molten lava when I test him—and they're more like pure gold when he's seconds away from coming inside of me—but *black*?

I've never heard of something like that happening before, and I already thought the *silver* was super freaky.

She's hiding? My alpha wolf pushes me to draw her out, almost like a challenge. With a casual toss of my blonde hair, I never take my eyes off of her as I drawl, "Yeah, well, from what I hear, there's a lot of things that the Wicked Wolf does that his victims don't deserve."

My comment was meant to be flippant because, well, that's just me. The way Elizabeth's head jerks up, her eyes wide and staring, makes it clear that she doesn't take it that way.

"Shh... you can't talk like that." She hurriedly waves her hands, her voice dropping to barely a whisper. The inky black of her eyes fades until they're back to the shocking silver. "Not here. The Alpha has eyes and ears everywhere."

Yeah. 'Cause that's not even a *tad* bit surprising.

She looks so incredibly spooked, though, that I feel bad for her.

Okay. Fine. No jabs at the Alpha so that I don't give my new roommate a heart attack.

Got it.

Another grin. This one's more to calm Elizabeth than anything, but it seems to work. "If you say so."

She shudders out a breath, tiptoeing around me, careful not to get too close. Swooping down, she grabs the suitcase nearest to her. "Come with me. I'll show you to your room."

The knock at the front door of the cabin has my inner wolf up and alert. As if making amends for slacking earlier, she tells me exactly who is out there right before Elizabeth pulls it open.

Christian. The Beta.

Ugh.

Behind him, I see that it's finally starting to get dark outside. I lost track of how long I've been at the cabin, putting my stuff in an empty dresser that Elizabeth pointed out to me, but it's gotta be at least six or seven by now.

Elizabeth's hand tightens on the knob. I can hear the metal squeak as she gives the Beta an innocent look. "Christian. What are you doing here?"

"You'll be dining with the Alpha tonight. I'm here to escort you."

Her shoulders immediately slump, but she covers it up with a small smile. "Thank you. I'll be ready in a moment."

His flat eyes turn toward me. "You, too."

Excuse me? "Oh... yeah, I think I'm gonna have to decline. Jet leg, you know? I just finished unpacking. I'd rather stay in if it's all the same. Thanks."

Christian purses his lips. "It's not. The Alpha was very clear. He wants you to see everything the district has to offer. Dinner included. Unless," he adds wryly, "you'd prefer to break your agreement with him so soon."

Right. When I've yet to set eyes on Trish, I've been separated from Jace and Duke, and he has to have my freaking phone.

That's something I noticed when I was unpacking. I'd had my phone turned off for the plane ride, tucked in one of my suitcases so that I didn't leave it behind in Accalia accidentally. Once I was alone in my borrowed bedroom, I immediately searched for it so that I could tell Ryker what was going on before he got too worried.

But it was missing.

I proceeded to throw everything I packed with me onto the floor in my panic, cursing up a storm when I realized that one of the Western Pack wolves must have gone through my things and taken it. Elizabeth eventually crept in to see what was going on, a look of understanding crossing her dainty features when she understood my mood.

Turns out, there's a strict 'no phone' policy in the Wolf District. The Alpha is dedicated to keeping his territory so secluded, they're not even allowed to have contact with the outside world. By me agreeing to stay, I gave up my ability to contact my mate.

Talk about not reading the fine print, huh?

That was almost enough to have me say 'fuck this' and leave. *Almost*, though, because I didn't come all this way to fail.

Twenty-five days. I gave my word. If I break it, it's about the same as me challenging Walker. And while I'm barely resisting the urge to shift and go for his thick throat, I have to remember that it's not just about me anymore. I still haven't seen Trish, though he swears she's being well taken care of. I brought Jace and Duke with me here, and I'm not going to do anything to jeopardize them.

It's not just the four of us here, either. I have Accalia to worry about, too. The Wolf District is clearly way bigger—and Walker a way bigger threat—than any of the other Alphas in the collective know. If I push the Wicked Wolf too hard, he could use my new status as one-half of the Alpha couple of the Mountainside Pack to attack us all instead of just me.

Luna damn it. I guess I'm going to dinner.

"Let me go get my shoes."

The Wicked Wolf of the West has a reputation that has only grown to a myth-like status over my lifetime.

By now, I've heard every rumor about him because of my dad. As the Alpha of Lakeview, he was determined to keep his pack protected from any prospective threats. When it came to my mom, though? He's always been fanatical about her safety. It didn't matter that she broke her promise of a mating to Jack Walker twenty-five years ago. My dad is devoted to her, and he's never been able to understand how the Wicked Wolf could let her go.

She was his fated mate, but Walker preferred to bed any willing—and, from the rumors I've heard, not so willing—females in his pack. No one was strong enough to say no to the Alpha, and they rarely did.

It looks like things have hardly changed. As Christian leads the two of us to the front table in the middle of the district square—he calls it the Alpha's table—I pass quite a few female shifters milling about. At least three of them reek of Walker. The only way to embed a scent that deeply into another shifter's skin is through mating. The more animalistic the sex, the stronger the scent left behind. It would only last a few hours unless he mated them again, and his unmistakable scent is notably fresh.

My stomach goes queasy. The Wicked Wolf's been a busy, busy male today.

I try desperately not to think about what—and *who*—he's been doing since I slammed my door in his face. He insisted that me and Elizabeth join him for dinner, but if I dwell too much on him hopping from bed to bed since I saw him a few hours ago, I won't be able to choke a damn thing down. And wouldn't that just give him the perfect reason to be offended?

The preening bastard is already seated at the elaborate table when we approach it. I see that there are four different serving dishes heaped with food, but only two empty place settings. One is set in front of Walker. One is directly opposite of him. A third seat is placed next to that one, making it clear he intends for me and Elizabeth to sit across from him.

Almost dutifully, Elizabeth takes the seat without a plate. With only one chair left, I sink into that.

Christian nods—or, you know, *bows*—at Walker before disappearing into the throng of packmates all eager to get a table near their Alpha.

Once we're seated, Walker clears his throat.

"You look lovely, girls," he says, and I'm pretty sure I'm not the only one who hears the slime oozing out of his annoyingly rich voice. Then, his gaze sliding over to me, he adds all too casually, "I tried my damnedest to take Elizabeth as my mate. Did she tell you? Sometimes I wonder if I should've fought harder to claim such a dark-haired beauty as mine." His lips quirk. "Guess you could say, I always had a thing for a pretty brunette."

Like, oh, my mom?

Did she tell you?

Can't say that she did. I talked to my new roommate for a little while before I started to unpack but, somehow, the topic of Walker wanting Elizabeth to replace my mother as his mate just never came up.

Huh. Imagine that.

CHAPTER 10

Keeping my expression neutral, I peek over at her. Unlike me, she can't hide how horrified she looks. She's smart, though—or, the snarky side of me whispers, she's *trained*. Quick as a flash, she drops her gaze, taking only a few seconds to completely lose the disturbed expression. Her hands are folded in her lap, her strange eyes downcast and demure.

Me? I boldly meet the weight of Walker's heavy, leering stare. There's a dare tucked in the corner of his smirk, and something has me re-running his words through my head again.

Tried my damnedest...

Should've fought harder...

My wolf's instincts—and what she can sense coming from the dark alpha she's facing off against—has the soft, pale hairs on my arms standing on end.

Add that to her look of horror and I know that the only reason why I'm not sitting with a mated couple right now is because Elizabeth said no.

A mate gets to choose. She didn't, but I've heard enough about the Wicked Wolf to know that he wouldn't have made it easy for her to refuse him.

Suddenly, the missing place setting makes a lot more sense. That, and his insistence that I take over her territory. Bastard thinks he's pitting us against each other, does he?

Then and there, I decide to make Elizabeth my ally. Especially since my wolf has this urge to throw my body between her and my bio-dad in a bid to keep her Alpha from forcing her into his bed.

He knows it, too. Worse, from the way the air surrounding our table goes thick with tension, I can sense he's enjoying himself immensely.

Pardon me while I puke.

With a lazy crook of his finger, Walker pulls his glass closer to him. It leaves a trail of condensation on the wooden tabletop. He swipes it with the side of his hand before picking up his glass in the most precise movement. With a grin that makes me want to rake my claws down his perfect face, he takes a sip, absolutely sure that he has full command of my attention.

Prick.

"Thirsty?" he asks slyly.

I can't stop myself from glancing down at the table

again. Next to my plate, there's a glass of water. But only next to mine.

Elizabeth doesn't get one of those, either, I see.

I seize the opportunity.

For some reason, my knee-jerk reaction is to protect her, but she at least chose to be here. In the Wolf District. Seated at the Alpha's table. Bowing down to the Wicked Wolf. She can have the glass.

Using the back of my hand, I shift it toward her.

Sorry, Elizabeth, but I've already made this mistake once before. I accepted a Coke poisoned with mercury from Audrey Carter and, boy, did I live to regret *that*.

Mercury—*quicksilver*—saps a shifter's strength, cutting us off from our beast. For the first time in my life, I wasn't an alpha wolf. Luna, I was barely a weak kitten. No claws, no fangs, no shift. It took the rest of the night until the worst of the poison wore off and I was myself again, but the hours of vulnerability in Ryker's basement aren't as easy to shake off. I pretend I have, even going so far as forgiving Audrey, but I only did that because she honestly believed that she was looking out for the good of the pack and Ryker when she poisoned me.

The monster who sired me? I wouldn't put it past the Wicked Wolf of the West to poison me just for shits and giggles.

My suspicion only grows when he *tsks* his tongue. "That was for you."

Yup. And now I *definitely* don't want it.

"I'll drink something later. Elizabeth can have mine."

"She isn't thirsty. Are you, Elizabeth?"

"No, Alpha."

His perfectly styled blond eyebrows lift as he nods at her. "Then give my daughter her glass back. Now."

The order isn't necessary. Elizabeth has already shoved it toward me before dropping her hands back in her lap. The perfect submissive wolf—only if she's truly a submissive, then I'm freaking Santa Claus.

"Of course, if you don't trust that my intentions are pure..." Walker nudges his own glass a few inches past his side of the table. "Here you go. Take mine."

Oh. I'm *fucked*.

What do I do? Swallow a doctored drink that might leave me defenseless? Or accept what he's offering me knowing that it's not as easy as simply quenching my thirst?

In shifter culture, sharing a meal with another wolf—or taking a sip from their glass—has a very special meaning. It's like you're agreeing to them saying: I will protect you. I will feed you. I will take care of you.

You're mine.

Now, I only went along with this sideshow because, technically, the Wicked Wolf is my birth father, and Christian made it clear I didn't have a choice. The poster child for deadbeat dads—with an emphasis on 'dead' since he would've been happy drowning me when I was a pup—it sucks having to admit that we share some of the same DNA, but if that allows me to explain away sharing a meal with him to my wolf, I'll take it. Plus, we're sitting among his packmates, and he did say it was a community spread. The food isn't *technically* from him.

The glass of water, though? It would be.

Just like following Christian and Elizabeth to the Alpha's table, I also don't have any choice about this. I saw him drink the water out of his glass so I highly doubt that he messed with it. Can I say the same about the one waiting for me?

Nope.

Damn it.

I snatch his glass, using my thumb to wipe the rim before I lift it to my lips.

He watches with a smirk as I drain half of it.

There. Happy?

Walker seems to be. Once I set the glass down, he gestures at the plates. There are steaks, potatoes, sausages, seasoned vegetables, rolls, and more piled up on the serving trays. The last one is topped off with a pile of cream-filled donuts that has my wolf and her sweet tooth eager for a bite.

"Go on. Eat up, my daughter. And then we can get to know each other a little better."

If those are his terms, I'd honestly rather starve. I

might've refused, too, if it wasn't for my wolf. She reminds me that, without fuel, I'll weaken quicker. Since being weak is absolutely unacceptable—and I already drank the water—I say screw it. I fill my plate, ignoring the way his honey gold eyes seem to glitter as I reach for the thickest steak instead of the donut my wolf is whining at me to eat first.

At least Elizabeth is allowed to pick at a roll.

I try to tell myself that it could be a strange quirk of being part of a pack. The Alpha always gets first pick of a meal, and the poor she-wolf is sitting with *two* alphas. Either she feels as queasy as I do, or her instincts are telling her she has to wait until we've been sated.

Whatever her reasons, I promise myself that I'm going to load up a plate when we're done. If it's more that Walker wants her as a fixture than a guest, I'll rely on my own instincts. I won't let a packmate go hungry, even if I have to pretend like I'm taking some of the food to go.

We eat in silence. Us shifters take our food seriously, and it's not like I really have anything I want to say to my bio-dad. Once our plates are clear, he waves his hand. A red-headed male appears suddenly at the side of the table. He clears the dirty plates, the remaining food, and our water glasses. All he leaves behind are the donuts and Elizabeth's half-touched roll.

Walker's smirk is back on his face. Jerk. From his reaction, I'm betting he figured out I was planning on packing up the rest of that and he made it so that I'd have to ask for more food if I wanted it. How much do you want to bet he'd get his rocks off making me beg for it?

It's the power that's the point. It's the need to have all of the control.

I can't forget that. Not if I want to beat him at his own game.

And I *will*.

He leans back into his seat, the perfect picture of a satisfied male. "I hope you were done."

If the company was better, I could probably put away another steak easy. "I couldn't eat another bite," I say sweetly.

Elizabeth's kitchen is stocked. I checked it out myself earlier. We can always eat later at the cabin if we want to, no strings attached. Considering how little of her roll she got down, she's probably banking on it. Dainty or no, she's a shifter, and shifters need to eat.

Too bad Walker doesn't seem to think dinner's over just because the food's been cleared away.

"I'm glad to have been able to feed you." *Gag.* "But now that we've eaten, I'd like to talk to you." He pauses for a moment, and it's clear he's making sure that I'm hanging on his every word before he adds, "About bonds. I want to talk to you about mate bonds."

In the seat next to me, Elizabeth stiffens. I guess his opening comment about him trying to claim her as his mate wasn't just to shock me, or to bring up the sore point of how awful he was to my mother.

This dinner really is about mates, isn't it?

He wants me curious. I purposely go for bored. "Oh? What about them?"

Like it did when we first met, his gaze goes straight to my mating marks. "When I heard that Loup failed me, I assumed you would go through with mating Wolfson. The Danvers girl later confirmed it. Still, I had hoped they got it wrong."

As if wiping off his stare, I run my fingertips over the jagged lines. Even though Ryker isn't here with me, and the distance has turned our bond from an unbreakable rope to a whisper of a thread, touching his marks almost makes me feel like he's sitting on the other side of me instead of across the country. I soak up some of his strength before daringly meeting Walker's eyes again.

"They didn't."

He makes a soft noise in the back of his throat. "Ah, but what if I told you that you didn't have to stay with him? That, in the Wolf District, you could have any male you wanted? Think about it. When you finally decide to make our pack your home again, you won't have to be lonely when Wolfson stays behind on his precious mountain."

My wolf snaps her jaws at what he's suggesting. I don't blame her. A bonded mate is for forever. Even *thinking* about being with another male after me and Ryker claimed each other is enough to make me want to throw up the entire dinner I just ate.

"I would tell you not to waste your breath. I'm happily mated, and nothing can change that."

He goes on as if he hadn't heard the first part of what I said.

"Don't be so sure about that. And, true, your next mate bond won't be a fated bond, but I've seen plenty of wolves enjoy themselves with a mate they've chosen as their own."

Did I think I was going to puke before? The only thing that keeps me from heaving—or saying something I'd regret—is my jaw clenching when he says, "Speaking of, how is my dear Janelle?"

My jaw isn't the only part of me that reacts. Hearing my mom's name in his voice has my fingers flexing, then forming a tight fist. I forgot that I was holding the steel fork in my hand. The metal creaks as the fork bends in half.

Whoops.

His eyes light up. I can't tell if he's amused or excited as he darts out his tongue, licking the corner of his lip right before he asks, "Does she miss me?"

That does it.

"Miss you?" I offer him a tight, meaningless grin as

I set my destroyed fork down on the tabletop with a *clink*. "Yeah. Sure. Like a bad case of mange, maybe."

His smirk slides off of his face, features twisting in a mask of fury so quickly, I suddenly understand why every shifter in the States warns of his temper.

Ah, great. Good going, Gem. You couldn't even make it one full day before pushing him past his fake friendliness.

Well, what did he expect? My mother is a Luna-damned saint. She put up with this cruel bastard for years, always just avoiding being tied to him for life. He hurt her, he cheated on her, he tried to force her to bond with him... he did everything a forever mate never would, and he has the balls to ask me if she misses him?

"Ruby. Don't you forget that you're here as my guest." His voice develops an edge as sharp as my claws, snapping on the last half of *guest* with all the force of a bear trap. "I invited you, and I can easily revoke that invitation."

"No, you can't," I retort. Might as well get this out of the way now while we're still pretending to get along. "You swore to the Luna."

"I did," he agrees readily. That should've been my first warning, because then he shifts in his seat, his focus on Elizabeth. She'd been so quiet, I almost forgot she was there, but he obviously hasn't. "Elizabeth, have you told Ruby why I keep you so close?"

Her expression goes stark this time, her silver eyes wide as she sinks in her seat. I get the feeling she was hoping that we had both forgotten she was still there.

Feeling a little guilty that I actually had, I decide to cover for her. Hey. It's not *her* fault she's stuck at the table with me and my dysfunctional sperm donor. "No. And stop calling me 'Ruby'. My name is Gemma."

He ignores that. Why am I not surprised?

"You're quite unique, my daughter." Luna, I *hate* how he keeps calling me that, but not as much as when he says 'Ruby'. Pick your battles, Gem. Pick your battles. "A female alpha. So rare, I never even thought it could be possible. You were part of my pack a whole year and I missed it. Then your mother stole you from me, made me believe I lost my chance at the future. I'm going to fix that, and if I have to, I'll use Elizabeth to do it."

"Alpha..." Her voice is shaky. "I don't—"

"Shut up, Elizabeth," snaps Walker.

Her mouth immediately clicks shut.

He laughs. There's enough pure enjoyment in the sound to send shivers coursing down my spine. "I was just telling my daughter that, unique as she is, she's not the only special one. You might not be a female alpha, but your gift is just as rare, isn't it?"

She knows better than to answer him with words. Instead, she gives him a slow nod.

He doesn't seem to notice how reluctant she is—or,

if he does, he doesn't give a shit. "The silver eyes give her away, you see. It's the mark of the Luna, and she's just as powerful. Having her near helps hide the district from my enemies. She conceals our scents, making us better predators. Elizabeth's nature even neutralize some alpha gifts," he adds, "but that's not all, Ruby. Do you know what else she can do?"

Gemma. "No."

And, suddenly, I'm a little worried to find out.

"One touch," Walker says. "One touch from my pet and Janelle's bond to Booker is gone. *Poof.* I'll finally be free to take my mate back, and all it will take is one touch."

Booker. *Paul* Booker. My dad—and my mom's chosen mate.

Hang on… is he really trying to say that Elizabeth and her weirdo eyes have the power to snap mate bonds?

Oh, *hell* no.

"You can't do that." Forget that, if I believe him—and I don't see Elizabeth jumping in to deny it—I've just discovered that something I took for granted as unbreakable might actually be broken. I won't let anyone come between my parents.

Especially not this asshole.

"Why not? The Luna gave Janelle to me. Maybe I want her back."

"She's bonded to my dad. They chose each other. *That*'s why not."

His canines punch out. It's the slightest loss of control before he purses his lips, hiding them from my sight. When he smiles again, his teeth are blunt and gleaming and infinitely more terrifying.

I can handle fangs. But the predator trying to pretend he's harmless? Yeah fucking *right*.

"And, like I told you, all it will take is one touch from my pet." Reaching out, he picks up the plate of donuts he hasn't touched yet, holding it out to me. "Dessert?"

I have to swallow the answer I really want to give him. He might have concealed his true nature as easily as he lost control, but I know what I saw. And I know better than to try my luck in defying him again, now that he's made it clear what leverage he plans on using to get me to behave.

And, okay, he might have pegged me correctly. Threaten my mom? Yeah. To save her from having to look at that smarmy, cruel face ever again, I'll be Good Girl Gem. I'll be whatever it takes to get these twenty-five days to pass as quickly as possible so that I can get out of here in one piece.

Hell if I'll be Ruby, the doting daughter, though.

I shake my head. And my wolf—who was salivating over the donuts earlier—curls her muzzle up over her fangs as she recognizes that he's far more dangerous than she first thought.

"Suit yourself."

And with one vicious bite, he tears the donut in half with canines that are suddenly longer than they were before.

Yeah, yeah.

Message received.

CHAPTER 11

I have to give myself credit. I make it through the rest of dinner only imagining gutting him in my head without actually doing it. Then, when Christian returns to walk me and Elizabeth back to the cabin, I keep a tight hold on my wolf's leash. No one knows that I'm on the edge of going feral.

But once we're inside and Christian is gone again?

I drop the damn leash.

Flexing my fingers, my claws shoot out. I have the points prickling the side of her throat, palm curved around the hollow, before Elizabeth has any idea that I was about to attack.

I don't know what the hell she is, but I know what she's *not*. She's not an alpha, so I at least have one advantage. When the Wicked Wolf used his dominance against her, she immediately obeyed. I'm not above doing the same.

"Tell me," I command, voice throbbing with the power of my alpha wolf. "Tell me who you are."

She barely dares to swallow. Her silver eyes begin to glow, a pleading look filling them, but that doesn't sway me.

I squeeze. "He called you his pet. *What* are you?"

"I'll tell you," she squeaks out. "I swear to the Luna, just let me go. Please! Don't hurt me!"

It's my alpha nature. Deep down, I'm a fighter—but I'm also a fierce protector.

One chance. Damn it. I'll give her *one* chance.

I release my claws, taking a few purposeful steps away from her before I lunge again.

Her fingers are trembling as she strokes her neck, probing the tiny nicks I left in her skin.

The way I see it, Elizabeth got off lucky. If she really is Walker's 'pet', if she works with him and is willing to do something that will hurt my mom, she got off very lucky.

She won't get that lucky again.

"I'm waiting," I snap.

"Okay." She swallows for real this time, more of a gulp, as she slowly lowers her hand. "What am I... honestly, I don't know what it's really called, but my mom always said our line was Luna-touched."

I blink, my wolf as puzzled as I am. "Is that supposed to mean something to me?"

"Not really," Elizabeth confesses. "As far as I know,

we're the only shifters who have these strange kinds of gifts. Everyone in my family who has one was born with these." With her pointer finger, she gestures at her silver eyes. "It manifests differently in each of us. I always thought the way I covered up a shifter's scent just by touching them was all I could do... but I discovered a couple of years ago that I was wrong. Sometimes, when I touch a mated supe, I can break their bond instantly."

"How?" It slips out without me meaning it to. "That's not possible!"

Even after Walker held that exact threat over my head, I guess I still couldn't bring myself to truly believe it—but though I can't tell if she's being honest right now, my wolf assures me that she is.

And then she goes on to explain her gift, and I wish she *was* lying to me.

"Oh, but it is. I wish it wasn't, but it is. If a mated pair isn't happy in their mating, if there's even an ounce of hesitation between either of them, all I have to do is brush their hand and... like the Alpha said: *poof*. The bond's gone, and it takes an awful lot to get the Luna to bless the same mating all over again." She glances away from me. "And that's if she's even willing to be persuaded."

"Holy shit." What else can you say to something like that? "I mean, whoa. That's some kind of gift you got there."

"It's not a gift." She was already shaking her head before I had finished my stunned statement. "You have to understand... it's a *curse*. It's brought me nothing but trouble. I even had to leave my home pack because of it, and when I came to live in California, I swore that I'd take the secret with me to the grave."

Yeah. I know all about those kinds of secrets—and how easily it is to let it slip in the heat of the moment. "What happened? How did you end up in the Wolf District in the first place?"

Her silver eyes darken to the color of mercury. "It was... it was an accident."

"Accident?"

"My life's been one big accident from puphood," murmurs Elizabeth. "Then I left my home pack... but I guess I was a lone wolf that wasn't really meant to be alone. When I stumbled on a shifter territory, I thought I could start over." With one more sharp shake, she admits roughly, "I was *wrong*."

Because the Wolf District isn't just any shifter territory. It belongs to Wicked Wolf Walker.

"He said he wanted you to be his mate."

She gulps, a shadowed look falling over her pretty face. "He did. As soon as he realized I was different, he tried to make me choose him."

Because the mate always chooses.

"But you didn't. He didn't force you to, either."

And isn't that a surprise?

"Only because I told him that I couldn't mate *any* wolf, not just him. That, with my 'gift', it's impossible for me to bond with another soul. Think about it. If my touch breaks bonds, how can I ever have one? Unless it's with a mate I choose... and I'll *never* choose him." For a moment, her silver eyes bleed black again, showing off an emotion I know too well. That's hatred, all right. The hatred she has for Walker that she must keep locked down deep inside. "He stopped trying to get me to agree after that, but I sealed my fate anyway. To you, this is a cabin," she says, gesturing around the living room, her voice sounding tired as the black begins to fade away. She sighs. "To me? It's nothing but a gilded cage."

Maybe it is—but I'm beginning to see that she hasn't had her wings clipped just yet. She might be small in stature, but she's pretty strong, too.

"There are other packs out there," I tell her pointedly. "You don't have to stay here, you know."

A hollow laugh. "Of course I do. He'll kill me if I don't. And even if he decides I'm worth more to him alive, he told me that if I ever betray him, he'll bring me in front of the rest of the Alphas and tell them I'm an abomination—and then *they* will kill me."

She says it so matter-of-factly, I hate to know how many times he threatened her with death in order to make her so beaten down. Something tells me it wasn't just once or twice. When he called her his 'pet', he wasn't kidding. He domesticated Elizabeth long before I was even on his radar.

As if I needed a reason to hate him any more than I already do.

I move toward her. She flinches—though her throat is completely healed, she's probably remembering what it was like to have me seconds away from slicing it open—but she's resigned enough to stay where she is.

I purposely meet her stare, showing her the power of my wolf. "Listen to me, Elizabeth. I don't know what you've heard about me, but I'll tell you this: I *am* a female alpha. If you want to leave with me when I go, I won't let him stop me. It's your choice."

"Gemma—"

"You heard him at dinner. You heard him talk about my mom. He kept her trapped here for three years. Do you know how disappointed in me she'd be if she found out I left you behind?"

"Three years?" echoes Elizabeth.

I nod.

A wistful sigh. "I've been here for two already."

"Twenty-four more days," I point out. "I'm walking out of here in twenty-four more days after this one. You want to come, I'll make it happen. But, until then, it looks like we're both stuck here together. I hope you're okay with that."

She casts a wary look over at the door to my

bedroom. I know what she's thinking. It's what a lot of shifters who don't know me very well think.

I'm not as delicate as she is, though I'm still pretty small. Tiny. Breakable. For Luna's sake, throw me a mini-skirt and a pom-pom, and I could pass for a high school cheerleader. No one ever guesses that I can be as impulsive or as vicious as I am. I've used that to my advantage one way or another my whole life.

Now she knows it, too. To Elizabeth, I'm probably as dangerous as the Wicked Wolf of the West is, even if I'm the one who is offering her her freedom.

I hate thinking that I have anything in common with Walker. I can't do shit about my genes; as much as I want to deny it, he *is* my birth father, so short of dying my hair and wearing colored contacts, I'm destined to be his twin in appearance. My level of dominance is something else I can't change. I'm dominant. I'm an alpha. It is what it is.

But I'm not heartless. And I'm not *cruel*.

I'll never hurt someone for the sake of seeing them in pain. I protect myself and what's mine. That's all.

"Promise me."

Something about my tone has her head whipping toward me, her expression still haunted. "Promise you what?"

"Promise me that, no matter what happens, you won't do anything to my bond. The one I have with my mate."

"I told you. I *can't*. It only works if either or both of the mated pair want it dissolved. I'm Luna-touched, Gemma, not the Luna. I can't create bonds, and I definitely can't break them if they're truly meant to be."

That's good to know—but it's not a promise.

I smile, making sure my fangs are showing. "Then it shouldn't be a problem to promise me that." When she hesitates, I decide to throw her a bone for scaring her so badly before. "Look. Here's the thing. If you promise me that you won't mess with my bond, I'll swear to the Luna that you have nothing to fear from me. I'll never hurt you. Understand?"

I know the moment that she does. Her eyes brighten, relief flooding through her strange aura.

"Okay," she says at last. "I promise."

"Then I swear." I let my smile fall away. "You don't have to be afraid of me."

My smile falls away, but hers slowly returns to her face. "I know that *now*, Gemma."

Know what else? Since we're going to be living together for a while...

"Hey. Call me Gem."

Sleep doesn't come easy that night.

Did I expect it to? No. Not even a little. Though I received Elizabeth's promise, I still can't get over the truth of her curse—because, yeah. If you ask me, that's one hell of a curse.

She seems like a sweetheart, though. Incredibly secretive in regards to her rough past, but once she recognizes that she has a possible ally in me, she's a lot more open when it comes to her feelings for the Wicked Wolf.

Spoiler alert: she hates his stinking guts.

I freaking *knew* it.

Elizabeth is a smart she-wolf. A survivor. After she warned me that there are eyes and ears everywhere, I start to pick up on what she means by the seemingly simple things she says. Once she realizes that I'm quick enough to get her code—and that I'm all aboard the "Walker sucks" train—she lets down her guard enough that the rest of the night isn't as awkward as it was when I, you know, had her by the throat.

She forgave me for that, by the way. Muttering something about how that wasn't the worst way someone reacted when it came to her gift, she tells me it's fine. It's not fine, obviously, but I let it go because it's just as clear that she's not the argumentative type.

We stay up way too late. That's on me. The jet lag I used as an excuse earlier started kicking my ass about an hour after dinner, but between wanting to learn more about the Luna-touched Elizabeth and subconsciously avoiding my empty bed, I kept her talking. Only when her eyes start to droop, her voice gone raspy from overuse, do I realize that I'm being a coward.

And I *hate* being a coward.

It's just… Ryker ruined me. There. I admit it. He ruined me because, once I started sleeping in the same bed with him, I completely forgot what it was like to be in one alone. The bed in Elizabeth's spare room is a twin, but it seems so huge without him there. The pillow isn't comfortable at all. My bond is a faint echo of what it is when he's close by, and I force myself to ignore it if only because it hurts, knowing we're apart, and that it's all my fault.

What's even worse is that I have twenty-three more nights of this crap.

Ugh.

I don't know how late it was when I finally fell asleep, but when I'm woken by a knock at my door, I can definitely say that I haven't had enough hours down. For a moment, still caught in a dozy world between dreamland and rageville, I blindly grab a pillow and chuck it somewhere over my head. It slaps the wall with a muffled *thump*.

The knocking doesn't stop.

Forcing my eyes open, I jolt in place when I see the unfamiliar surroundings. In the borrowed room, I have a small bed and a dresser. That's all. But it's not *my* bed and dresser, and it takes me longer than it should to remember where I am. When I do, I growl under my breath, throwing back the thin blanket Elizabeth lent me. I ended up falling asleep in my t-shirt and jeans last night so at least I'm dressed enough to confront the shifter who's about to lose a paw *because they just won't stop fucking knocking.*

My hair's a blonde rat's nest. My shirt's crooked. I trip over one of my boots in my haste to get to the door. Snarling, I kick it out of the way, barely reacting when the force of my kick has the tip of the boot leaving a crater in the wall.

Oops.

My face is contorted in an angry expression when I yank the door open. I warned my new roommate that I wasn't much of a morning person and she still decided to wake me up. Way I see it, she deserves the snarl.

I really thought it would be Elizabeth out there. She's the only one who has a right to be in this cabin, and it never dawned on me that someone else would invade it.

But it's not Elizabeth. She's standing a few feet behind the male shifter, nibbling on her pointer fingernail nervously. No doubt she feels my annoyance mixed with my wolf's dominance slapping her in the face as I brace the doorway, claws scraping its jamb.

I blink. Something about the black-haired, light-eyed male is familiar. The cleft in his chin, too. I feel like I've seen him before, but I've set eyes on so many shifters since I arrived at the Wolf District yesterday that it's possible I cataloged him in passing, then completely forgot about him when he wasn't a threat to me.

That's when his aura seems to clear the last of my hazy, angry drowsiness, knocking me the rest of the way awake.

It's an *alpha* aura.

Oh, yeah. That's right. I *do* know this guy.

What was his name again?

Ah!

"Theo. What the hell are you doing here?"

His eyes are pretty much laughing at me as he takes in my appearance. "Good morning to you, too, Gemma."

I'm not in the mood. Flipping him the bird with one hand, I try to tame my wild blonde mane with the other as I keep the scowl in place. "Yeah. Yeah. What do you want?"

"It's a new day. I thought you'd like to see your... friends."

Smart wolf. At the last second, he didn't call them guards the way that his Alpha did.

I take a deep breath. This early in the morning, it's hard for me to go from pissed off to pleasant. Ask Aleks. We got along amazingly mainly because he's a vamp and, well, I've never been much of a morning person no matter where I lived. It's one of the reasons why I chose to work at Charlie's when I needed a job. Bar hours were right up my alley.

Add that to a stressful situation, an unfamiliar—and empty—bed, and little sleep, and he's lucky that I barked first before I bit.

Okay. *Okay*. He's here to bring me to see Jace and Duke. Friends... I wouldn't necessarily use that word about Trish, but I'd like to see her, too.

Besides, this is Theo. If it was Walker offering, or even his grim-faced Beta, I might've said no out of pure spite. But it's the friendly alpha who, so far, is the only wolf I've spoken to in the district who hasn't, at one point, really ticked me off.

Exhaling roughly, I force myself to smile. "Give me ten minutes to change and freshen up. I'll be right out."

"Take your time. There's no rush."

For him, maybe.

For me? Yeah. The prospect of seeing my packmates, of making sure that they're getting on all right... it has me rushing back to my room.

There's a small bathroom attached to it, with a shower stall and a sink. Grabbing the first change of clean clothes I can find, I dash in there. No time for a shower, but I scrub my face, splash water in my hair so that I can wrangle it into a ponytail, slather on fresh deodorant, and brush my teeth. Once I'm as presentable as I'm going to get in a handful of minutes, I change my clothes, then shove my shoes back on.

When I leave the room, I find Elizabeth on the couch, Theo standing over her with an affable look on his handsome face. From what I can tell about her in the short time since I've known her, she looks way more relaxed, even if she can't shake her perpetually guarded nature.

Hmm. Maybe my instincts are spot-on for a change and he's one of the good ones here. My mom told me that most of the wolves in the Wolf District were decent shifters in a shitty situation. They didn't necessarily agree with the way that the Wicked Wolf ran things, but their paws were tied. The lower-ranks—the deltas, the gammas, the omegas—they need a powerful Alpha in charge. And if there's one thing no one can deny, it's that Walker *is* powerful.

Plus, Theo doesn't set my wolf off the same way that some of the other Western Pack wolves do. Maybe it's because he seems kind and friendly, and his alpha wolf isn't trying to play dominance games with mine so far. In fact, my wolf seems to think of him more as another ally than an enemy, and I trust my girl more than I trust myself.

"Okay," I announce. "I'm ready."

Theo turns slightly. His attention is on me now even as he addresses Elizabeth. "You want to come with us?"

She shakes her head. "No, thanks. I think I'm gonna go back to sleep."

Lucky. If it wasn't for Theo's tempting offer, I'd still be getting some extra z's of my own.

"Maybe you can join me for lunch later in the square." Then, almost as an afterthought, he glances at me. "You, too, Gemma. If you want. No pressure."

I get the vibe that he's being a generous host if only to make up for my bio-dad's well-earned reputation. The way he was looking at Elizabeth before, it's easy to see where his interest lies. He probably asked me because he doesn't want to be rude.

In a flash, I remember how Elizabeth told me last night that, because of her curse, she can't form a bond with another shifter unless she *chooses* to. Though my ability to sense when someone is lying doesn't seem to work the way it should around her—probably because of that same curse—I think she's exaggerating a little. Maybe she can, maybe she can't, but she definitely didn't want to bond to Walker.

Not that I blame her.

But Theo... he seems like a cool wolf. And if I bite off more than I can chew and I can't figure out a way to get her out of here, if he takes her as his mate, maybe *he* could.

"We'll have to see," I say eventually. I'd prefer not to cockblock him if I don't have to. If he wants a quiet lunch with Elizabeth, there's no reason I have to tag along. "But can we go see my packmates first?"

"Sure. They're actually in a cabin not too far from

here. I'll take you right now." He waves at Elizabeth. "I hope I'll see you later."

Elizabeth makes a noncommittal noise in the back of her throat as she returns the wave.

I wait for Theo to head toward the door first before flashing Elizabeth a thumb's up behind his back. Her lips curve in a small smile that's fleeting, but I know it's there.

After that, my focus is entirely on making sure I can remember how to navigate my way to where Duke and Jace are staying.

When Theo says it's not that far, he's got it in one. Within ten minutes, he's guiding me toward a row of three cabins. I know immediately which one belongs to my guards because there they are: Jace is sitting on the porch in front of the cabin, knees bent to his chest with his arms wrapped around them while Duke is pacing restlessly in front of him.

Thank the Luna.

As I rush toward them, I can't help but do a double-take, just to make sure that I'm not seeing things wrong. Something about the big, dark-haired shifter wearing a hole in the grass has me having a hard time believing that it's him.

But it is. That's Duke, all right.

The pacing... now, that *is* different.

Jace is normally the one who can't be contained, burning off all of his excess dominance by constantly moving. He's not an alpha, not quite, but he's not a true delta wolf, either. Some blend of the two, he's a born soldier. A guardian.

Duke, on the other hand, is built like a brick house. He has a tendency to loom, and he's so stingy with his words, it's like each one costs him a dollar. A good male to have at your back, so solid and unflappable that he let me change his freaking name from Jack to Duke without even a blink, but now he's pacing?

Something's *wrong*.

CHAPTER 12

"Jace! Duke!"

As soon as they recognize it's me, Jace jumps to his feet. Duke pauses mid-pace, though his eyes never stop moving, as if he's searching for something he can't quite find.

My jog becomes a sprint as I leave Theo in my dust. Jace meets me, while Duke lumbers toward us, his thick body a bundle of electric nerves that snap and spark at me as I close the gap between us.

I look at him first. "What's going on?"

I look at Duke, but it's Jace who answers me.

"They told us to wait here for you." They... it doesn't take a genius to figure out who *they* could be. Especially since no one has mentioned my packmates since Walker forced us to be separated yesterday afternoon. "Are you alright, Alpha?"

I never thought I would actually be happy to hear one of my guards use that title in regards to me, but I am if only because it means that *they're* okay. Out of the corner of my eye, I see Theo wince. Yeah, yeah. I'm not the Alpha of the Western Pack, so it probably weirds him out to hear me called that, but tough shit. I'm part of the Alpha couple of Muncie, and these two are my responsibility.

"I'm fine. What about you guys? Are you good? They treating you all right?"

Jace nods, his long hair falling into his face. It's not enough to hide how frustrated he is by the situation we're in, and I understand why when he says, "They took my phone. Duke's, too. They gave us a place to hang out in, then told us to stay, like we're a pair of fucking dogs or something, and that we should get comfortable. I mean, what's *that* about?"

Get comfortable... probably because no one has told them that I agreed to stay here for twenty-five days yet. And if *I'm* staying...

"Yeah," I drawl, not quite sure how to tell them myself. This is another one of those band-aid situations, isn't it? Say it quick, get it over with. Okay. Here goes. "About that... I kinda had to extend our visit a little."

"A little?" Jace gets a wild look in his eyes, but he forces it away. "How long is a little?"

Oh, boy. "Twenty-five days total," I admit. Then, before either of them can say anything, I quickly add, "It was the only way to get the Alpha to promise we could bring Trish back with us."

I don't know what it was that I said. Her name, maybe? Could be. All I know is that, suddenly, Duke is gripping me by the shoulders. It's a gentle grip, not even a little bruising, but the look in his golden shifter's eyes has me wondering how close he is to breaking since, unlike Jace, there's no shoving that stark emotion out of sight.

"Alpha! Have you seen her yet? Have you talked to her?"

I'm so shocked by his unexpected reaction, the answer comes out as a gasp. "What? No. Not yet. They haven't told me where she is, but—"

"Come with me. I know where they're keeping her!"

What?

ONCE WE REMEMBER THAT HE'S THERE, THEO TRIES TO convince us that we should wait until the Alpha gives us permission to go see Trish. Ha. Even if I wasn't so determined to see her with my own eyes, to prove that she was safe, there's no stopping Duke. Theo might be an alpha, Duke a delta, but my packmate is huge. He's prepared to bulldoze past Theo to lead the way to Trish, and I'm okay with that.

I have no idea why he's so determined. When we discovered Barrow took off with a bleeding Trish, Duke was as angered as the rest of our packmates at the Wicked Wolf's dare. And, sure, he was the first to volunteer to come with me, but I thought that was more to do with him being pledged to me as my guard than anything else.

I'm, uh... beginning to think I was wrong about *that*.

As far as I know, there's only one way a male shifter can reliably find a female: the same way Ryker could find me in Muncie after I finally took off Aleks's charmed fang and stopped drinking his enchanted tea.

Holy shit. Is it possible that Trish Danvers is Duke's mate?

There's no time to ask. I tell Theo we're going to see Trish, and despite his trying to get us to stay at their cabin, he knows which way the wind is blowing. He joins the three of us as Duke unerringly crosses through dense forest, past countless other rows of grouped cabins, until we find a structure that's built more like a shotgun house. It's long and thin with a single entrance—and a shifter in his skin prowling in front of the place while wearing an expression that just about screams "guard duty".

"There," Duke says, not even a touch out of breath after the sprint he led us on. "I saw her last night. The guy guarding before wouldn't let me in to talk to her, but I saw her. They've got her in a cage, Alpha. She's in her fur while locked in a Luna-damned cage."

I whirl on Theo. The alpha has the good grace to look a little ashamed.

I jab him in the chest with my pointer finger. "You want to explain that?"

"It's for her own safety," he says, an apologetic tone to his voice. "She didn't want to be a guest, but the Alpha couldn't let her leave. She threatened to hurt herself. No one wanted to see that, so she's in a locked room. That's all. The Alpha provides her with plenty of clothes. Food, too. She eats," Theo assures me, "but she prefers to stay in her shifted form."

Of course she does. If I was a delta she-wolf that was abducted by one of my own packmates, dragged across the country after being attacked, and told I was nothing but a bargaining chip being used against a female who has issues with me over the male I wanted and could never have... yeah. I think I'd stay in my fur, too, where I could do a lot more damage if I had to.

There's something else that Theo doesn't mention but that—as a female—I immediately think of. Shifters only mate when we're in our two-legged, human forms. It's one of those lines we just don't cross.

We only hunt and eat raw prey while we're in our fur, and sex is saved for our human bodies.

If Trish shifts back, it'll be a lot harder to stop any male from trying to force her to mate. In her fur, the risks are much smaller, and she has her claws.

Credit where credit's due. My old nemesis is as much of a survivor as Elizabeth.

Behind me, I can just about feel the heat of Duke's fury warming my back. Pretending I can't, I keep my own tone pleasant as I say, "If all that's as you say, then it won't be a problem if I go in and let her know that we'll be taking her home soon. If she knows we've come for her, she might not be such a danger to herself anymore. Don't you think?"

Theo doesn't have a retort for that. I guess the Alpha's brainwashing only goes so far because I'd bet anything I had that his earlier response was dictated to him specifically by Walker. That prick was never going to let me see Trish. At least, not for a couple of more days. Why, when he knows that part of the reason I'm staying is because I'm committed to keeping her safe?

Theo doesn't have a retort, but he does nod.

"Good," I say, patting him in the chest where I'd just been poking him. "That's settled. We're going in."

The only thing stopping Duke from bursting inside of the narrow building is knowing I've taken the lead. As a delta, he's wired to listen to me, to follow the more dominant wolf, even though I can sense him bristling to take down the guard and let himself inside where Trish is locked up.

I hold out my hand, telling him to hang on as I notice that Theo is making eye contact with the guard. He stopped his pacing, taking up position near the entrance.

We'll go through him if we have to, but I'd rather not start any more trouble if I can avoid it. "You gonna call off your guard dog so we can go inside?"

Theo hesitates a moment before bluntly asking me, "Are you really a female alpha?"

Weird question. I was pretty sure everyone knew the truth about me by now, and unless he wants me to pull rank on the other wolf, I can't see why he's bringing this up at this very moment.

I nod. "If it matters, then, yeah. So... can we go in? And have a little privacy?"

"I'd heard rumors that you existed, but I thought they were all exaggerating." He says it more to himself than to me. "I never thought I'd really meet someone like you. It's incredible."

Oh, come *on*. I don't have time for this. Besides, he's after Elizabeth. She's just as incredible as I am.

Right?

Suddenly, I'm not so sure. Not about her being incredible—because that curse is definitely *something*—but about Theo being interested in her.

I saw the way he was looking at her earlier. But the

way he's sneaking peeks over at me now? I've seen a lovesick expression that looked just like that when Aleks was still trying to convince me to choose him over Ryker.

Ah, *Luna*. My luck can't be *that* bad, can it?

When Shane first revealed his true colors, he told me about the bounty on my head. For more than two decades, my bio-dad believed my mother's lie: that I died as a pup, drowning in the river that separated the Lakeview Pack's former territory from the Wolf District. I still have no idea how he figured out that I was alive, or that my name was changed, but he did—and then he offered a shit ton of money to any wolf who could tame me and bring me back to him so he could use a quirk of my birth to make him more powerful.

Despite hiding out for twenty-five years, I'm here now—but Theo is already an alpha. Shane wanted me to mate him if only because shifter lore says that any male who mates a female alpha becomes an alpha in his own right. There's nothing I can do for Theo that's any better than what Elizabeth can do, and I'm mated. She promised to leave my bond alone. I'm completely off the market. He's chasing a dead end.

Or maybe I'm just reading too much into the whole thing.

Please let me be reading too much into it...

Either way, he knows I'm an alpha, too. Just like how Christian tested me yesterday, it's like he was only after confirmation of that fact. Fine. If he really needs me to, I'm not above using my alpha nature to command him if I must. To make sure Trish knows we're here to save her—and to keep Duke from wolfing out—I'm getting us in there *with* some privacy.

Before I have to resort to using my wolf, though, he nods. "Five minutes. I can distract Brendan for five minutes. After that, I should probably be bringing you back to the cabin."

Five minutes? I'll take it.

We wait for Theo to say something to the other wolf, Brendan. The guard looks notably confused, but he nods and steps away from the front door. Once he does, Theo gestures for us to head inside. Without a moment to waste, the three of us do.

Immediately, I understand what Duke meant when he said 'cage' before. I guess I thought he was so upset, he was making it sound worse than it was.

Nope.

Trish Danvers is literally in the first room of at least four, complete with a set of iron bars that prevents us from getting any closer to her.

In her shifted form, she's a beautiful white wolf. She's curled up on the carpet, ignoring the couch that the space has in favor of staying on the floor. Her eyes are closed when we enter, but when Duke murmurs her name—*Patricia*—they spring wide open.

Did she sense him? Or was she faking?

There's no way to know because, despite the way her golden eyes brighten in recognition, she stays in her fur.

I move past Duke so that Trish knows I'm here, too. I'm probably the last person she wants to see, but it's important that she knows I'm in her corner. If I am, then so is Ryker, and knowing your Alpha has your back is enough to give strength to any packmate.

"Shift," I order her. "We have so much to talk to you about, but only five minutes. I need you in your skin, Trish."

Duke immediately spins, giving her his back. When Jace doesn't, the big shifter reaches blindly behind him, grasping Jace by the shoulder before wheeling him around next.

That... that's very interesting.

We're wolves. Whether we're in our fur or our skin after a shift, we're naked. It's completely natural, just a fact of life. It's rarely sexual, until a mate or physical attraction between two shifters is involved.

And Duke knew where to find Trish...

I wait a few seconds, but she stays right where she is despite my order. Cocking her head slightly, she gestures her muzzle at the bars, as if saying she's locked in there.

Oh. I understand. Until she's out of the locked room, she's not taking any chances.

Unfortunately, I can't open the cage to let her out. Not yet, at least. Not when I've been here for such a short amount of time with so many more days to go. I plan on getting her out as soon as possible, but I can't right now. Knowing I only have a few minutes left, I explain that to her—explain my agreement, the time limit, what kind of game the Wicked Wolf is trying to play—and I swear to the Luna that I'll get her home again.

She can understand me in her wolf form. I know that. It doesn't change how shitty I feel about leaving her behind bars when our five minutes are inevitably up.

There's no sign of Theo yet, but I doubt that'll last. Trish perked up when I made my vow, and though she's curling herself up on the floor again, settling back in, I hate how much I wish I could trade places with her if only to make sure she's not suffering because of my bio-dad's fixation on controlling me.

"I don't want to leave here by herself," I mumble under my breath. "She shouldn't be alone."

"She won't be." I'm not even a little surprised when Duke clears his throat before offering, "I'll stay here with her."

"Really, Duke? You will?"

He nods, shoulders set as he braces his feet against the floor. "Let them try to drag me out."

"And I'll stay with you."

Know what? I'm not surprised by Jace's offer, either. But as much as I appreciate his wanting to protect me, my wolf has another idea.

"I need you to do something else for me, Jace. Can you do that?"

"Anything you want, Alpha."

"I need you to go back to the pack."

Jace stiffens. "And leave you alone? No. I'll do anything, but not if it puts you at risk."

Okay. I'd be lying if I said that I thought he'd jump at the chance to get out of the Wolf District while leaving the rest of us behind. He's no coward, not even when he's up against such big odds. The fight with the rogue vamp in Muncie proved that.

It still doesn't change how we have to play this, though.

This trip was a trap. It's *always* been a trap.

But I have Walker's promise, I tell myself. I'll be okay—I just need Ryker to know that.

I've got to break Trish out. I won't stop until I make sure she and Duke are safe again on our own territory. But since she's locked behind bars and he isn't kidding about having to be dragged away from her, I can't save them just yet—but I can make sure Jace isn't in danger.

Not only that, but someone has to warn Ryker. He has to know what's going on.

"They took our phones," I remind him. "Without them, there's no way I can tell Ryker what kind of mess we're in."

No doubt my mate already guesses that I'm in over my head, but neither one of us expected that I'd be forced into agreeing to stay here for twenty-five days without any contact. And my mom? She knows I can take care of myself, but she's probably worrying a hole in her living room since I haven't been able to let her know I'm okay. Last either of them heard, the three of us were heading into Western Pack territory. It's been radio silence since then, and even though it hasn't been a full day yet, it's gotta feel like an eternity to my anxious omega mom and my protective alpha mate.

"But, Alpha—"

I hate to do this, but I have no choice.

"You pledged yourself to me. You gave me your loyalty. Believe me when I say this, Jace: I need you to go back. Do you understand? I need you to tell Ryker what's going on. And I'm not ordering you. Okay? I'm asking you. Please go."

Jace shudders out a breath. "I will, Alpha."

Good.

Theo looks noticeably taken aback when I step out of the cage—sorry, I overhear Brendan referring to them as protective holding cells—with only one of my guards. Before he can ask, I tell him about Duke's decision to stay behind with Trish.

"What? Oh, no. I don't think—"

"She's Mountainside. She belongs to my mate's pack," I say haughtily, emphasizing 'my mate', just in case. "I'm responsible for her, and it's my duty to make sure she's safe."

"Safe? She hasn't been in any danger since she crossed our borders."

It's not a lie, and I don't need my alpha sense of telling when someone is being dishonest to know that. Of course she's in no danger. Trish immediately chose to give her wolf control so that she could have a barrier against being hurt, and she's locked up inside of a cage. A pretty cage with a carpet and a couch, sure, but she's not free to come and go.

"Doesn't matter. Duke will keep her company." I pause. "Unless there's a reason why he can't?"

Theo opens his mouth, then closes it. He shakes his head. "No. I'm sure it won't be a problem."

"Good." *Phew*. "And Jace is leaving, too. We have a flight tomorrow that I obviously won't be on, but there's no reason he can't make it."

"Oh. Are you... are you sure? I don't think the Alpha—"

Yup. I'm positive.

"Your Alpha is right," I say, and how I don't choke on those words, I'll never know. "A wolf of my rank doesn't need any guards, and if he really wants to convince me to trade my loyalty to his pack, I need to be free to explore on my own without a shadow. There's no reason for Jace to stay." A small smile plays on my lips. "Unless we're not guests. But the Wicked Wolf wouldn't *lie* to his *daughter*, would he?"

Theo purses his own lips for a moment. His nostrils flare, obviously trying to find some way to answer that in a way I like without being disloyal to his Alpha.

"Of course not. You're... you're an honored guest."

He is clearly trying to be the good guy. Hey. For as long as he wants to act as if he's on my side, I'm going to take it. And if I have to use my status as Walker's "daughter" to get what I want... welp, I'll do that, too.

For my mate. For my pack.

I'll do *anything*.

"I'll see you in a few weeks, Jace," I tell him. *Now get out while you can.*

He looks from me to Theo and back.

"Count on it, Alpha," he vows.

JACE IS SAFE.

Duke is using his protective nature for good to protect someone who needs it.

Trish isn't alone.

And, once Jace makes it back to Accalia and fills Ryker in on what's going on, my mate will understand why I felt forced into staying longer than any of us wanted to.

Not bad for two days' work.

I'm feeling a little more hopeful the next morning. Even better, there's no early wake-up call, so I also feel rested and in a much better mood than I did the day before.

Too bad it doesn't last.

Elizabeth and I are just discussing whether we should cook in her attached kitchen or head out to the community spread for breakfast when, all of a sudden, Christian returns to our cabin.

I hate how there's something about this place that throws off my wolf. And not in the normal ways—how being in an unfamiliar place has her on edge—but how her senses seem... dulled, almost.

Normally, she can sense an approaching threat from a football-field's length away. Now? She doesn't jump to her feet, prowling uneasily around the inside of my chest until a split second before the insistent knocks sound.

Throwing me an apprehensive look, Elizabeth answers the door, bowing and backing away from the

Beta when he announces that the Alpha wants her brought to him.

Again.

I feel bad for her. After our heart-to-heart, I know that she's as trapped here as I am, only I've got a countdown to my way out while Elizabeth's captivity is a lot more open-ended. With Walker's threat to turn her over to the other Alphas terrifying to the Luna-touched she-wolf, I get it. She doesn't know that she'd probably be a lot safer with any other Alpha than she is with the Wicked Wolf, but I haven't had enough time to get her to believe that.

With a sad look thrown my way, she immediately follows behind Christian. Something about this scene tells me that this isn't the first or even second time that Elizabeth has been dragged in front of Walker like she really is his pet and he's the master. I only hope she was telling the truth when she said that she's convinced him that she wasn't worth mating. Being his pet is bad enough, but being forced to fuck him because he's the Alpha and he ordered her to?

My jaw goes tight as I watch her go. At the beginning of this mess, my goal was to bring Trish back to Accalia and find some way to get my bio-dad off my back. Now, though? After watching the way he—and his right-hand wolf—treats her, I'm determined to save her from this place. If she really wants to escape the district, I'll do everything I can to make that happen.

Just not today, Luna damn it.

Soon, though. Soon, I promise her silently.

Once Elizabeth is waiting for him outside, Christian turns to me. I already have my hand wrapped around the doorjamb, ready to slam the door shut with the other, when he opens his mouth.

"Ruby—"

My fingers tighten.

"Gemma," I correct.

I'll correct them all a million times if I have to. I don't care. I'll never willingly answer to that Luna-damned name while I have the choice.

His expression is as granite as it was when he appeared in our doorway. "I understand one of your packmates requested to stay with the Danvers girl. The Alpha wanted me to let you know that, as a favor to you, he's allowed it."

My stomach sinks. A favor to me? It's what I wanted, but that still doesn't sound so good.

"So Duke gets to stay with Trish? Is that what you're telling me?"

"You could say so." The tiny smirk that suddenly cracks his stone face should've been enough of a warning, but I'm a little shook when Christian explains, "The Alpha didn't put the big wolf in the same holding cell, but in the one next to her." His dark eyes lighten ever so slightly. "I hope that satisfies you."

Is it possible that my stomach could drop any

lower? 'Cause, right now, that sucker is halfway to China.

Freaking great. I pulled rank to get Duke to keep Trish company, and what happened next? I just landed my only ally in this place in a cage.

Good going, Gem.

Good freaking going.

CHAPTER 13

I wait the rest of the afternoon to see if Elizabeth is going to come back to her cabin.

When hours go by and there's still no hint of her, I decide it's about time to go for a walk. I need to do something to stop me from wondering about what's happening to her, or to my packmates.

Besides, the wolves here are so eager to prove that I'm a guest, not a prisoner. Might as well hold them to it. My stomach has been growling for a while, too. A bite to eat might help my anxious wolf, and it's probably a good plan to chow down before Walker decides to host another dinner for me.

As soon as I step outside of the cabin, I'm a little startled to discover someone is standing about ten feet away—and that I had no idea until I moved outdoors. He's staring at the front of the cabin, but as soon as I pull the door open, he freezes as if he never expected me to come out there.

Blue-black hair. Light golden eyes. The cleft in his chin.

And four jagged claw marks that go from temple to jaw.

They're angry and red and, holy shit, just looking at them makes my cheek twinge in agony.

I'm rushing toward him before I even realize I've moved.

"Theo! What the heck happened to you?"

His hand slides up to his face, fingers spread to cover the marks.

As if that's going to make them any less obvious.

In the Lakeview Pack, I grew up with my Aunt Corrine's boys: Devin and Max. They were a year older than me, and super protective of their "omega" cousin. They treated me like I was super fragile, as if I was made of spun sugar, while occasionally beating the shit out of each other because, at the end of the day, that's what shifters do. Add in the fact that they were brothers and it was inevitable.

So, yeah. I've seen marks like that. Sometimes Devin got in a lucky hit, sometimes it was Max, but until they healed any injuries from their sibling squabbles, they often had a few fresh scars covering their skin.

As a shifter, there are only two ways to actually bypass our regenerative properties and leave a true scar: mating marks, and a shifter tattoo. Unless he treats the marks with a blend of silver and herbs, Theo's face will heal. Considering the raised ridges and jagged flesh are more of a purpley-pink, I know it's a fresh injury; from this morning, at least. Claiming marks turn white when a shifter chooses to keep them, and a shifter tattoo shimmers with the silver shoved into the wound to make it permanent. Those marks are neither. In a few hours, there would be no sign he was carved up at all.

No wonder he's trying to cover it up. He never meant for me to see them.

Now, it could just be that he's a vain alpha. After living under Wicked Wolf Walker, I wouldn't be surprised if some of my bio-dad's vanity rubbed off on his packmates. Something tells me that there's more to it than that, though.

"What happened?" I ask again when he doesn't answer me.

"It's nothing—" My look of disbelief has him changing his story halfway through. "Just an accident. Really. I was sparring with one of my packmates and it kinda got out of hand."

Yup. Still a lie.

He's totally lying to me.

It's hard to explain to a non-shifter, but certain emotions—and some actions—have a scent. Like how fury smells like a fire burning, happiness smells like cotton candy, and dishonesty stinks like rotten milk.

The ability to tell when someone is lying to me is one I've had my whole life. My dad—my real dad, Paul—has it, too. So does Ryker. I figure it's an alpha thing, which means Theo should also have it. But if that's the case, why would he think he can get away with such a blatant lie like that?

Then again, my sniffer has been a bit on the fritz since I crossed into Walker's territory. I'm beginning to think that Elizabeth has something to do with that. Like how she can somehow cover up a shifter's innate scent—but not their aura—being around Elizabeth has made it harder for me to tell when someone's full of shit.

Or maybe it's just when I was leery of her and Walker's answers. Because I'm not having a problem with telling that Theo is lying his ass off.

"A sparring accident? Who were you sparring with?"

"No one you know."

Lie.

Lie, lie, lie.

I blink up at him.

Theo coughs, then looks away. "Anyway, don't worry about it, Gemma. I deserved it, and I know what

I did wrong. It won't happen again."

"Mm." That part, at least, is true. "So what's up? What are you doing out here? Elizabeth isn't home."

His gaze darts back to me. The way his eyes shadow over next is a sure sign that I wasn't supposed to call him out on that, either.

Oops.

"I wasn't looking for Elizabeth." He wasn't? Ah, *crap*. "I had some free time and Christian told me that you were alone. I thought I'd stop by, make sure the perimeter was safe for you."

Right. Because he wanted to be gone before I noticed his claw marks.

I blink again, slower this time. "You do remember our conversation from yesterday, right? You know. When I admitted that I was a female alpha?"

"I remember."

"Great. So why, exactly, do you think I need a bodyguard? Unless," I add, daring him to lie to me again, "you know something I don't know. Because I only said I would stay because the Alpha promised me that me and my people would come to no harm while we were here. That hasn't changed, has it?"

Theo hurriedly shakes his head. "Not at all."

Damn it. If Walker reneged on our deal, I could use it as an excuse to demand that he release Trish and Duke before the three of us hauled ass out of here.

"What about you?" he asks, changing the subject. "Were you heading somewhere?"

"Yeah. I was hoping to get something to eat."

I could've grabbed something from the kitchen, but it didn't seem right to do that with Elizabeth gone. Besides, I like the community set-up for food that this pack has. It's never easy to navigate meals when accepting them from the wrong shifter might send the wrong message. The buffet laid out for any packmate in need is probably the only upside to staying in the Wolf District.

It also gives me an excuse to continue to get a feel for this place. If Walker is all for keeping me secluded in Elizabeth's cabin under the guise of "privacy", stubborn Gem is all about walking around, seeing what life is like for the different ranks in the Western Pack, daring him to stop her.

Give me one reason, Alpha. Give me one single reason that I can take with me when I leave. I'll tell Ryker and he can bring it up at the next Alpha gathering in July. That might be more than a half a year from now, but if the Alphas can finally get some insider knowledge on how the cruel Alpha abuses his packmates, maybe the Wicked Wolf's three-decade reign over the Wolf District will end at last.

Claws crossed.

Oblivious to my machinations, Theo gives me a friendly smile. "I can eat. I'll join you."

Since I can't think of a reason to tell him no, I figure it's okay if he tags along with me. "Sure."

We make it halfway to the district square before a bearded delta with dark skin and copper-like eyes flags us down. I have no idea who this guy is, but Theo greets him warmly, so I figure maybe he's another one of the good ones here.

"Where are you going, Theo?"

Theo gestures to me. "I was bringing the Alpha's daughter to the dinner spread."

The delta wolf—Theo called him Joshua—raises his eyebrows at that before quickly shaking it off. "Not now. The Alpha has called a pack meet."

"What? When did that happen?"

"About an hour ago. Where in the Luna's name have you been?"

I can answer that. From the red that tinges Theo's whole cheek, I'm betting he was doing a perimeter check around mine and Elizabeth's cabin for longer than he wanted to admit to.

"Busy," is all he says. "Where's the meet?"

"It's at the pit," Joshua answers, an excited edge to his baritone voice. "Now come on. You two aren't gonna want to miss this!"

I have no idea what's going on, but I'm kind of stuck on the word 'pit'.

What the hell is the pit?

So it turns out that the pit is just what it sounds like. In a part of pack territory that I haven't had the chance to explore yet, there's a stretch of land that's about as big as a football field. There's no grass, just dirt, and it's dug out so that it's about a foot below ground level.

We follow Joshua to the pit, though he leaves us to find a good spot along the edge—at least, that's what he told Theo. It looks like nearly all of the adults in the pack are already here. A majority of them have built a wall around the pit, so I can't really see what's in there until I tiptoe closer and a few shifters trip over themselves to let me through.

I'm not really too impressed with the pit. No. My attention is drawn to something that's built beyond the earth. With four steps leading up it, there's a platform that rises more than two feet off the ground. It's pretty clear it's designed to let whoever's on the platform have an even better view of the dirt without having to be a part of the crowd.

Makes sense when I get a better look at the platform.

In the middle of it, there's a.... well, there's no way around it. It's a throne. A freaking throne. In the middle of the platform, there's an iron-wrought throne that the Wicked Wolf lords in like he's some kind of king.

There's an empty seat next to him. Catty-cornered to the throne, about a foot behind the second chair, there's a third one. Elizabeth is sitting in it, her hair tucked over one shoulder, body turned just enough to make it clear that she'd rather be anywhere other than where she is.

"Ruby," booms Walker when he spies me staring at them. "There you are, my daughter."

"Gemma," I automatically correct. I desperately want to add, "And I'm not your daughter," but if there's anything I've learned since I've been here, it's when to pick my battles.

He ignores my retort which just proves I was right; I instinctively know that he never would've tolerated the second comment, especially with his pack as witness to it. Waving regally at the empty seat, he says, "Sit down."

As if I have a choice.

Theo's face might be ruined right now, but the marks don't do much to hide the look of disappointment that flashes across it. "Alpha's calling for you."

Yeah. I heard him.

"I guess dinner's gonna have to wait."

"Maybe, if you still have an appetite, we can eat later?"

I cock my head. Why wouldn't I still have an

appetite? Sure, going anywhere near Walker is sure to kill it, but I'm a shifter. Before long, I'll be ready to eat again.

Theo doesn't give me the chance to ask. With a wave, he separates from me, moving to join the crowd circling the empty patch of dirt just below Walker's pretentious platform.

Actually, I notice as I reluctantly move around the circle, heading toward the foreboding chair, it's not quite *empty* empty. While every other packmate is in their skin, there's a wolf prowling around the east side of the circle in his dark grey fur. From his size and aura, I can tell it's another delta wolf shifter; from the frothing at the mouth, I know he's a hair away from turning completely feral.

What the—

I feel the weight of Walker's gaze on me as I trudge toward the platform. Being rude would be a mistake, so I nod at him, then plop myself in the empty seat. Almost immediately, I turn to face Elizabeth.

She blanches when she realizes she has my sole attention.

Oh, come on. I thought we were past this. So long as she stands by her promise not to fuck with my bond, I won't use my more dominant wolf against her. She has no reason to be afraid.

Well, except for the asshole sitting next to me.

"Hey." I keep my voice as soft as I can make it.

Gentle, too. I almost sound like Omega Gem again. "You all right?"

Elizabeth glances at the back of Walker's head. Her eyes dim, but she nods.

I don't buy it. "What happened to you today? I know you left, but—"

"Shh," Walker interrupts, hushing me. "Turn around. You're just in time. The show's about to start."

Show? What show?

I get the answer a few seconds later. When I do? I just about fall out of my chair.

He walks out of the trees, but he's not alone. Two shifters in their skin... big, brawny brutes... walk right behind him, making it seem like he's a dead man walking.

Or, in his case, *un*dead man walking.

"Oh, no."

No.

Aleks.

No.

It's him. No denying that. It's *Aleks*.

What in the name of the Luna is he doing here?

His eyes find me immediately. In the daylight, the pale color of his irises seems closer to silver than green. Just like Elizabeth, I think. Funny that I never realized how similar their eyes look until right this very moment.

I only hope his skin is slathered in sunscreen.

Though vampires turning to dust during the day is nothing but a myth, they're still very sensitive to the UV rays. Without the proper protection, his skin could be burned to a crisp in no time. We're in California, after all. The trees that surround the district might block out some of the sun, but it can't be enough.

And, shit. Look at me. He's standing between two of Walker's biggest goons. No glasses. No shoes. The gentle elegance I know so well is gone, a twist of boredom tinged with defiance settling on his normally gorgeous features. His cheeks are gaunt, his clothes obviously a few days old. With Aleks, there's no illusion that he's a guest.

There might not be any chains on my friend, but hell if he isn't a prisoner, and I'm worried about freaking *sunscreen*.

My heart stutters in my chest as I finally realize what's going on.

The platform. The arrogant throne. The panicked wolf pacing at one side of the dirty, circular pit. Aleks being led to the other side.

The ring of shifters that keeps either from getting out.

And Walker's flippant hush, plus the way he said the show's about to start...

As far as I can tell, the Wicked Wolf of the West has the honor of fighting the most Alpha challenges. Growing up, I'd heard rumors—rumors that my mother would have a fit over if she knew they reached my ears—that he would pick a fight with whatever wolf pissed him off that day, acting as if the lower-ranked shifter challenged him over some perceived slight. It was his way of being a pack-sanctioned murderer. A freaking serial killer who then turned around and made his packmates applaud his kills.

If I'll say one thing for Walker, he's not a coward. Most of the time, he was the one walking into the pit—and when he did, he was always the wolf who walked back out of it. But, when he was feeling particularly bloodthirsty, he would force two of his wolves to fight to the death in front of him.

The show's about to start...

A vampire versus a shifter would be one hell of a show to a sadistic bastard like Walker.

I want to get up and go to Aleks. I don't know what it'll cost me—probably more than I can pay—but I can't let this happen. With the way things are between us right now, this is probably just another move on the chessboard for the Wicked Wolf. Somehow, he found a way to involve Aleks in his sick game. Whether he knows what this vampire means to me or not doesn't matter. I wouldn't want to sit here and watch anyone have to fight a nearly feral wolf.

Especially not my best friend.

He's still looking at me. Then, almost as if he knows what I'm thinking, he gives his head the tiniest shake.

No. He's telling me no.

As if that's going to stop me.

I shift in my seat. I'm just about to get up when, suddenly, his gaze slides from me to the female sitting just behind me.

His pale eyes bleed to a shocking red in an instant. With the whole crowd watching, Aleks's fangs shoot out, longer than I've ever seen.

Behind me, I hear a gasp. I spin around, following Aleks's unblinking stare to Elizabeth.

She looks like she's seen a ghost.

Honestly, I feel the same way.

What is going on here? Why is he down there?

What is he even doing in California?

It has to be because of me. That's not even a self-obsessed thing—it's fact. This is Aleks. If he's here in the Wolf District, it's because I am. That's not what has me so confused, though. Say Aleks found out I was here; possible, especially after I sent Jace back to Accalia. There's a huge difference between him knowing I was in the Wolf District and him ending up in the pit, about to fight a challenge against a wolf shifter.

Before I can understand how this happened, Walker clears his throat. My head swivels back to him just in time to see him lift his arm, holding out his palm.

The crowd falls silent.

His smirk is enough to have me curling my fingers beneath me to hide my furious claws.

"For tonight's challenge," he announces, deep voice echoing, "we have a parasite. Our ancient enemy. Let's see what it takes to kill him." He drops his arm. "To the death!"

Ryker told me once that Aleks had thrown their fight.

At the time, I didn't want to believe him. Mainly because, back then, I wanted to think the worst of Ryker. Watching him brutalize Aleks definitely helped me with that—which, I later discovered, was exactly why the vampire did exactly what Ryker accused him of. He wanted me to hate Ryker, and playing the victim worked.

Some part of me still wasn't so sure that Aleks would've been able to handle Ryker even if he wasn't holding back. I've seen Ryker take on another Fang City vampire; after the vamp threatened to stick me with a silver dagger, Ryker ripped his freaking head off. Then there's the vampire I killed myself after he just missed tearing out Jace's throat. They weren't that big of a challenge to either of us.

And, if I'm being completely honest, I'm a shifter. A

wolf. I'm always going to think my kind of supe has the edge.

Within seconds of the fight beginning, I quickly change my mind. Who knows? Maybe we only found it easier to dispatch those vamps because they were low-level bloodsuckers and me and Ryker are alphas.

Aleks is Cadre. He is one of the most powerful vampires in Muncie. And, as I watch him take on the snarling wolf, there isn't a single doubt left in my mind that Aleks let Ryker carve him up the way he did.

This isn't a challenge. It's not a fight, either.

It's a Luna-damned *slaughter*.

When Walker announced "to the death", I bet every single shifter in the district was convinced that it would be to the vampire's death. If so, they were wrong. Aleks shows no mercy. In less than two minutes, he's disabled the wolf's hind legs, gouged out one eye, and, as the finale, hoisted the twitching, defeated beast by the neck before plunging his fangs past the fur, past the muscle, sucking so deeply that the shifter is nothing but a desiccated rug by the time Aleks is done.

He drank an entire wolf shifter, and after he was done, my former roommate threw him to the dirt before wheeling around, looking for another target.

I watched in a mixture of horror and pride. Part of me couldn't reconcile this monster with the Aleksander Filan I've known for over a year. Then again, if someone threw me in the pit and told me to fight for my life, I'd do whatever it took to survive. Aleks did. That definitely deserves some pride.

He won. Thank the freaking Luna. I don't know what I would've done if I had to watch Aleks hunted in front of me—

I've barely had half that thought when Walker calls out for his Beta.

Christian is one of the wolves ringing the pit. "Yes, Alpha?"

"Shoot him."

What?

Christian pulls a gun out of Luna knows where. One second, his hands are empty. The next? He has a heavy-looking pistol that spits out bullets faster than even my shifter's eyes can catch.

He's a fucking marksman, too. In about six seconds, he's put a bullet in Aleks's left thigh, his left shin, his right thigh, his right shin, and his right shoulder just as Aleks shoots his hand out.

The first bullet stopped Aleks dead in his tracks. By the time he had four in him, he collapsed to his knees. The one in his shoulder took away any chance that he could grab one of the nearby shifters before his whole body locked up.

There's only one thing that can do that to a supe, and especially a vampire.

Silver bullets. Christian shot Aleks full of silver bullets.

And now I know exactly how Walker got his paws on my friend.

Pumped full of silver, even a vicious vampire is as docile as a lamb.

CHAPTER 14

I'm still standing on the platform, shocked and a little sickened at how Christian riddled Aleks full of silver bullets before a pair of shifters picked him up and carried him away from the pit.

The oozing slickness of Walker's aura slides over me. I jerk in place in time to see that he's sidled next to me.

Don't puke, Gem. Don't *puke*—

"What did you think of my little display?"

He sounds so pleased with himself. And to think I already believed I hated him more than it was possible to hate another shifter. Looks like there's no end to my hatred when it comes to him.

I won't give him the satisfaction of hearing me say that. So, swallowing back the bile that rose in my throat, I shrug. "So you found a rogue vamp and sacrificed one of your wolves to him. Am I supposed to be impressed?"

"Ah, but he wasn't rogue when we found him. In fact, he was very... refined before, even after we caught him lurking on the edge of my territory. Refused to tell us what he was doing, but he was very classy with his 'fuck you'. It's why I decided to keep him alive."

"Right," I say wryly. "You decided to keep a vamp as another pet, and then you had him fight a shifter's challenge where he could've easily died. Then, when he didn't, you pumped him full of enough silver to kill him anyway. Why not just pull off his head while you're at it?"

"Careful, Ruby. If I didn't know any better, I'd think you're siding with one of the corpses over your own kind."

"I'm not, and it's Gemma. Remember?"

His lips thin just enough to know I've struck a nerve. *Good.* "Now, I know you spent time living among the bloodsuckers, but any daughter of mine would always choose her people over the undead."

Walker's deep voice is strangely light, almost as if he's trying not to let the threat creep into his tone while we still have an audience. But the way he talks about Aleks... when I saw my old roommate stride out into the middle of the pit, my immediate thought was that he was only there because Walker knew our history.

I... I'm not so sure now.

Well, if Walker thinks he's just some vamp, I'm not going to be the one to enlighten him otherwise. Especially since Aleks must have gone to great lengths to cover up what he was doing breaching the Western Pack's border as a vamp on his own. Even though I've got no clue what Aleks is doing here, I'd be purposely obtuse if I pretended it wasn't because of me.

Great. Another captive of Wicked Wolf Walker who only has me to blame for their predicament.

I keep my own voice cool. "I'm just trying to understand what the point of that was."

Walker grins. "Training."

Excuse me?

"I don't get what you mean."

"It's very easy to understand. I want my pack prepared. If they can't win against a captive vampire, they would've succumbed in a true battle. At least, here, my other wolves will learn not to make the same mistakes. After all, every day we live, it's another day of war with the fanged monsters."

He's... he's not *wrong*. And I'm not talking about the derisive way he says 'fanged monsters' like that.

Technically, the Claws and Fangs war never ended. I'm not sure how it could. For as long as supes have existed, our two communities—shifters and vampires—have been at odds.

They think we're no better than our beast. Shifters think they're parasites.

It's always been that way.

Two hundred years ago, the silent war turned brutal. History differs on what really set off the war— the vamps claim an Alpha attacked one of their own, the pack at the center of the first battle claim a vamp murdered an Alpha's mate—but, for decades, there were terrible clashes that left countless packs decimated and hundreds of immortal vampires staked and beheaded.

Eventually, the Alpha collective at the time approached one of the most powerful Cadres and they brokered a sort of treaty. The vampires got their Fang Cities, the packs got their territory, and lines were drawn... until I drove into Muncie and found a savior in Aleksander Filan.

Since then, there has been a shaky truce, but that's another topic that all depends on who you ask. It doesn't change the fact that, at our core, we're old enemies.

Then there's me. I spent a year living with my vampire roomie. We were proof that the two peoples could get along, and that's without me getting into the whole "Aleks was convinced I was meant to be his mate" thing.

He saved my life. I have no doubt in my mind that the Nightmare Trio would've killed me that first night if it wasn't for him. No way in hell will I stand here and let anything happen to Aleks.

I have to be careful. I can't really believe that Walker really has no idea who Aleks is—I'm banking on him being totally aware but trying to see if I'll confess first—but on the odd chance that he does think it's one big coincidence, I can't let him learn about my ties to Aleks otherwise he'll never survive the next bout of "training".

I work hard to keep my expression neutral. For a second, I look away from Walker, using the excuse that I'm checking on Elizabeth—only she's gone. Sometime after the challenge ended, she must've stepped down the backside of the platform, slipping away.

Lucky.

Walker is still waiting for me to say something else. So I do.

"How long will the silver keep him weak?"

Walker raises his eyebrows at my question. "It took him a few hours to expel the bullets after we caught him. So at least that long. Why?"

Okay. Here goes nothing. "I'm curious. He might know some of the vamps I met in Muncie. I'd like to go talk to him if I can."

I wait for him to call me out on my blatant bullshit —but he doesn't.

His shifter's eyes flash. "And you're asking me?"

If that's what he wants to think... I nod.

His expression turns thoughtful. "You know you probably could've... mm... persuaded young Theodore to sneak you in. Of course, I would have had to bloody that handsome face of his again, but he should consider himself lucky that that's all he got for being foolish enough to betray me."

Well, that answers my question from before, doesn't it? I wondered how Theo ended up with those vicious grooves in his cheek. Now I know.

Of *course* it was Walker.

"But," he adds, "since you did ask me, I think a meeting could be arranged." Raising his hand, he gestures for his Beta. "Christian?"

Christian is still holding the gun when he marches over to the bottom step of the platform. "Yes, Alpha?"

"My daughter wants to see the parasite. Take her."

I let the 'my daughter' slide. What if I snap at him again and he changes his mind? No, thanks. Getting to talk to Aleks is more important than how icky I feel whenever Walker reminds anyone that his blood runs in my veins.

"Oh, and Christian?" Walker's heavy gaze lands on me even as he tells his Beta, "Don't forget to bring more silver bullets. You never know when one of the bloodsuckers will go rogue and need to be put down for good. And you must understand how much I'd hate to have to do that to your roommate, my daughter."

I gulp and say nothing.

Yeah. I understand, and in more ways than one.

How many cells are in this place?

That's the first thought I have when Christian leads me to the south side of the Wolf District. He calls the separate structure a jailhouse—because of course this place has a freaking *jailhouse*—and leads me to the entrance. Inside, I see at least five different cells that stretch the length of the room in a single line.

And when I say cell, I *mean* it.

The room I find Aleks in is about the size of my old bedroom back in his apartment. It has three solid walls, no windows, and a row of gleaming silver bars that make up the cell door. A massive lock is built into the center. It doesn't take a genius to know it's turned shut.

Just like when me, Duke, and Jace went to see Trish, I refuse to let Christian follow me inside. I expect him to pull the Beta card, but he doesn't. He just flashes the gun, a silent reminder that he's armed, before telling me he'll be within earshot in case I need him.

Translation: *I can hear everything you say, and be sure that I'll be reporting back to my Alpha.*

I might've been more worried if Walker hadn't already made it clear that he knows exactly who Aleks is. Because of that, there's no reason to be cagey or to find a way to hide how I know him.

Good thing, too, because the best of my acting days are behind me. When I see Aleks sitting on the cement floor, his back up against the thin, blanket-loss cot, nothing can stop me from rushing forward.

My fingers come within inches of wrapping around the bars between us before my inner wolf snaps a warning and I realize that, if I grab them, the pure silver will singe the skin right from my fingertips.

I gasp, yanking my hands back, and bring my fingers to my lips instead.

I hate it, but I guess I understand. If Walker really believes that he's preparing for the next Claws and Fangs war, then of course he's going to want to keep Aleks contained. With Trish, he could play it off like he was doing what was best for her, the way he kept her protected behind bars.

Not Aleks. The silver in the bars makes that obvious.

A pit of anger mixed with shame forms low in my gut. The silver bullets were one thing; after the way Aleks defeated his challenger, nothing less would've kept him from rampaging through the rest of the pack if a vampire's bloodlust got the better of him. But there's only reason why Walker would toss him in a cell with silver bars: he wants his supe prisoner to *hurt*.

"Oh, Aleks..."

His head shoots up. His pale skin is flushed, probably from the meal he just ate, and his eyes had reverted from the raging red back to a soft, light green. Still no glasses, but at least he looks like the Aleks I know and love.

Except for the blood staining his shirt and the bullet holes riddling clothes, that is.

"Gem. What are you—" With some effort, he starts to climb to his feet. "Are you—"

"Don't get up for me," I plead, cutting him off. In my mind's eye, I can still see the bullets tearing through his pale skin. The ruined clothes aren't helping. This close, the wrinkled, blood-stained fabric reminds me of Swiss cheese.

I can't keep the look of horror from twisting my features. Holy shit. How many times has Walker ordered him shot?

His face softens. Despite my pleading, he keeps going until he's on his feet again. "I'm all right. And I'd rather stand in your presence."

Why does he have to be such a freaking white knight? "Aleks," I say pointedly, trying not to sound hysterical, "you were *shot*. You need to rest."

"I'm fine." When I start to argue, he waves at the floor of his cell, pointing out the silver bullets he must've already expelled from his body. "Really, Gem. The bars are no picnic, but I can at least stand."

That's another reason for the bars. Regular bars

would be no match for his vamp strength. Silver bars? It would sap his energy and burn his skin at the same time.

This really is a jail for vamps.

"Gem." It's his turn for his softly accented voice to turn pleading. "Tell me you're okay."

That's Aleks for you. A plaything for the Wicked Wolf and barely recovered from being shot—*again*—and all he's worried about is me.

I know him. Unless I assure him that I'm as safe as I can be, I won't get a word out of him. In his own way, he's as stubborn as a shifter.

Tell him? Sure. I can do that.

Speaking as quickly as I can, hoping that if I spit it out I can overlook how guilty I feel and how upsetting it is to see Aleks behind bars, I tell him all about what I've experienced since I arrived in the Wolf District with Jace and Duke. I tell him about how Trish is in her own version of a cage, how Duke is with her, and how I sent Jace back so that there was one less person Walker could use against me.

I specifically don't mention that, now that I know Aleks is here, that number has increased by one again.

He listens to everything I say, interjecting every few sentences to either ask a question or to make a comment. The more I talk, the harder the edge of Aleks's jaw becomes. He's furious on my behalf which just makes me feel *worse*.

By the time I get to the part where Walker told me that Aleks's fight to the death was considered "training" for another Claws and Fangs war, his eyes are starting to bleed back to red again.

"Głupcy," he spits out angrily.

The whole time I was talking, I was wondering when he'd slip into Polish. "What's that mean?"

"Idiots," he translates for me. "Fools."

Fitting.

I choke out a laugh that, honestly, sounds more like a sob. "How do you say 'asshole' in Polish?"

"Dupek."

"Dupek," I echo. "That's fitting, too."

Aleks actually smiles. It's the tiniest curve to his lips, but with him trapped in this hellish space, it's something, at least.

"I know how they caught you. Walker told me his scouts caught you poking around their territory. I don't get it, Aleks. What were you even doing here?"

I haven't seen him since the night I told him I was bonding myself to Ryker. He wasn't in the apartment when I went to visit him, and even if he picked up my scent on his return, that doesn't explain how he just so happened to stumble upon the Wolf District while I was its unwilling guest.

"Your wolf came to see me."

I don't think I could've been more shocked if Aleks

said he sprouted a pair of wings and flew from Muncie to the Wolf District.

"Ryker?"

He nods. "He's smarter than he looks. He requested a meet through Roman, knowing that I wouldn't be able to refuse. I was out of town, visiting an old friend, but when Roman calls, you come. Your wolf wasted his time, though. When he told me what he wanted, I would've agreed even without the Cadre getting involved."

"What did he want?"

His pale eyes lock on me. "Wolfson didn't trust this Alpha, and he had good reason not to. He wasn't able to leave his pack, but with Roman's blessing, we all decided I would come watch over you."

Okay. That makes a little more sense. I don't have to like it—and I can save that argument for when we're out of this crazy place—but that sounds exactly like something Ryker would do.

He must've been desperate to keep my safe if he went to Aleks of all people to ask for help. If I didn't know he loved me already, that right there would've proved it.

Luna, I need to get back to him.

Later. No matter what it takes, I'll be with Ryker soon. I'm not worried about that. No. I'm worried about *Aleks.*

"How long have you been here?"

"I took the next flight out after you and the other wolves left. I was only a couple of hours behind you when they first gunned me down." Aleks snorts. "Silver bullets. Those were banned after the last great war. I suppose it's my fault for believing the dogs would stand by their word."

Though it's one of the worst insults a vamp could use against a wolf shifter, I ignore the way he called the Western Pack dogs. If they caught him the same day I landed here, that means he's been in this silver-lined cell for two full days now.

Hell, yeah, I think they're dogs, too.

Dupek dogs who use silver bullets.

I shake my head, my claws getting caught in my hair as I shove it angrily out of my face. "This is crazy. I can't believe he kept you in here for so long before he threw you in my face. And, shit, Aleks... I'm so sorry." There's no reason to say what for because we both know he wouldn't be in this mess if it wasn't for me. "I'm so, so fucking sorry."

"Don't be. It's not your fault." I wish it wasn't. "Besides, he miscalculated. He wanted me thirsty. Before tonight, I haven't had a sip of blood since I left Muncie. Either he thought I'd be weak or my thirst would rule me. He never counted on me being in complete control."

I believe him. Aleks might have looked a little out of it when he saw me, and he looked a *lot* out of it when he noticed Elizabeth on the platform, but he was totally in control—up until Christian started shooting him again.

"Why would he do that, though?" I'm speaking more to myself than to Aleks. "I don't get it."

"It's like you said, Gem. He wants another Claws and Fangs war."

My puzzled expression must give me away because Aleks drops his voice before adding, "Roman's only one leader. Muncie, one Cadre. But I've been alive a long time. I have friends. Contacts. If anything happens to me, he could very easily get the war he craves."

It takes a lot for me to admit to any kind of weakness, but the idea of anything happening to Aleks scares me. There are only a few feet between us, but because of the silver bars and the huge lock, it might as well be a world away.

That doesn't stop me from impulsively shoving one hand past the narrow bars. I get too close to the bar on my left side, the silver burning a raw strip down my entire forearm, but if it means I can touch Aleks, that I can prove to myself that my friend is still okay, it's worth the pain.

"I'll get you out of here," I swear. My fingers graze his hard chest. "I promise you."

Aleks takes my hand. For a split second, I think he's going to bring my fingers to his chilled lips and, I don't know, kiss them or something. But he doesn't. He gives them a gentle squeeze before carefully, carefully guiding them through the bars again.

"Don't you worry about me. I've been through worse, and I'm not about to let some mangy wolf take me down. Not now that—"

Aleks stops talking.

I wait a second before prodding, "Now that what?"

He shakes his head. "It doesn't matter. The only thing that does is that you keep your head. You hear me, Gem? We'll get out of this together."

Yes.

Yes, we will.

CHAPTER 15

Christian is gone, and so is his gun.

That's the upside. The downside?

Theo is waiting outside of the jailhouse, a gun that looks like the twin to Christian's clasped loosely in his grip.

As soon as he sees me, that I'm in one piece and Aleks hasn't found a way to break through the bars and suck me dry, he quickly gets rid of it. I'm not really sure how, maybe he sticks it in his waistband or something, and all I can think about is what the silver bullets would do to his dick if the gun accidentally went off.

It would be a much funnier thing to think about if it was still Christian with the gun. Like, *boom*, there goes his nuts. The stone-faced Beta would totally deserve it.

Theo, not so much.

I keep my voice calm. Cool. "Waiting for me?"

He nods. "Christian told me you went in to see the vampire. When the Alpha called for him, I offered to stick around so I can escort you back to your cabin."

Why am I not surprised?

I jerk my chin at him. "Face looks better."

"Thanks." He lifts his now empty hand, running it over his cheek. The faint scar is a vast improvement over the jagged marks from earlier. Give it another hour and he should be completely healed. "I'm glad you like it."

I blink. Um. Okay. I definitely didn't say that.

Theo drops his hand, gesturing in front of him. "Come on. I'll take you home."

Part of me wants to point out that I'm only borrowing Elizabeth's cabin because Walker conned me into agreeing that I would stay, but that it's definitely not my home. That it'll *never* be my home. Before I give in to that urge, though, I notice how everyone is staring at me as we move through the Wolf District.

That's not new. Ever since I came here, I've been the center of attention. Why wouldn't I be? Between being Walker's "long lost daughter" and a female alpha, I'd be more worried if they pretended I wasn't here.

But there's an edge to their stare that has me glancing up at Theo as I ask, "Are you walking with me because you're protecting me or protecting them?"

He gives me an impish grin. "A little of both, I'd bet."

Yeah. That's what I thought.

We walk together in silence. I have half a mind to tell Theo that I can make it back to the cabin on my own, but then I remember how bad his face looked earlier. Walker obviously discovered that Theo was the one who let me and Duke in to see Trish. If I hadn't pulled rank on him, he never would have, but I did so it's partly my fault that Walker lashed out at him like that.

At least now I know why he was eager to lie to me about the injury. He didn't want to me to know that he was hurt because of me.

Don't get me wrong. I blame Walker completely for his attacking Theo. I mean, what kind of Alpha turns on his own wolf for something so harmless? If anything, he should've come after me—but, I'm guessing, he won't do that while he still believes he has a chance to convince me to stay here of my own free will.

After that? I'm thinking all bets are off.

Huh. Seems like I answered my own question already, too. What kind of Alpha would do that? The same kind who would throw one of his wolves at a furious vampire and smirk when the vampire drained him to the quick.

A shiver courses down my spine.

I never saw Aleks feed before. At least, not from a

live donor. That's something he did on his own, almost as if he was careful not to rub his being a vamp in my face. Like, logically, I knew Aleks didn't survive on blood bags. It's just... that was hard to watch, and I'm a shifter who can eviscerate a deer during a hunt.

Theo picks up on my shiver. He doesn't know me, though. He has no idea what's going on in my head otherwise he never would've said, "If their stares are bothering you, let me know. I can tell the Alpha and you can be sure he'll stop them from doing it."

Right. And then he'll grab one of them and throw them at Aleks the next time he feels like having some "training".

I shake my head. "It's okay. Let's not do that."

"Why not?" Theo sounds surprised. "He wants you to be comfortable here. Wouldn't that help?"

The only thing that'll help me is Walker letting Aleks out of that cage, releasing Trish into my care, and letting me and Duke take her home.

I don't tell him that, though. I just shrug and keep on walking. Besides, we're quickly passing the more crowded district square, heading out toward the private cabins built along the edge of the territory. I can already see my borrowed cabin in the distance.

I notice he doesn't offer to stop by the late dinner spread. He must know he was right. I really did lose my appetite.

I just want to bury my head under a pillow and hide for a few minutes. That's all.

And then Theo says, "He's really not a bad guy, you know," and I actually stop for a second so that I can stare at him in disbelief.

"Are you kidding me? When I saw you a couple of hours ago, it looked like someone had sharpened their claws on your cheekbones. *He* did that. Good guys don't do that."

The skin might have already closed over the wound. Doesn't matter. Just from the depths of the ridges and how long it was taking for the alpha wolf to heal was a huge clue that it wasn't a surface swipe. Someone had cut him down to his freaking *skull*.

And I should know, too. When Shane went for my cheek the night I refused to accept him as my mate, it took almost an hour before I stopped bleeding. Another two before I could talk without ripping open the scabs. By morning, there wasn't a single sign of his vicious attack, but the ache lingered the rest of the day.

Theo still has a mark. And, sure, I'm an alpha. I heal quicker than a lot of wolves just because of my rank. But isn't Theo another alpha? Besides, that doesn't change the fact that Walker blatantly confessed to cutting Theo open earlier because he felt like Theo "betrayed" him, and now Theo is *defending* him.

I have to remember that. No matter how nice Theo seems, he's part of the Western Pack. His loyalty is to his Alpha, not me, and no matter how he tries to sway me to his side, I can't fall for it.

Twenty-two more days. I only have twenty-two more days.

I move ahead of him, closing the gap between me and the cabin. Then, with my hand on the doorknob, I glance behind me.

He opens his mouth.

I let my wolf peek through my eyes.

His mouth closes with a soft *click*.

"Take care of yourself, Theo."

"Good night, Gemma."

"Night."

Elizabeth never returns to the cabin.

The cabin seems so empty without her, and it takes me a couple of days before I realize why that bothers my wolf. I grew up a beloved member of the Lakeview Pack. Between being the Alpha's adopted daughter and presenting myself as an omega, there was always someone nearby to keep me company. It was the same when I moved to Accalia as Ryker's intended. That first month, Ryker might have kept his distance, but I was definitely a curiosity—and that's not even counting how Shane was always around.

Probably should've realized something was up

then, now that I think about it. But I didn't, mainly because I was so focused on trying to figure out why Ryker was ignoring me. Something else the manipulative Shane had a paw in.

Dickhead.

Even when I was a lone wolf in Muncie, I wasn't exactly *alone*. I met Aleks my first night in the Fang City when he saved me from becoming vampire chow. He invited me to move in as his roommate right away. Apart from the weeks when Aleks left the apartment when he needed space, I've never really been on my own.

And now I am.

It's so weird. The morning after Aleks's fight, I found a new wolf standing guard under the same tree where I saw Theo the day before. It was so obvious that he was watching me, though he doesn't do anything to stop me when I walked out of the door to finally fetch some breakfast in the square.

Good. The mood I was in, I might have bitten his head off instead.

Elizabeth was there, eating by herself. She waved when she saw me approach, then invited me to take a seat opposite her while I scarfed down some of the community pancakes and bacon. But when I asked her what was up with her not returning to the cabin, she was quick to change the subject before admitting that Walker decided I deserved my own cabin. Instead of finding me an empty one, I got Elizabeth's, and she got moved to a different one closer to where the Alpha lives.

Of course, I didn't think that was fair. Not only because I hate watching my bio-dad tug on her leash like that, but because I was fine sharing her space. We had a lot in common—both of us hating Walker for one—and I liked being able to ask her her insight on the inner workings of the Western Pack.

I offered to see if I could change his mind, maybe try to get Elizabeth to move back in with me for the rest of the time I'm in the Wolf District. But, see, that's the really weird part. Her silver eyes darkened to a deep metal grey as she hurriedly shook her head. Then, glancing behind her to make sure no one was paying any attention to our conversation, she muttered under her breath for me to please let it go.

So I do. It goes against every instinct my wolf has, especially since I could sense how distraught she was, but I let it go. I tell her I'll see her around, and then I spend most of my time in the cabin, hoping to avoid Jack Walker.

I hadn't seen him since the night he gathered the pack together to watch the challenge. Based on what Aleks told me, I know that was only the beginning. Walker will expect to parade his captured vampire out sooner than later, but he's going to want to starve him a little first. Anything to make the show more entertaining, right?

Three days pass. I only run into Elizabeth one other time, and she finishes her meal quickly when she sees me heading her way. Before I reach her table, she's already standing up from the table with an apologetic expression on her haunted face.

Something's going on. My wolf is in total agreement with me, too. With Duke locked in the cage next to Trish's, Aleks trapped behind silver bars, and Elizabeth obviously avoiding me, I feel more alone than ever—and considering I've been sick with missing Ryker since I left Mountainside, that's saying something.

The distance is fucking awful. I purposely avoid reaching for the bond deep inside of me because it's so painful; it feels like a tease to grab it, knowing that I'm stuck here while he's back in Accalia. Still, I'm getting to the point where I'd do just about anything to see him again. I even think about demanding my phone back if only to hear his voice for a few minutes. Sure, I let them get away with sneaking mine out of my luggage as part of my agreement to stay. Don't care. My wolf is desperate for her mate, and so am I.

I busy myself in the solitude of the cabin. Elizabeth has a television, so at least I can make myself mindless binging a show. She also has a stacked bookshelf full of countless types of genres for when I need a little quiet.

I curl up on the couch and keep myself content, ignoring the ever-changing rotation of wolves keeping watch over the cabin.

Walker's agreement said I had to stay in the Wolf District for twenty-five days. It didn't say I had to pretend like I actually planned on joining his pack.

Six days down. Nineteen to go.

I get away with hiding out for those three days before a gentle knock sounds at the front door of my borrowed cabin.

My wolf is already up, pacing around inside of me as her ears flick to and fro. Neither one of us needed the laughably gentle knock, either. The dark, oozing aura preceding this particular wolf slaps at us from more than fifty feet away. It's almost stifling with him now that he's so close.

I have no clue what Walker is doing out there. I'm guessing it has everything to do with me purposely staying out of his sight these last few days.

The bastard hunted me down.

Freaking wonderful.

I set my book down on the couch. Refusing to answer the door isn't an option. With everything I know about Walker—everything I've learned since I've been here—the knock was just his way of giving the appearance of being polite. If I refuse to answer, he'll kick in the door.

"Coming," I call out. Then, steadying my nerves so

that he can't sense how much I loathe the idea of him entering my personal territory, I pull the door open.

He marches into the cabin like he has every right to. "Ah, there she is. My lovely, lovely daughter."

Don't puke, Gem, I tell myself again. It's become a constant refrain around him.

It's also a struggle. There's something in the way he's looking at me that makes my stomach turn. Before, when we met, there was always a dare written in the lines of his ruggedly handsome face. Later, the hint of a challenge, almost like he's daring me to defy him.

Now, though?

I've seen that look before, and it sure as hell doesn't belong on any male who wants to tell his pack that he's my father.

His gaze lingers on my face way longer than I'm comfortable with. When he finally glances away, looking around the empty room, I take the opportunity to put a couple of feet between us.

"Elizabeth isn't here."

There's a predatory look in his honey-gold eyes that I notice even as Walker smiles. He's watching me closely again, waiting for my reaction as he says, "I know. I thought you might want some... privacy."

That's exactly what Elizabeth had said. As much as I didn't like it, it does make some sense. Privacy is an Alpha's privilege. Just like how the Alpha's cabin in Mountainside is set apart from the rest of the pack,

Walker made a show of respecting me being a female alpha by kicking Elizabeth out of her cabin so that I could be alone.

At least, that's what I thought—until Walker slams the door behind him.

I gulp. The action is reflexive. The last thing I want to do is show this wolf any fear, but there's something about the way his strong body looms over me that has my back up.

If I step away from him, it'll be a retreat. An act of submission. If I don't... yeah. There is no *don't*.

I move out of his reach.

"Is there a reason you're here?" Besides being a creepy, leering bastard?

"Of course."

But he's not going to just come out and tell me, is he?

Forget it. "By the way, how's Aleks?"

We're beyond pretending that I'm a stranger to the vamp he captured. I guessed that he knew all along, and even if he hadn't made that clear with the "roommate" jab, I'd put a hundred down that either Christian or Theo filled him in on the talk I had with Aleks.

"The leech? He's fine. Getting ready for the next bout of training, if you really want to know. But enough about him. Let's talk about you."

"Me?"

"You've been here for almost a week. I was just seeing if you wanted to revisit my offer."

Riiiight. His *brilliant* idea that, if he could get me to set foot on his territory, I'd never want to leave.

As if I would leave my mate behind.

As if I'd ever betray my real mom and dad like that. *Please*.

"To stay here? Uh. No. Sorry."

I'm so not sorry—and he knows it, too.

"Oh?" Walker prowls around me. There's no other word for the way that he moves around me, circling me. I know better than to allow a monster like Walker at my back and I turn slowly, tracking him. "What if I sweetened the pot?"

Hmm. What's a nice way of saying that there isn't a single thing he can give me that would make me want to spend one minute longer around him than I have to?

The friendly, affable father figure facade he tries to sell is just that: a facade. This prowling alpha wolf, eyeing me as if searching for a weakness, for some spot to attack... this is the true Wicked Wolf.

I have to remember that.

Even my wolf is warning me not to piss off the unpredictable Alpha. Just because he's trying to be nice at the moment, I can't—I *won't*—let myself be fooled. The darkness that clings to him like a shadow is too thick, the gleam in his eyes too much of a warning.

Stay on guard, Gem. Don't let it down.

"Like what?"

There. Nice and safe and to the point.

He grins. And I know that he's pure wolf, that there's no vamp in him, but those fangs... whoa.

"Whatever you want."

Too bad there isn't a single thing I want from him.

"You're special," he goes on to say. "So special that I spent twenty-five years looking for you. I never believed that my blood would be erased so easily. You were a fierce and protective pup. I should've known you were something when you challenged me as a tiny whelp, and now look at you. A female alpha. Do you know what you could do with that power?"

Do I? Considering a lot of the rumors about a female alpha have proved to be true when it comes to me, I've got a pretty good idea. Am I going to admit that to Walker?

Not a chance in hell.

CHAPTER 16

"I don't want power," I tell him. "I'm happy with what I've got."

All I've ever wanted was my happily-ever-after with Ryker. So long as the Wicked Wolf was standing in my way, I thought I couldn't have that. I know better—a fact I'll happily admit to Ryker that I was wrong about when I get back home—and now all I have to do is survive Walker's cruel games so that I can grab Trish, Duke, and Aleks and get the hell out of here.

If only it was that easy.

"What if you could have more?" Walker asks. "Think about it. I've always known my line was strong, and I sired a female alpha. What could you do next? Now, let me make this perfectly clear: I want you to stay in the district. Can you imagine the sort of pups you could bear for me? With the right mate, you'll be the second coming of the Luna, the mother of a new, better race of shifters. A wolf queen with a legion of alphas to do your bidding."

Okay. This went off the rails real fast. What is he talking about?

"The right mate? I already have the right mate," I remind him. "My *fated* mate."

Oh. Walker doesn't like that answer, does he?

He recovers quickly, though, pulling that Hollywood-fake grin back to his face. "I said the *right* mate. Everyone knows the Wolfson line is weak. Look how easy it was for a beta wolf to take out the Alpha. The Mountainside Pack is a generation away from being nothing. I won't allow my daughter to sully her blood with a *Wolfson*."

"Too late," I shoot back, probably more gleefully than I should considering he's sounding pretty maniacal right now. "Shane didn't stop the Luna Ceremony." As a reminder, I tug on my shirt, showing off Ryker's mark. "I claimed Ryker and he claimed me. You can't change that."

"I can't," Walker agrees, "but we both know that Elizabeth can."

"Only if me or Ryker is okay with it."

"And you will be. Take it from an Alpha that knows. Fate doesn't always work out. Reject Wolfson, and you can have any other male you choose for your children. You don't even need to bond with them to have their pups. I'd prefer it, too. The more males you take, the wider the genetic pool, the stronger our pack will be."

Okay. Did I think he was crazy before?

Because *this*?

This is fucking nuts!

Put aside how I would never, ever willingly give Ryker up. Why would this prick think that I'd *want* any of what he's trying to offer me? I get itchy just knowing that my four wolf guards have pledged their life and loyalty to me. A... what was that? Legion of alphas?

Oh, *hell* no.

"Thanks, but I'm gonna have to pass on that. I think I'll stick with Ryker."

A muscle jerks in his cheek.

My wolf arrows her ears back, muzzle curling to show a hint of fang. She senses the way the air in the cabin suddenly grows thick with tension and immediately reacts.

That's okay, girl. My fingers flex, my body getting ready to shift. So do I.

As if he could care less about the threat I represent, Walker shrugs. "It might not be your choice. You would do well to remember that."

I go cold before asking in a careful voice, "What do you mean by that?"

"Just that, right about now, my Beta is sitting down with Wolfson and giving him the same offer I gave you. Only, in his case, it's not about a new mate. It's about keeping his pack from being decimated by mine."

What?

How?

It's bad enough that he just put that out there. He's not even hiding what lengths he'll go to to get me to agree to his insanity. Threatening the entire Mountainside Pack to get what he wants? I believe it.

But how is Ryker being taunted with the same threat?

I thought Christian was his Beta. But that can't be right. I just saw Christian a couple of hours ago, lurking outside of my window in between two other wolves I didn't know. Unless Walker could get his paws on some kind of supersonic jet, there's no way that Christian was able to trade the Wolf District for Accalia to approach Ryker with my bio-dad's latest madness.

"I have to say, Christian might seem grim, but he can be very persuasive when I order him to be. I'm sure he'll make it so that Wolfson can't refuse."

So it *is* Christian.

What the—

Understanding dawns. It's a fucking *terrible* understanding, and I'm praying to the Luna that I'm wrong when I guess, "Ryker's here. In the district. Isn't he?"

"Arrived this morning."

"Where is he?" I demand. Forget being cool. I have visions of Ryker behind bars, Ryker being forced to challenge another wolf, Ryker being torn apart by Aleks if my sadistic father *really* wants to destroy me... ah, Luna. He literally just said that Aleks is getting ready for his next training. *No.* "Where's my mate?"

For the first time since I met him, the tiny jolt of pleasure I sense coming off of him seems genuine. I did the one thing I told myself not to: I let down my guard, proving that Ryker Wolfson is my true weakness. I've been able to play it as cool as possible until now, but the thought of losing my mate because of my bastard sperm donor?

It's my breaking point—and I just made sure that Walker knows that.

He takes another couple of seconds to drink in my obvious terror before he says in a smug tone, "Another Alpha accepted my invitation to visit my territory. Of course I have to show him around, pay him the respect the shifter community has denied me for too long. I'm sure he'll be by soon—unless he decides he'd rather go back east."

Without you.

He doesn't say that part out loud. He doesn't have to. Whatever his reasons were, Ryker is known as the Alpha who rejected his fated mate. We might be fully bonded now, but if either one of us decides to sever our bond, Elizabeth could use her strange gift to break it.

Luna, I hate Walker. I hate him more than I've hated anyone in my life. The way my claws unsheathe inside of the fists I didn't even realize I'd formed tells me that my wolf feels the same way.

The tips of my claws pierce the meat of my palms. Blood perfumes the air. Walker makes a display of breathing it in as I fantasize about going for his jugular.

If freaking *only*.

"Tell me, Ruby. Have you noticed the wolves hanging around your cabin?"

He deserves an extra slash for the way he accentuates that damn name as he suddenly changes the subject.

Walker wants to pretend he didn't just make it obvious he intends to separate me and Ryker? Okay. Two can play that game.

"Uh, yeah. Can't miss them." It takes everything I have to keep my tone deceptively casual. "It's obvious you have them watching me."

"That's where you're wrong, daughter. They're not watching you. They're waiting for you to invite them inside."

Keep it casual?

Not anymore.

"What? *Why?*"

"Because they know what mating you will do for them. They're lining up to be the consort to your queen. The father to your pups. Don't fool yourself. They'd kill for that privilege, and it's time you know that."

You've got to be fucking kidding me. I thought he changed the subject, but I was wrong. And what he just told me is taking this whole thing way too damn far.

Keeping him in my sights, I cross the room, heading for the nearest window that looks out to the front of the cabin. Pulling the curtain back, I peek outside.

A familiar figure is leaning up against the same tree. He straightens as the curtain twitches, his head turned toward me.

Theo.

I let the curtain drop.

I don't think it's a coincidence that he's the wolf out there waiting. How much do I want to bet that he's the first stud Walker has in mind?

"It doesn't have to be any of them, either." His voice creeps up behind me—or maybe that's just him. "You know that Janelle abandoned me before we could be fully bonded. That left me in a bit of a predicament. An Alpha without a mate. I've never lacked for bed partners"—*Ew, ew, ew*—"but it could be that it's finally time I settled down for good."

Disgust turns to fury in a heartbeat as I whirl on him. "You can't have my mom—"

"Maybe I'll send Elizabeth on a trip to Lakeview," he muses cruelly. Then, as if that latest threat of his wasn't already awful, his golden eyes turn molten. "Or maybe I'll decide to try out the younger model instead. After all, I've already proven I can sire a female alpha. Imagine what I could sire with one as its mother."

In a split second, the disgust returns. Ten-fold.

Only a lifetime of concealing my true self keeps me from giving away just how repulsed I am as soon as I realize what he means. If he's saying what I *think* he's saying...

The leer.

The prowl.

The empty cabin.

Oh, Luna. No. *Fuck* no.

He thinks he's so slick. To make matters worse, he's picked tonight of all nights to talk to me about this.

The Luna is still a few hours from rising, but I've been pushing against her pull for days now. I'm not worried about moon fever—I have plenty else to worry about—but to suggest I turn my bed into a revolving door on the threat that he might want a turn...

His lips curve just enough to have my stomach clenching even tighter. I want to hurl so bad, and the bile burns the length of my throat as I clamp my jaws shut, keeping it back.

I won't give him the satisfaction of throwing up on him. Bastard wants a reaction. He wants to make me squirm. Mom might not have gone into detail on all of the ways he tortured her while they were mates, but even as coddled as I was, a girl picks up things. He'll probably get off more on how sick I suddenly am than anything he's ever done in the sack.

Purposely rearranging my features into a neutral expression, I pretend to think about it for a moment before I give my head a little shake. "Thanks for the offer, but like I said, *pass*."

"Very well." His lips curve just a touch higher. "Enjoy your privacy, Ruby."

Fuck you.

I almost spit the words out. They're on the tip of my tongue. Prick deserves to hear them, too, but after his not-so-subtle threat, I'm not about to give the sick bastard any ideas.

Instead, I force my own smile. "I told you. Call me Gemma."

Hell if he gets to call me Gem.

As soon as Walker leaves, I lock the fucking door.

Will it do any good? I highly doubt it. It's not a shifter-proof doorknob, not like the one that Ryker installed on his basement door during his year-long struggle with moon fever. One quick snap and anyone can enter the cabin while I'm alone.

Welp. There goes any hope that I'm sleeping tonight...

I give my head another, harsher shake. Later. That's a problem for Later Gem to deal with. I have something more pressing to deal with at this particular moment.

Now that I know that Ryker is here, I reach for our bond. I hadn't let myself do that the whole time I've been in the district because it was too much of a temptation. Screw that. If he's here, I'll be able to tell with one quick tug.

I'd be a huge fucking idiot if I took the Wicked Wolf at his word. I tug, and when I feel him sending reassurances down the line, I nearly sink to my knees.

It's strong.

It's *real*.

Ryker's here. He's really here.

I don't know why; Walker says it's because Ryker accepted his invitation, but that doesn't sound like my mate. The whole reason he didn't join me on this trip in the first place was that someone had to stay behind in Accalia. He shouldn't be here—but he is.

And, if Walker was telling the truth about that, then he's currently being offered the chance to break our fated mate bond.

My hands are trembling. Sometime after Walker

left the cabin, my claws retracted. Bloody tracks run down the inside of my palms from where I unknowingly pierced myself. I rub them against my jeans, my heart pounding a mile a minute.

Though I'm sure he'll think the worst, I close off my half of our bond. With him being so close, I can't risk him picking up on how much I'm suddenly freaking out.

He loves me. When he tells me that, I believe him. I believe him when he says that he's wanted me since he was seventeen and he knew in an instant that I was meant for him. But I also know that Ryker is fanatically loyal to his pack. He might've seen Trish Danvers as an unfortunate sacrifice, but what would he do if the Wicked Wolf really does threaten the entire Mountainside Pack?

Would he agree to let Elizabeth touch him then?

No. My head shaking turns almost violent. *No.*

Ryker would never break our bond.

I believe that wholeheartedly. He wouldn't reject me again. He has to know I'd never survive it.

He wouldn't...

Right?

THE NEXT FEW HOURS ARE LUNA-DAMNED AWFUL.

He's here. No denying that. I keep tugging on our

bond, making sure that it feels as close as it did a couple of minutes ago, and I keep getting the same reassurances sent down the line to me. I can't quite trace him—another mystical barrier that the Wolf District seems to have—but so long as it feels this close, I know he's here and that he's all right.

I don't know what to do. I pace around the cabin, wearing a damn hole in the floor, hoping, praying, *wishing* that Ryker would show up. When my nerves get the better of me—and my wolf urges me to check—I peek out of the window. Theo was replaced by Christian almost immediately after I saw the back of Walker, but the last time I looked I saw an unfamiliar blond packmate lurking out there and I jerked the curtain closed so quickly, I tore half of it off the curtain rod.

My wolf is furious. Now that we know what they're doing out there, she has the instinct to chase them away from our territory. She's already chosen her mate, and she's willing to fight off any poachers.

It might have been easier to rein her in if it wasn't for the moon. Night falls, with the Luna rising. Every inch of me feels electrified, and I'm hot. Like really hot.

Like, *suffering from moon fever*, hot.

Damn it.

I refuse to head out of the cabin. Control is tentative with the moon ruling me, and I tear through Elizabeth's kitchen, hoping she has some ice cream to cool the burn. Luckily, I find a pint of some local brand,

and I scarf it down. It helps a little, and the half-gallon of milk I chase it with makes it so that I can dare one last peek outside without worrying I'll go feral on the latest male who actually thinks he has a chance with me.

Lifting up the torn curtain, my heart skips a beat. My wolf goes from deadly to docile in an instant.

The moon shines down on the most beautiful sight I've ever seen.

I don't know how I missed him approaching the cabin, but he's there. With a deadly stride, and a warning that prickles against my wolf from even the inside of the cabin, his long legs are eating up the ground, heading right from me. He's dressed all in black, his dark eyes beaming like a pair of headlights in the dark. A stuffed duffel bag is gripped in one hand, the other clenched in a fist.

Rushing for the door, I throw it open.

His head jerks up. He looks so fucking sexy when he seems ready for murder, but the way his expression softens when he sees me?

I melt like butter.

"Ryker!"

My mate freezes. The duffel bag drops from his suddenly slack hand. A pulse of pure relief coupled with love slams into me as he holds out his arms in an open invitation.

I don't even hesitate. I run right to him, throwing

my arms around his neck as my inner wolf yips gleefully to see her mate.

He closes his arms around me, pulling me up against his chest as he bows his body over mine. His hair tickles my cheek as his lips go unerringly to the jagged white lines that curve around my throat.

Ryker's mark.

I shudder out a breath as he nuzzles it gently. He kisses it, laving it with his tongue, before he lifts his head.

For a few poignant seconds, we just stare at each other. I can't believe he's here. This is all I've wanted for ages now, just to have him close, but when Ryker grips my chin in his claws before slanting his mouth over mine, I realize that I was wrong.

This is all I've wanted.

The kiss is hot, heavy, and possessive. It also doesn't last anywhere near as long as I like. All too soon, he's breaking it. I want to initiate another one, but before I do, he glances over his shoulder, unerringly looking at the tree where I've had so many guests lately.

Shit. He probably is catching all of the different male scents laying over each other. And, from the way his expression shadows over, he's not happy about it.

No one is standing there now, but I should know that that's probably going to last. Plus, I've learned that there are eyes and ears everywhere in the Wolf District.

Privacy is a joke, and one that Walker seems to think is funny.

Dick.

At least there's some semblance of it in the cabin.

Grabbing Ryker's hand with both of mine, I start to pull him toward the cabin. He has just enough time to snag the duffel that he dropped at his feet before he lets me guide him all the way inside.

CHAPTER 17

Once the door is shut and laughably locked, I can't keep it in anymore. "I can't believe you're here! What are you doing? I thought you were staying in Accalia... how did you even *get* here?"

I spit out my questions rapid-fire. For some reason, that erases the dark look on his handsome face, replacing it with a heart-stopping grin.

"I took a plane," he says, answering my last question. "After Jace told me what was going on, I made all the arrangements I could. Warren wasn't happy, but I reminded him I'm the Alpha. He agreed to be acting Beta one more time on the condition that, when we go home again, I let him stay retired."

Fair enough. Warren earned his retirement, and my wolf settles a little when she hears Ryker say that *we* are going home again.

But that only explains how he made it to California.

"What about the Wolf District? How did you find it?"

"Jace told me how. It was easy. Actually, the hardest part was figuring out the rental car."

My jaw drops. "Hang on—you *drove*?"

His grin widens. "With a roof and everything. I left it on the edge of the Wolf District this morning when I arrived, but when we leave, I'll drive you back to the airport."

I... I can't believe it.

Shifters have a tendency to be claustrophobic, though that's not a word any of us will ever admit to. Our wolves need to be free to run, to roam, to use their senses. Being trapped inside a metal box takes that away from us. It's for that exact reason I drive a Jeep, so that I have access to freedom even when I'm driving.

For a wolf like Ryker, the cramped quarters of the plane would've sucked, but it couldn't be helped. It was the quickest way to cross the country, and time was of the essence for both of us to have to make that trip.

But a full-on car? Instead of running the whole way from the airport to the woods?

I know why he did it. Until it was too late, the Western Pack wouldn't have been able to sense him creeping toward their territory. Torture for Ryker, and he did it all for me.

Even more impressive when you realize that this is probably one of the first times he had ever actually operated a vehicle on his own.

We rode in my Jeep together one time and he nearly bent the bar out of shape, he was so uncomfortable driving around in a car—and it wasn't because of me since I'm a freaking awesome driver. It was one of the only escapes I had when I was still playing the part of Omega Gem, and my Jeep was one element of control that I clung to to quiet my alpha side.

The control... that's what Ryker's deal is. The freedom and the control, and he sacrificed all of that to show up in California to be greeted by an enemy pack trying to convince him that he should give up his mate.

Obviously, he refused. I mean, he's already dropped hints twice that he plans on leaving *with* me, and he accompanied his statements with another reassuring pulse through our bond. But I don't understand... I would've guessed that, if he refused, Walker wouldn't have let him stay in the Wolf District regardless.

But he's here. And that makes me wonder: how the hell did pull that off?

"I didn't know you were here," I tell him. "Not until Walker showed up at the cabin with some crazy idea that we should break our bond." I wait for him to tell me that that was impossible, and when he doesn't, I know that Walker told the truth: he did have Christian make the same offer to Ryker. I gulp, my voice going a little thick with emotion as I add, "I refused. Obviously. But he said you were here, that he was giving you the same chance to be free of me."

Ryker's eyes flash. For a heartbeat, he wears the same flat, neutral expression he calls up when he wants to hide what he's thinking. I haven't seen it in so long, but whenever I do, I'm thrown back to that fateful night in the den when I accused him of rejecting me in favor of Trish Danvers and he didn't deny it.

Tears burn my eyes, but I'm stubborn enough not to shed them. I blink them back, waiting for Ryker to finally say something.

He nods. "Yeah. The Beta tried something like that when I got here."

I can't take it. I wait a few seconds, then prod him with a harsh, "And? What did you say?"

"I told him to go fuck himself, then demanded he take me to my mate before I have Walker looking for his next Beta."

I let out a shaking laugh as I imagine how Christian reacted to Ryker's retort. He has to know about the Wicked Wolf's tendency to go through Betas the same way people go through underwear. Plus there's the undeniable fact that Christian only got the gig because Ryker killed Walker's *last* Beta.

I think it's a laugh. From the way Ryker sucks in a breath, he hears a sob.

Okay. It's a sob. It's totally a sob. One of relief, yeah, but that doesn't change what it was.

My knees buckle. Before I can even drop a few inches, he's there, arms around me, pulling me up against his chest. It's a tight squeeze, a hug that would have a human's bones groaning in protest, but it's the type of embrace that comforts both me and my inner wolf.

I don't realize until right that very moment how I spent the last few hours convinced that Ryker would've at least thought about breaking our bond.

Now that he says that like it never even crossed his mind, I just about collapse.

I'm an alpha female. Headstrong, impulsive, and reckless, I've been on my guard ever since I crossed into my sperm donor's territory. Just like how I told myself again and again to show no fear, I refused to let them scent any weakness coming from me. I had to be strong.

With Ryker, I don't have to be anything but *his*.

In the beginning of our courtship, I kept up my guard. After spending so long pretending to be an omega, it was nice to be an independent, fierce alpha. I was snarky. Flippant. I put up a wall around my heart, forcing him to find a way past it. Then, when he did, I still kept him at arm's length if only because I didn't want him to break my heart again.

When I finally allowed myself to admit that I loved

him, the guard came crashing down. Of course, I had to erect it again since I've been in the Wolf District, but with Ryker holding me closely, I let it crumble once more.

"I was so scared," I confess. "I know I shouldn't be. I fucking *hate* that I was, but the truth is, I just kept thinking 'what if'. What if you decided it was too much trouble being mated to a stubborn alpha who doesn't listen? What if you realized that I wasn't worth risking the pack? What if—"

"I would never," he murmurs into my hair, stroking my back, comforting me as I spill my guts out to him. "Even if you lost your mind and decided to live here for good, I'd stay. You're it for me, Gemma. You're home. Nothing's gonna separate us."

Sighing, I tighten my hold on him.

I wish I could believe him. I really, really do. And, if it wasn't for the situation we've found ourselves in, I *would*.

But I'm not so sure I can.

My alpha quirk of being able to scent deception has been wonky ever since I arrived in this cursed place. I'm pretty sure it has something to do with Elizabeth. If her strange gift has her able to hide another shifter's innate scent—not to mention breaking a freaking bond with just the touch of her hand—how hard can it be for her to mess with my wolf in other ways?

Theo proved it's not completely broken, but even though he's an alpha, his dominance is nowhere near Walker's or Ryker's. Half the time, I suspect my bio-dad is flat-out lying to me. Could Ryker be?

Know what? It doesn't matter. Even if he's completely full of shit, I'm just grateful he said the words at all.

Ryker Wolfson is my mate. Walker had to know that us mating again would be inevitable as soon as he allowed for us to be together, whether that was his intention or not. It doesn't really make sense, especially after his threatening trip to the cabin earlier, but I'm not about to look a gift horse in the mouth.

Luna, I missed Ryker so damn much.

I hate that being here the last week and a half has made me so suspicious. Reuniting with my mate should be a joyous occasion, but Walker taints it by what he tried to sell both of us earlier this afternoon. He doesn't want me with Ryker, but he's here. Why?

I know why my mate has come after me. His wolf would never have let him leave my safety in Aleks's hands if he could help it, and once Jace informed him of my agreement with the Wicked Wolf, it probably was only a matter of time before he decided he couldn't stay away.

I don't know what that says about the Mountainside Pack. He mentioned that he convinced Warren to take over begrudgingly, but it's easy to see that it cost him. Is he saying that I'm worth the price? I so want to believe that, but it's tough. Our mating has already been full of way too many ups and downs in only the last year and a half.

And now he's here, on the night of the full moon, when Walker could've easily shoved him in another silver-lined cell if he wanted to keep us apart after my mate refused his offer.

That's the suspicious side of me. Walker has his reasons. I'd be a moron not to realize that.

What could they be? And how is he using Ryker against me?

Based on his visit from earlier today, all he wants is for me to go ahead and start popping out more female alphas like me for him. He wasn't wrong when he said that two shifters can procreate without being fully bonded—I'm a perfect example of that since my mom got knocked up by that bastard without him ever committing to her—but it's rare. Not *creating female alphas* rare, but it has very low odds.

Mating with your fated mate? Odds jump. If he's your *bonded* fated mate? Odds jump even higher.

And if you bang repeatedly under the Luna's watchful gaze after she's blessed your mating? There's a very good chance there'll be a bun in the oven after that unless certain precautions are taken.

Stuck here, I haven't even thought about any kind of shifter-friendly birth control. Why would I? I expected to spend this full moon far from Ryker, and despite Walker's insane suggestion, I'd rather die than let one of the Western Pack wolves put his dick anywhere near me.

And if I don't get my hands on Ryker's, I might just lose it.

Then again, that prick did make it clear he hates the idea of my pups being bred with Ryker. And while I want to enjoy my mate a little longer before I start thinking about adding to our family, if the Luna wills it, she wills it.

I don't care. Nothing can stop me from showing Ryker how damn happy I am to see him again.

I need this male more than I need air to breathe. The hug soothed something jagged inside of me, the kiss made me feel like I'm home even in this strange place, but I need him.

All of him.

Pulling away from his embrace, I slip my hands between us, reaching from the hem of his shirt. When I start to yank it upward, Ryker circles my wrist with his hands, pausing me.

From the way I feel his fingers trembling against my skin, I know it's taking everything in him not to help me fling off his shirt. The moon will be riding him just as hard, and while our separation was rough on the both of us, knowing that Walker's endgame was to split us up probably has Ryker's wolf desperate to prove that I'm still his mate. After all, I know I won't feel whole until he's buried deep inside of me.

In a low voice, meant only for me, he says, "We have an audience."

I sense my eyes going the color of molten lava as I glance up at my mate through the fringe of my lashes. "So?" I don't bother to keep my voice down. "If they want to be within earshot, they're responsible for what they hear. It's the full moon. You're my mate. If they don't want to hear me fucking you, they can get the hell out. You're mine, Ryker. I'm yours. You think I give a shit if we have an audience?"

It's never stopped us before. The first time either of us mated, we did it outside, for Luna's sake. We're wolves. Mating is, at its core, a biological urge. Whoever's out there—whether it's Theo, Christian, or any other wolf who thinks he's male enough to tame me—had to have known I'd want to reconnect with Ryker. Knowing they're out there isn't about to stop me.

Unless Ryker isn't down with the public display...

He's never had a problem before. We've mated in the back alley behind Charlie's where any supe in hearing range would've known we were at it; in Muncie, the vamps probably curled their lips and thought, *Wolves,* before going on their way. We christened my Jeep when we couldn't wait to make it back to the townhouse before our wild natures took us over. The Fang City park. Beneath the trees in Accalia.

Every freaking room in the Alpha's cabin besides the den.

But this is the Wolf District. An enemy Alpha's territory. Walker's already played his hand, letting us know he plans on breaking up our mating no matter what he has to offer us. We might have refused him so far, but I guess I can see how flaunting our mating in his face by spending the night of the Luna fucking Ryker like we're a pair of Energizer bunnies is probably not the best idea.

Then again, maybe he shouldn't have allowed Ryker to come see me when the Luna's pull is so damn irresistible.

Not that I'm complaining. And if my mate decides we should focus on taking care of Walker instead of our own urges, I get it. It's fine. I feel like I'm crawling out of my skin with the urge to jump him, but not if he thinks we should wait.

He still hasn't said anything.

My wrists go limp. The hem of his shirt slips out from between my fingers.

"Okay. I get it. I can hold off if you can—"

In one fluid motion, Ryker replaces my grip on his shirt with his before tugging it over his head.

"I never said I could. I just wanted you to be aware that, when I claim you tonight, it's not just Walker's sentry who's gonna hear it. I'm going to make sure this whole fucking place knows you're mine."

Ryker's chest is heaving. My marks on his skin seem to glimmer in the light of the cabin—or maybe that's just me. His wolf is peering at me through his gaze, looking at me like I'm a freaking steak and he hasn't eaten in weeks.

That's okay. I'm *starving*.

"You talk tough, big man," I tease. I'm panting a little in anticipation, rising up on my tiptoes as if I can't get any closer to him. "Prove it."

"*Gladly*."

He's an alpha wolf. I should've known better than to dare him—and maybe I did. Within seconds, I've forgotten about anyone else except for my gorgeous mate. He makes it easy by stripping down to nothingness before helping me shuck off my clothes.

There's a bed somewhere behind us. Do I care? Not even a little. As soon as we're both naked, I place my hands on Ryker's shoulders, leaping up until my legs are wrapped securely around his waist. His warm, callused hands support my bare as easily as I press my tits against his chest.

His thick, heavy erection is stuck between us. It sprang to life as soon as he freed it from his jeans, so I know he's as ready as I am. I'm sopping wet, my body crying out for him, but when I shimmy into the perfect position to let my powerful mate nail me, I slow down a little. As he watches me unblinkingly, a rumble in his chest making me feel like I'm vibrating, I reach between us to position his cock against the opening of my pussy, but I don't sink down on him.

Ryker wants to claim me? I swallow my dominant urge as I realize that I'm perfectly okay with that.

In a throaty voice, I order, "Make me yours. *Again*."

One month ago, I told him to mark me. Some mates do it with a bite. Others unleash a claw, slicing gently in a place that has meaning to the bonded pair. Not us. When I finally gave Ryker free rein to mark a part of me as his, he used four claws to rip a tear around the curve of my throat and down past my collarbone. It was a blatant mark of possession, and Ryker's way of making sure every fucking person I ever met knew I belonged to him.

Shifters are a strange race. If anyone else was ever able to cut me like that, my reaction would be to gut them next or—like I did to Ryker—go for their heart. But knowing it was a way for Ryker to show me how desperate he was to mark me as his, I relished in the pain and the long, white scars that he left behind.

Now, trapped in dangerous territory, perfectly aware that there really is no such thing as privacy here, I give him permission to do it again.

As Ryker jerks his hips, burying his cock to the hilt inside of me, I moan at the sudden feeling of fullness. It's so good, so *right*, and I'm just about to start riding him when he opens his mouth wide.

Out of the corner of my blissed-out eyes, I notice

his canines are extended. Before I can understand why, he pulls his cock part way out of me before slamming back home—right as he sinks his fangs into my shoulder.

My scream starts out high-pitched before turning throaty. Ryker didn't just make me his by mating me during the height of the Luna. Oh, no. He just gave me a second claiming mark as if to prove that nothing—and no one—can come between us.

He's rocking in and out of me, pistoning his hips as he keeps his fangs where they are. It's like he's desperate to keep us connected in any way that he can.

I know exactly how he feels.

Our connection is undeniable. It always has been, and I realize at this very moment that it always *will* be. I don't have to worry about him rejecting me. In so many ways, Ryker Wolfson has made it clear that we're a bonded pair.

Forever mates.

Nothing will *ever* separate us.

As my orgasm begins to build, Ryker all-consuming in his quest toward dominating me, I have just enough sense to release my hand from its death-grip on his shoulder; my weight is nothing to him, and he's strong enough to keep me pinned on his length even without me using his body to ride him. I flex my fingers, tapping into my keening wolf. My claws suddenly appear.

I moan his name.

"Mine," he grunts. It's muffled, since he's refused to take his fangs out of my flesh just yet, but even if I didn't know what he was saying, my wolf understands the message coming from his.

I belong to him, just like Ryker Wolfson will always be *mine*.

When I angle my hand the way I want it, I press the tips of my claws to his shoulder blade. One quick swipe and I slice through his skin. His blood fills the air.

The rusty tang of it has me coming around his cock.

Ryker finally rips his mouth free. Throwing back his head, he lets out a howl that shakes the whole damn cabin. The scent of his blood might have made me orgasm, but knowing that I marked him as my mate on purpose has him shouting out his pleasure. The marks he wears around his heart represent the time I repaid him for "rejecting" me by threatening to rip out his heart. He kept them because he always knew he wouldn't stop until I was his mate, but in the last month, I never actually marked him on my own.

And now I have.

Because he'll always be mine, and I'll do anything to keep him.

CHAPTER 18

My cheek is pressed to Ryker's sweaty chest. I've got one arm thrown over his waist, my fingers absently playing with his side.

He's rumbling with pride, the vibration tickling my skin. I smile because hell if he doesn't deserve to be proud.

We finally made it to the bed that's been designated as mine. It's still the one in the smaller room, mainly because I don't feel comfortable mating in Elizabeth's bed. It's a twin, so we had to be a little flexible during that last round, but that's okay. It gives me an excuse to lay directly on top of him like his blanket while we recover.

His claws thread through my hair. It's a tangled mess. He snags a few knots from root to end, murmuring a soft apology every time he does.

I squeeze his side. No apologies necessary, babe.

The moon is still controlling us. Beneath me, Ryker's cock is twitching, already semi-hard. No doubt he'll flip me to my back and hook my ankles over his shoulders again when the need gets too strong, but he's still in control.

I take advantage of that to ask him something that's been bothering me.

Propping myself up on my elbow, I lay my hand over his heart, running my fingers over the marks circling his nipple. "Hey. Question. Didn't Jace tell you I agreed to twenty-five days?"

That duffel is an overnight bag. It's bulging, but it's nothing like the suitcase I packed when I planned on being here a few days. Luckily, the pack commissary provided me with a couple of extra changes of clothes when I ran out so I wasn't forced to re-wear my used clothes without washing them first. I'm sure they could do the same for Ryker... if it wasn't for how he keeps mentioning his plans to make sure that we get out of here as soon as we can.

Somehow, I don't think his plan includes either of us finishing out the rest of the twenty-five days—and I'm right.

With a barely muffled snort, he says, "You agreed. I sure as fuck didn't."

"But, Ryker—"

"No *buts*, sweetheart. What, did you think I only came here to check up on you, then I was leaving? I'm an Alpha. Leader of a pack. I get forty-eight hours on an invite, then it's considered a challenge. I'm leaving the day after tomorrow, and you're coming with me."

His jaw is set, his eyes an even darker shade of gold.

He expects me to argue. And, okay, that's definitely something I would normally do.

Normally.

Right now, I'll take any excuse to get the hell out of here. But I can't leave alone, and I make sure he knows that.

He knows about Trish being locked in a cage, thanks to Jace. I hurriedly explain that she's not the only one we have to break free. Duke's locked up, too, and so is—

"Oh, Luna," I blurt out suddenly, slapping him in the rock-hard abs. "Aleks is here, too."

How could I forget about him? It's been days since I've seen him, and though I've been obsessing over what's happening to him, I decided it wasn't worth the risk to try to see him again. Eventually, Walker's going to resort to using him against me, but he hasn't yet and I'd like to leave it that way as long as possible.

Ryker brushes my messy hair out of my face. "I know. Even if Walker didn't rub it in, a vamp's scent tends to linger." He's not wrong. I'm used to it, but to a wolf, vamps have a very unusual cold, dead scent. "My wolf picked it up on the edge of the territory where I entered this morning. He did exactly as I asked. Maybe he's not as big an asshole as I thought he was."

Coming from Ryker, that's high praise indeed for Aleks.

"Look at you." I nudge him in the rib before dropping my palm to curve over his side again. "You made a friend."

Ryker purses his lips. "Maybe an ally," he admits after a moment.

Hey. I'll take it.

Beneath my hand, he suddenly stiffens. And my mind might be in the gutter—it usually is when a naked Ryker is involved—but I don't mean his cock.

I immediately rise to my elbow again. "What? What's wrong?"

His hands go to my waist. He lifts me up as he raises his upper body, scooting back so that he's leaning up against the headboard. Once he's sitting, he maneuvers me so that I'm tucked in his lap.

Only then does he ask, "Is Filan the only bloodsucker in Walker's territory?"

Weird question considering how on-guard he's suddenly acting, but I answer him. "As far as I know. Why?"

"Because I just realized something."

Uh-oh. "What?"

"Hold up. Let me ask you another question first."

At my nod, he says, "How often did the Lakeview Pack host other Alphas?"

The answer to that is simple enough.

Never.

My dad was super careful to guard my secret. He couldn't risk someone figuring out that I was different, or for someone to recognize that I looked too much like Jack Walker. I was allowed to attend the annual Alpha's gathering that took place every summer, but that was the only exception. I was Paul Booker's daughter, even if our names didn't match, and he rarely let me out around the other Alphas while I was there.

Which was perfectly fine with me since I got to spend the time with the Alphas' families—including Ryker Wolfson.

"He didn't."

"That's what I thought. And there's our problem. When an Alpha is invited to another's territory, there's... pomp. Circumstance. Ridiculous traditional shit. For those forty-eight hours, I'm actually a guest, and Walker's made it clear he intends to treat me that way. He's hosting a big dinner tomorrow night before my time's up, and some kind of entertainment." Ryker rolls his eyes. "It's a way of showing me his power so that I don't try to push my luck and stay past the forty-eight-hour deadline."

"You keep saying forty-eight hours," I point out. "I

don't get it. He made me promise I would stay for twenty-five days, but you only get to be here for two?"

"It's the same thing I told you before, sweetheart. You're an alpha, and you're my mate, but you're not an Alpha of a pack."

That's true. I'm an alpha wolf, and part of the Alpha couple of the Mountainside Pack, but I don't lead my own. Not that I want to, but when he talks about pomp and circumstance and things like dinner and a show of might... Walker *did* do all of that for me.

I had the dinner with him and Elizabeth. The challenge where I was forced to watch Aleks destroy one of Walker's packmates. My own cabin.

And maybe he's treating me like an "honored guest" because he's determined to show his pack that I'm his long-lost daughter. Could be. Could be that he's also eager to put on a show for the rest of the Western Pack, parading me around as a rare female alpha.

Or maybe it's something else...

I huff out a breath. "Do I at least get to go to this dinner and a show?"

Ryker's eyes flash. "You're my mate, Gemma. I'm not going anywhere without you. Never again. Even if he didn't request your presence"—he gives an angry snort when he says that—"he couldn't have stopped me."

Good.

For once, I'll let our outdated lore and tradition

work in my freaking favor. If that asshole thinks my only worth is in having pups and being pretty, I'll let him think that.

I survived one dinner with him. With Ryker at my side, I can totally survive another.

As for the show of might...

I'm absolutely positive I know what Walker's going to do tomorrow at the dinner. He wants to put on a show in "honor" of Ryker's visit? It'll be another chance for him to trot Aleks out, and I'll be damned if I'm not there to make sure it doesn't end up a challenge between the two males who mean the most to me.

Ryker must guess the same thing. Why else would he ask if Aleks is the only vamp in Western Pack territory? If it's a wolf versus vamp showdown, Aleks would have to be one of the fighters.

I just hate to find out who the other one is.

I WISH I COULD SAY WE CAME UP WITH A BRILLIANT PLAN to rescue Aleks, save Trish, and get Duke out of his cage before tomorrow night's dinner. Instead, with the full moon riding us and our separation longer than either one of us expected, we don't leave the cabin.

The cabin? Heh. We barely leave the *bed*.

Together, we go through almost all of the food in Elizabeth's kitchen. Such vigorous sex really amps up our already considerate appetites; with Ryker next to me, my hunger for him turns to hunger for food. With a teasing jab to my hip bone, he points out that I lost more weight than I probably could've afforded to. With shifter metabolisms what they are, I need a shit ton of calories just to stay my size. The few meals I skipped did more harm than good, and he makes sure I'm stuffed—in more ways than one.

In between mating and snacking, we cuddle together in bed. Ryker demands to know everything that's happened since I sent Jace back to Accalia. I tell him nearly everything, tamping down my wolf when she realizes what I'm keeping back.

Though we talk at length about Walker's plans, I can't bring myself to tell Ryker about the Wicked Wolf's twisted threat. I let my mate know that he has this grand vision of making me the next Luna, and how Ryker has no part in that vision, but I keep the truth about his future for me to myself. I know Ryker. If he finds out that Walker wants me to sleep with his packmates—and I'm not even letting myself think about *him*—to start popping out pups, Ryker will lose it.

I wouldn't blame him, but until we're out of the district, I need to keep him safe. I already have Trish, Duke, Elizabeth, and Aleks that I'm worried about. I'm desperate to keep Ryker out of my bastard of a sperm donor's machinations.

The next morning, we eat breakfast, share a shower that's not as quick as Ryker promised it would be, then get dressed. Ryker pulls on his black jeans and a plain black button-down shirt; as the visiting Alpha, he has to make a tiny bit of effort not to piss off the Wicked Wolf.

Not me. I pull on a wrinkled pair of jeans that barely pass the sniff test, a shirt that's cut low enough to show off Ryker's mark on my neck, and a pair of sturdy boots. I pull my hair back in a neat ponytail, swipe some glittering brown eyeshadow on, and, as a final touch, take my golden chain out of its hiding place.

Ryker's expression turns heated when he gets a look at me. I'm not sure what turns him on more: me wearing his gold-plated fang between my boobs, or the curve of his claw marks standing out against my skin. When he gruffly pulls me toward him for a deep kiss, I figure it's both.

No amount of showering is enough to wash his scent from my skin. It's embedded into mine the same way it's been since we were fully bonded, but I absolutely smell like he's been rubbing against me all night. Which, yeah, he has. In so many ways, he's marked me, and it doesn't take a genius to figure out what he's doing. Without words, he's proving his claim to me. Any wolf who passes us will know that I belong to him. He falls short of pissing on me to mark his territory, but considering how often he came inside of me last night, it's not necessary.

Between the fang, the mark, and my scent, I'm a walking billboard that says: PROPERTY OF RYKER WOLFSON.

It goes both ways, too. One sniff and the females in the Western Pack would know that Gemma Swann owns that delicious male—and I wouldn't have it any other way. Walker wants to insist on acting as if Ryker is any other Alpha, that's fine with me. We made our own stamp on the situation.

All through dinner in the district square, we have the eyes of every single packmate on us. Walker invited us to join him at his table, but Ryker politely declined. Because he was polite, my bio-dad couldn't do shit to demand it—not when the visiting Alpha is technically his "equal"—and the two of us take a small table as far away from him as possible.

I do feel bad when I realize that he commands Elizabeth to take the seat meant for me. She looks even smaller and frailer than when I saw her last, and it leaves me unsettled that, while Walker eats plenty, Elizabeth's plate stays empty.

Speaking in tones meant only for Ryker, I point him out to her. Just in case, he needs to know who Elizabeth is. It's one thing for him to hear from Christian that the Western Pack has a member who could do the impossible, but I think the message really hits home when I point her out and remind him not to let her touch him.

Supposedly, her gift only works when one of the two bonded mates wants out of the mating. Ryker might insist that the two of us are it for each other, that it was a "'til death do you part" sitch with us, but I can't stop thinking about Elizabeth's warning from the night I was forced to eat with Walker.

It doesn't always have to be a conscious decision. If one of the mates has doubts, if they aren't fully committed to the bond, it could still snap. Did I want to risk that happening with Ryker?

No. No, I did not.

He gives me a strange look when I remind him to keep his distance, but instead of asking me about it, he nods. "Don't worry, sweetheart. I will."

Don't worry... that's easier said than done.

Though part of being an alpha means showing that you aren't afraid of anything, that you are in constant control, I can't help but sneak peeks at their table. At one point, I notice that Theo has replaced Elizabeth across from Walker. He's leaning in, whispering intently to the Alpha, and I get a bad feeling about that.

I knew I shouldn't trust him.

Ryker's just finishing his steak when he follows my gaze. Dropping his fork, he nods over at the table. "Who's that?"

"Theodore Michaels," I mutter. "Theo."

"Theo."

Ryker's voice is suddenly flat.

I turn to look at him. His voice is flat, and so is his expression.

My back goes up. "Yeah. Theo. Why?"

"Nothing."

As if I believe that.

I kick him under the table. When he raises his eyebrows over at me, I give him a look.

He shrugs. "I saw him standing outside of your cabin last night. My howl sent him running away, but his scent was all over the perimeter. He's been watching you a lot, hasn't he?"

It's my turn to not want to answer his question.

"Walker has a lot of wolves watching me," I finally answer.

"Mm."

"What's that supposed to mean?"

Ryker opens his mouth, but I never find out what his noncommittal noise means. Before he can say another word, a sudden shout has everyone's head shooting that way—including mine.

"Attention, everyone!"

We all turn to look toward the Alpha's table. Walker is sitting in his seat, a secretive smile on his face, while Theo has moved to stand in front of it.

He's the one who yelled out. He's not an Alpha, but

he's still an alpha wolf, and his command is enough to draw the attention of most wolves regardless of how loud he yelled.

Once he's sure all of his packmates are looking at him, Theo clears his throat. Then, to my shock, he raises his voice even louder to call out four words that have my wolf suddenly up and pacing inside of me.

"I challenge the Alpha!"

In his determined shout, I can all but hear the capital 'A' in Alpha. But it's not Walker. Theo would never challenge the Alpha of *his* pack.

Still, he said Alpha. So, if not Walker, then—

No. He can't possibly mean—

I swivel, searching for my mate.

That same fucking awful neutral expression is on his face.

He knows he's been challenged, too.

Shoving back his chair, Ryker meets Theo's stare head-on. "I accept."

Damn it!

CHAPTER 19

Ryker was right. After dinner, Walker had planned to host another challenge between a delta wolf and a very thirsty Aleks. That's put on hold, though, the moment Theo challenges Ryker and my thick-headed mate accepts.

I know why he did it, too. No matter what, Ryker couldn't really win. Either he accepts and there's a risk he could lose his life, or he refuses and he *definitely* loses. Based on Theo's challenge, the black-haired alpha is challenging him for his place.

He wants the Mountainside Pack, and he wants me. By defeating Ryker, he has a claim to both.

And I really should have seen this coming.

I didn't do what Walker wanted me to. I didn't fall for Theo's good guy act, and I refused to invite him inside no matter how many times he walked me home or was suddenly hanging around the cabin. When

Walker told me I could have whatever male in the pack that I wanted, even I was quick enough to realize he was referring to Theo, but I refused, then spent the night fucking Ryker before showing up to the dinner with my mate.

Walker can't challenge Ryker. At least, not in the first forty-eight hours. After, he could, but would he? When his whole act is predicated on me deciding to join him of my own free will? I don't know about you, but murdering my mate isn't the way to endear me to anyone.

But passing the job onto a loyal wolf who told me once that he was looking for a mate like me?

Yeah. I *really* should've seen this coming.

As soon as Ryker accepts the challenge, we're forcibly separated. I'm ready to fight tooth and claw to stay with him; Ryker, knowing the proper procedures involved in an Alpha fight, kissed me quickly before disappearing with Christian and Brendan. Once he's gone, I whirl on my bio-dad, who only smirks and tells me that I'm more than welcome to join him on the platform.

Though I'm furious, I tell him I'll be there. After all, the platform has the best view of the pit.

I don't even get the chance to take my rage out on Theo. The second he issues the challenge, he disappears, too. I don't see him or Ryker again until I follow the crowd from the district square to the dirt pit where I watched Aleks fight four nights ago.

I'm one of the first to arrive, my wolf spurring me faster as if I can meet up with Ryker first and save him from his challenge. Though I could easily snag a spot along the edge of the pit to watch the fight, I stubbornly take the same seat I had last time. Walker wants me right there when Ryker goes into the pit?

Fine with me.

I'm not too worried about Ryker losing against Theo. I've seen him in action during a challenge where the other wolf thought they could steal his claim to being my mate, and though I'd be an idiot to underestimate the fact that this *is* a challenge to the death, I have faith in Ryker.

I don't have faith that this fight will be fair, though.

It seems like forever before Ryker and Theo are led to the pit. Each one is in his skin, wearing the same clothes they had on when I saw them last. The only difference is that they're barefoot which, yeah, doesn't bode well. A barefoot shifter is a sure sign that someone plans on shifting, so just because they're in their skin now, that doesn't mean it won't change.

Ryker jumps into the pit first, cracking his neck and rolling it around on his shoulders as he gets loose and limber.

Theo's friendly, flirty expression is gone, replaced by a darkness that I have no idea how I missed before this. He drops into the pit, glaring at Ryker before he glances over at the raised platform where me, Elizabeth, and Walker are sitting.

Talk about déjà vu.

Like the afternoon when he hosted the brutal fight between Aleks and the wolf my vamp roomie easily destroyed, Walker is sitting regally in his iron-wrought throne. I'm to his left, Elizabeth sitting just behind me. I don't know where she disappeared to during dinner, but when Walker showed up at the pit about twenty minutes after I did, she was trotting dutifully behind him.

She murmurs something to me as she moves to take the seat behind me, but it's so low, not even my wolf catches it. I just nod, though, then give my complete attention to the pit.

Theo's gaze finds me. I show him my teeth. His eyes go from gold to fiery orange and I have to work hard to hide my sudden disgust.

Ew.

He breaks the stare first, looking from me to Walker. Unlike when his eyes were completely focused on me, he dares a peek over at his Alpha, then darts away.

It's enough. Walker nods royally at Theo, the benevolent lord giving permission to his subject.

And, just like that, the challenge begins.

Theo strikes first. Bounding on his feet like some

kind of wannabe boxer, he moves into Ryker, slamming his fist into his cheek. Ryker takes the hit, using it to get a gauge on just how strong Theo's wolf is. His forehead creases a fraction, and when Theo throws another punch, Ryker catches it.

A crack splits the air, a howl tearing its way out of Theo's throat as Ryker squeezes, crushing his hand. Once every bone is pulverized, Ryker shoves Theo away from him, watching closely as his challenger hits the dirt.

A fight doesn't have to be to the death. In a regular challenge, in a pack run by a non-psycho Alpha, to submission is an honorable end. Theo challenged Ryker, Ryker proved he was the stronger wolf. That could've been the end of it.

It isn't.

Theo is desperate for his prize. I can see it in the curve of his spine as he forces himself to his knees, broken hand hanging limply at his side. The bones will start to knit together immediately, though there's no way that hand will be functional during this fight.

His hand won't be. But a paw?

In the blink of an eye, Theo goes from skin to fur. In a re-run of the challenge where Shane gave up fighting in his human form, Theo goes wolf right before he starts loping toward Ryker.

My heart lodges in my throat.

In an explosion of his black clothes, Ryker shifts

just in time for Theo to sink his fangs in the meat of Ryker's foreleg.

I gasp.

Ryker throws him off. As a human, the two were of a similar size; as a wolf, Ryker is notably bigger. Theo lunges at him, hoping to get in another lucky bite. My mate dodges him, using his muzzle to flip Theo up and over and onto his back.

With his jaws snapping and his dark gold wolf's eyes determined, Ryker goes for Theo's exposed belly. A single whimper tells the spectators that Ryker did some damage—not to mention the blood that fills the air—but Theo kicks out, sending Ryker flying.

My mate lands on his side for a single bounce before he's up again, going for Theo's throat. He locks his legs around his opponent while Theo does the same thing to him. After that, I can't really see what happens, though Luna knows I can sense it in so many other ways.

Fur flies. Canines gleam in the setting sunlight. The grumbles that began the close-quarter battle die out, the only sound claws scraping against bone as the two of them attempt to eviscerate each other.

When the air suddenly stinks of expelled bowels, I know that one of them has.

Suddenly, it's over. Two wolves might have entered the fray, but only one wolf limps away from it.

My heart soars even as the familiar dark wolf extricates himself from the body of the wolf he put down.

"Ryker—"

"Will fight another challenge," Walker says, cutting me off.

No, he fucking won't.

"Ryker!" I yell again. He's limping, but he's already making his way closer to me.

"Christian, don't let him out of the pit."

I don't even have to look to know that Christian has pulled his trusty gun out.

"No—"

It's the only word I get out before Walker rises from his seat, gesturing to someone in the crowd. "There's more than one wolf willing to fight for the privilege of having you. I won't let him win."

What?

Relief subsides as anger overwhelms it.

"The challenge is over," I snap at him. "Ryker's the victor. Deal with it."

"No, Ruby. I won't." He points a shaking claw at me. "If you don't want him to fight for you, then we'll do it the hard way. Elizabeth. Take her bond."

He's furious, but so am I.

"You can't do that," I snarl.

"Do it!"

I sense Elizabeth shifting in her seat. I spin on her, just in time to see her hand reaching for me.

"Don't you dare." I lace my voice with all the power of my wolf. "Don't you fucking dare."

It doesn't work.

Her silver eyes dim as she bites her bottom lip. "I'm sorry, Gemma," she whispers, raising her hand. Like her eyes, her fingers seem to glow.

"Don't—"

She does it. Before I can use my reflexes to stop her, she grabs my wrist in an iron grip.

My wolf is screaming inside of me, terrified that I'm going to lose Ryker.

She told me that one half of the bond has to give permission. It's not as easy as me or Ryker saying yes or no. With her gift, she's tapped into the Luna. She knows if either one of us has regrets or doubts.

I don't. Even when I was on the run from Ryker, hiding out from him, I think I always knew that there would never be another male for me. It's why I never entertained the idea of giving Aleks a shot at wooing me, or how I missed the warning signs that wolves like Shane and Theo were giving me. It's always been Ryker.

I would never give him up.

But what about him?

If the bond snaps, it'll be because he doesn't really want me. The final rejection, it wouldn't matter if it's possible that another one could be formed in its place after Elizabeth snaps it. Breaking our bond would break me.

Her hand feels like fire on my skin. I brace myself for what's going to happen, but despite the few outcomes I've dreamed up, what happens next is nothing like what I expected.

Elizabeth lets out a short shout as her odd eyes suddenly roll to the back of her head. She yanks her hand away from me, her whole body jerking as if she's been electrocuted. Her hair stands on end. Her skin glows. A piercing, keening sound spills from her open mouth before she drops to the platform, crashing into the chair behind me.

Before I even think to move to make sure she's okay, a terrible sound echoes through the air, reaching deep inside of me and freezing me so suddenly, it's like he found an off switch again.

It's a spine-chilling roar. As a shifter, I instinctively recognize it as if it's some bone-deep memory. That roar is the battle cry of a murderous vamp.

Once I shake it off, I glance down at Elizabeth. She's splayed out on the ground, clutching her wrist. Her eyes are closed, though, and her breathing is slow. She's alive, but barely. Whatever she just did, it nearly killed her.

"No!"

Leaving Elizabeth where she is, my head whips around again.

Walker's handsome face is contorted in an ugly rage.

Hate fills me at the same time as it fuels me. Later, I'll admit to Ryker that what happened next hadn't been my intention before I turned around and looked at the bastard. The way he's staring at me as if this is all my fault does something to flip my switch. The whole time I've been in the Wolf District, I was careful not to be too impulsive, too reckless, too much like the Gemma Swann I've always been.

He wanted me to be Ruby Walker. No fucking way. I'm Gem. I'm an alpha.

And this has been a long time coming.

Shoving the chair aside, I break the stare. I hear him order me to come back to him, but that's not going to happen. Like, really? He just tried to forcibly break my bond after gleefully drinking in my fear as I watched Ryker in a fight to the death.

He deserves this. He deserves *all* of this.

His hand-picked alpha being dead.

His pet being injured.

His captive vampire, who is clearly enraged and will be out for blood. I might not understand what's going on between Aleks and Elizabeth, but I know that it's only a matter of time before Aleks gets revenge for what happened to him—and her.

His whole pack has watched as his grand plans

have fallen apart, too, which seems like poetic justice to me.

And now...

Welp. Might as well add something to the list.

He deserves to have his daughter finally challenge him. Because, if I challenge Walker, then any other challenge is postponed. I won't have to sit and watch as he sends wolf after wolf to fight Ryker in the hopes that they'll eventually take him down.

As if he can sense what I'm about to do, he calls out my name.

Sorry, my mate. You fought twice for me. It's my turn.

"I challenge the Alpha," I announce, jutting my chin out as fire blazes in my eyes. "I challenge the Wicked Wolf of the West."

CHAPTER 20

The entire crowd has gone eerily silent. And maybe it's because I'm so in tune with my mate, but all I can hear is his heavy breathing as he comes down from his kill and not a damn thing else.

Theo deserved his brutal end. Every shifter in the district knows that. Understands that. Don't challenge a dominant wolf unless you're prepared to risk your life.

And... I am. Why else would I throw the gauntlet down and challenge the Wicked Wolf like that? Not because I'm suicidal, or because I want to throw my future with Ryker away. Nope. It's because, deep down, I know that twenty-five days would never be enough for the cruel Alpha. Twenty-five *years* wouldn't be enough. Like Elizabeth and Trish, I'd be trapped here.

Another prisoner. Whether it was a gilded cage or a silver-lined cell, he wouldn't stop until he got what he wanted.

Ryker stopped him from selling me to the highest bidder when he accepted his challenge. Theo is dead, but we both know that there's always another wolf willing to tame a female alpha. Shane was the first one. Theo, the next. And now that it's clear that not even a bonded mate is sacred to Jack Walker...

I really have no choice. Either I risk my life now in an alpha challenge or I go back to living it while looking over my shoulder, always waiting for his next move.

And there would be one. No doubt about that. Whether he made off with another packmate, harassed me in Muncie, found another vampire that was willing to help him wage the next Claws and Fangs war... he would never stop. Until he got what he wanted from me, he'd keep pushing and pushing.

It's time to push back.

As I stand there, staring at the smirk slowly growing on his face, I think of my mom. Of how just the memory of this bastard still terrorizes her more than twenty-five years later. Of my dad, who will never come out and admit it, but who regrets not finishing Walker off when he had the chance, even if my mom didn't want him to.

I think of Trish, caught in the crosshairs of the Wicked Wolf's plan. Of Elizabeth, who fell for his sociopathic charm only to be trapped under his claw these last few years. Of the close to one hundred and twenty Betas who deserved a better Alpha, and the packmates who suffered with him as a leader.

I think of Ryker, who is a shining example of what a true Alpha is like, and who will probably be chomping at the bit to interfere in this fight, to stop me, but who won't because he understands that I'm an alpha, too, and this is my challenge.

Desperation mingled with pride and another emotion I can't quite place comes pulsing down our bond. I can't look down in the pit. I sense him, I know he's there, but my gaze is firmly on Walker. I don't even freaking *blink*. Even if the words weren't enough, the prolonged eye contact with a dominant wolf is as much of a challenge.

Now all I need is for him to accept it.

It's not just an alpha challenge—it's an *Alpha* challenge. The only one who can answer it is Walker, and once I threw the challenge down, there's no taking it back unless he refuses it. And if there's one thing I know about my bio-dad, it's that he's never once refused any of the countless challenges he's been in.

He steps down from his platform. Like me, he keeps his eyes open as he returns my stare. Mine are burning. I want so badly to blink, but I know I can't. One of us will have to first. It's inevitable.

Walker clears his throat.

You could hear a pin drop. Even Ryker controls his breathing so that there's no missing it when Walker holds out his arms and says, "A king versus a goddess reborn. It should be an interesting challenge." His eyes —the same ones I see when I look in the mirror—flash in anticipation. "I accept. Clear the pit."

I always guessed that the Wicked Wolf thought of himself as a shifter king, with his packmates as his subjects instead of the shifters he's supposed to protect as Alpha. The goddess crack is obvious. As a female alpha, my mom always warned me that other wolves would see me as the Luna reborn. An interesting challenge... yeah. I think he's right about that.

I hunch my shoulders, mimicking Ryker's pose from his challenge. My fingers flex, my claws unsheathe, and I wait for Walker to make his first move.

Out of the corner of my eye, I see Christian and Joshua jump down into the pit and approach Ryker. He's bristling in ill-disguised rage as they reach for him. Shaking them off, he leaps out of the pit, lurking on the edge so that he can't miss a second of what's about to transpire.

Now, according to pack tradition, the form that a

shifter begins the challenge in is supposed to be the one they stay in. There are exceptions, and I've already been witness to a couple of them.

During my Luna Ceremony, Shane started in his skin, but when it became obvious that Ryker was holding back, he snapped and shifted. Ryker never did. At least, not completely. Up until the moment that he tore his ex-friend apart, I really believe that Ryker thought Shane was worth saving. So he engaged in a partial shift, turning his hands into powerful paws with lethal claws, like what I'm doing now, and that was still enough for him to win.

Only minutes ago, Theo pulled the same stunt. He could have chosen fur right away. Instead, he struck out with his human hands before shifting as a wolf. I'm almost positive that he heard about Ryker and Shane's challenge and expected my mate to treat him the same way.

Yeah. That didn't happen... and now Theo is dead, too.

Watching as the Alpha steps easily into the pit, I have to wonder: how is Walker going to react?

I don't know, but I'm ready for it.

He gives me an appraising look, then takes a few lazy steps toward me. I know what he sees, and I know that—despite me being an alpha like him—he's not even a little worried about this challenge. Why would he be? He has a good foot of height on me, he has at least a hundred pounds more in muscle, plus decades of battle experience. He's also a born killer and a sadistic bastard. He threatened to drown me once when I was a pup. What's going to stop him from putting me down now that I'm an adult?

Nothing. And, seconds later, he proves it.

Walker doesn't even pretend that he's staying in his skin. In a burst of exploded clothing and boots, a massive wolf takes his place in the pit. In his shifted form, he's almost twice my size, but if I thought that meant he would be notably slow, I'm totally wrong.

Powerful legs bunch as he launches across the pit at me.

I have just enough time to give control over to my wolf before he's on me. As a human, he could've gone for a vital organ immediately; as a wolf, I'm smaller, quicker, and more feral. He wants to fight in his fur? He might be huge, but in this form, I have at least *some* advantage.

He should've hit me. If I was already shifted, I could've easily dodged his leap, but he had the advantage there. The split second it took me to switch forms was enough to make me a sitting target. He *should've* hit me—but he doesn't. He soars over my head, landing hard.

Harder than he thought, I'm sure. Prick is playing around, showing off his fangs instead of using them.

He purposely missed his chance to finish me off quickly by leaping over my head like that, slamming into the ground with his paws.

I'm going to make him pay for underestimating me.

Pure adrenaline has me spinning around and leaping onto his back before he can dig himself out of the hole he made. I don't waste time with shows of aggression. Snarling? Nope. My fangs have one use right now, and bearing them to make a statement is just a waste of time.

Clinging to his thick neck, I try to clamp my jaws around his throat. Damn it. He's too big, my wolf too small; ripping out his throat is impossible with my bite-span. I do manage to get my fangs into the thick muscles of his shoulder, tearing with as much force as I can. Hot blood spills into my mouth, the air filling with the scent as I do some damage, but I know instinctively it's not enough.

Even so, knowing that I drew first blood flips the switch inside of Walker. Instead of toying with me again, he goes just about feral. He whips his head, slamming his muzzle into my ear, knocking me on my side. Snapping his jaws, Walker leaps, but my smaller size comes in handy. He's a big bastard. Me? I'm *quick*. I dodge him, my paws scrabbling in the dirt as I wheel around.

Walker snarls, spit spraying as he bares his fangs at

me for real this time. He goes low, haunches rising as dominance pours off of him.

Any other wolf would back down. They would lie down in submission, showing the Alpha their throat, praying to the Luna above that he'd take mercy on them instead of putting them down.

Not me. My birth father has thirty years of experience on me, more than a hundred challenges under his fur, but as my wolf samples the scents on the air, I notice something.

Jack Walker is the only one bleeding.

The perfume of his pain energizes me. It makes things clearer.

Suddenly, I know how I can win this fight.

I can't get his throat all at once. My mouth isn't big enough. But if I can keep biting chunks of it when I get the chance, that might just work.

Of course, he's not going to stand there and let me attack him repeatedly. Once he's figured out my plan, he waits for me to dart closer, slashing at me with his claws every time I get in reach. It isn't long before my blood joins his, but I ignore it. Adrenaline courses through me, shoving the pain to the back of my mind as I focus on taking him down bit by fucking bit.

I'm determined. The sounds of the crowd fall away until all I can hear is Walker's breathing, the frantic thump of his heart, and my mate spurring me on—

"Come on, Gem. You can do it."

Gem. For the first time that I can remember, Ryker is calling me *Gem*.

"I know you can, sweetheart. Finish him."

I know how fucking hard it is to stand on the sidelines, watching your mate fight for their life, knowing that you can't interfere. I've had to do it twice now, and it wasn't any easier the second time. Ryker's probably got an iron grip on his wolf, forced to be a spectator so soon after coming off his own deadly challenge.

I know you can...

Ryker has faith in me. If for no other reason than to prove him right, to prove that I'm strong enough to be his mate, I have to end this.

Now.

If his packmates can get away with it, so can I. Sprinting away from him, I put a little space between us. I let him think I'm retreating, but right as Walker wheels around, ready to chase, I shift to my skin.

I make sure to keep my claws, though.

He's a two hundred pound wolf, yeah, but it's much easier for me to handle him in his fur rather than as a human. I might look petite. My small stature, my pretty face, and my long blonde hair always made others think of me as Little Miss Shifter Barbie. It was worse when I pretended to be an omega, but even though everyone here now knows that I'm an alpha, there's only one shifter present who isn't shocked when I manage to catch the wolf lunging at me.

Walker expected to plow into my human body; even with my legs braced, a direct hit should've been more than enough to send me flying if he got his paws on me. I have no doubt that he planned on rending me, clawing me wide open as soon as he could. Once I was down, my throat would be next, and my bio-dad would repay my challenge by slaughtering me in front of my mate.

That's not what happens.

I time it perfectly. As he leaps at me, I lift my arms, snatching him out of the air. One hand has his upper jaw clasped in its grip, the other gropes for his lower jaw, my shifter strength stopping his momentum dead as soon as I have him by the fangs.

Walker's powerful legs swing behind me. I refuse to let go of his muzzle knowing that, if I do, he'll bite any part of my naked human body that he can reach.

I'm already a bloody mess. Shifting brings a new wave of pain as my wolf retreats inside, leaving my weaker human body to deal with the gouges, the gashes, the furrows that cover so much of it.

I can heal, I remind myself. So long as I keep him from giving me a fatal wound, I'll heal.

With a sickening crack, I yank both halves of his jaw, dislocating it instantly. The shock of the pain stuns him for a heartbeat, but it's enough. Letting him dangle with a one-handed grip, I flex my fingers, positioning my claws just so before I gouge a huge chunk of his throat. Blood drenching my fingers, I throw him to the dirt.

He lands with a thud. On impact, he bounces, then immediately shifts back to his skin, gurgling on his blood.

I watch him coolly as I stride toward him, towering over his fallen body.

I'll heal. A wound like that, he probably will, too, if I give him the chance.

I should kill him.

When I don't, he shifts from his side to his back. Lying flat, Walker lifts his hand. I watch as he forms a fist, punching himself in the mouth. He swings from the opposite direction of his hanging jaw, knocking it back into place with another ear-splitting crack.

The skin is already slowly knitting together. Blood still dribbles from his throat, welling against his collarbone. He wiggles his jaw, checking to see that it's on its way to healing, and then he grins. His eyes flash, too. There's a dare in their depths, and a cockiness to his smile. It's such a contrast to his ruined neck that, if I kept my gaze on his face, I would have no idea how close I came to killing him during the fight. Left alone, he'll heal in minutes, but those are a few minutes I have where Jack Walker is at my mercy.

"What are you waiting for, Ruby?" His voice is ragged, thanks to the hunks ripped out of his throat. "Do it. Finish the challenge."

He doesn't think I have it in me. And I get that. After I broke his jaw, I could've easily slashed at his throat more than the single time I did it. I could've even split his jaw open, or broken his neck. He knows I have the strength now.

I could've done it.

But I didn't.

It's not because he's the bastard that sired me. I could care less that his blood runs in my veins. To me, Jack Walker is nothing but a sperm donor. That's all he'll ever be.

To the rest of the shifter world, he's more than that. For Luna's sake, he was halfway to becoming a shifter king to his pack.

Someone has to stop him.

Killing him would turn him into a martyr. Worse, it would only add to my own legend. Gemma Swann, female alpha, the one wolf bad enough to take down the Wicked Wolf of the West.

No, thanks.

Besides, I've got a better idea.

I drop to my knee at his side. He expects me to finish my attack on his throat, and I'm willing to bet that he has some way to block me. Doesn't matter. When my claws slash out at him, I don't aim that high.

I jab my hand at his bare chest, claws slicing right into his pec. With a practiced shove, the tips of my claws come within centimeters of piercing his heart.

Surprise, surprise, he actually has one, and it would be so freaking easy to rip it out.

But I don't do that, either.

Instead, I smile, and then I give him a single order: "*Yield*."

CHAPTER 21

What else can he do really? I've wrangled him into submission. Unless he wants to risk shredding his own heart, he has to stay in the dirt. I could kill him, or I can force him to accept that I beat him in the challenge.

"You're soft," the Wicked Wolf taunts, spitting out the words so that he doesn't move his chest any more than he has to. "Janelle was soft, too. She didn't let Booker go for the kill twenty-five years ago, and now you're hesitating, too, Ruby. Like mother, like daughter."

He says it like it's an insult. Like comparing me to an omega wolf with a heart of gold is the worse thing he can do.

But that's the thing. I *wish* I could be more like my mom. Be good and kind and caring.

Yeah, right. And the way he uses my dreaded birth name like that again?

He has it coming.

I tighten my grip so that he knows I'm deadly serious. The crowd falls away again as I purposely meet the hatred in his stare. Of course he hates me. He's probably hated me from the moment I was born and my protective mother sacrificed everything to hide the fact that I was different. He hated me for being an omega then, and he hates me now for being an alpha out of his control.

And, Luna, he's going to *loathe* me for what I do next.

"I won't kill you. I won't have to. And if that makes me my mother's daughter, there's nothing else I'd rather be. Because maybe I'm my dad's... my real dad, that is... I'm my dad's daughter, too, because there are worse things than dying in a challenge."

"Yeah? And what's that?"

"Losing it with plenty of witnesses."

The only reason Jack Walker was able to retain the title of Alpha after he lost the challenge to my dad was that he *let* him. Paul could've claimed the victory, then taken everything from Walker. His title, his pack... his power. He didn't, though. Because all he wanted was to keep my mom safe, he told Walker to leave and never come back.

My dad's a good man. Me? I'm a teensy bit more vengeful than that.

I don't need him to yield. For my own ego, it would've been nice, but I don't need it. He's flat on his back, my claws tickling his beating heart. Sure, he could survive his ruined throat so long as it heals. But could he survive it if I pull his heart out of his chest and show it off to the Western Pack?

No. I know it. He knows it. Every freaking shifter watching with bated breath knows it.

"I win," I announce. I don't take my eyes off of him just yet, mainly because I want to see the look on his face when I add, "But I don't want the Western Pack. I belong to Mountainside, with my Alpha mate."

All he wanted was to trap me here. As his servant, as his captive, as his broodmare popping out pups in the hope that one of them would be another female alpha like me, Walker orchestrated everything to get me to return to the place of my birth.

What better way to really drive home my victory than to reject it?

I won't be its Alpha. Now that the Wicked Wolf lost his challenge—and there isn't a single shifter who would refute his loss—he can't be its Alpha. No self-respecting pack would follow an Alpha who was bested in a challenge.

To me, this is the best revenge. I don't have to take his life. I just have to take his pack from him.

"Kill me," he demands. "If you don't, I'll rise up again. And next time? I won't let you win."

Let me win? Please. Even if he did, that only proves my point. He's weak. No dominant wolf would ever *let* a challenger win.

I slide my hands out of his chest before slowly getting to my feet. Walker stays down. With a small smile that is as vicious as one of his, I give him my back.

I wipe my bloody claws along the side of my thigh. I'm already stained with red, streaked with gore. It doesn't make a difference to the mess of my battered body, but I feel no pain.

Know what? I actually feel pretty damn good as I search out Ryker. On the edge of the pit, he's watching me with such open affection and pride and, okay, *lust* that I nearly laugh. Put me in a sundress with curls and I barely turn his head. Have me nearly rip a male's heart from his chest and he looks at me like I'm the most amazing female in the whole world.

My Alpha mate. I wouldn't want him any other way.

I count to ten inside my head, making sure that none of his former packmates are looking to challenge me next. The fact that Walker doesn't try to attack me while my back is turned makes it obvious that I've bested him. If only for right now, I've won.

When no one seems willing to try me, I look down

at my bio-dad again. He's propped up on his elbow, glaring at me with such heat in his gaze, my skin nearly sizzles.

Oh, this is going to be *fun*.

"Challenge laws. You know them. We all know them. Any Alpha that loses isn't fit to be Alpha."

His honey-colored eyes darken, losing any of the humor that lingered. "You wouldn't dare, Ruby. You wouldn't *dare*."

Huh. Maybe if he hadn't called me Ruby one last time, I would have just run him off like I was planning to. But now?

I gave you that wound, asshole. Time to rub a little salt in it.

"You're not the Alpha anymore. That means you better get the hell off of Western Pack territory. If you go now, I promise you safe passage for a time, but after that? I just don't give a shit what happens to you."

I'm not worried about him sticking around. While most Alpha challenges are to the death, those that end in submission all have the same outcome. The loser beats feet pretty quick otherwise any other wolf could finish the fight if they choose to. And after the way that he treated his packmates and his Betas over the years, I'm sure there are quite a few itching for revenge.

I think about how much it sucked watching Ryker fight a challenge only to turn around and make my mate suffer the same thing.

And then there's the howl of rage when Elizabeth fell that I know had to belong to Aleks.

Yeah... I don't have to be the one to kill him. He's signed his own fate.

He knows it, too.

Still, I'm not ruthless. I can be fair.

"You wanted to keep me here for twenty-five days? I'll give you twenty-five seconds to get out." A vicious grin tugs on my lips. "Tick, tock, dickhead."

He doesn't need twenty-five seconds. In less than five, he's shifted to his wolf, back on his paws. With one powerful leap, he clears the pit, bounding over the platform, before racing toward the forest in the distance.

Good freaking riddance.

I WAS RIGHT WHEN I THOUGHT THAT A FEW MEMBERS OF the Western Pack would want to see him off. They shift and tear after him as soon as I count down from twenty-five, and you can bet that it wasn't to say farewell to the former Alpha.

Though I guessed how they would react, I can't stop myself from shifting back to my fur and running with them. Ryker catches up, running at my side as we follow after him ourselves, neither one of us willing to take their word for how far Walker got. I'd been burned by believing I could always tell when someone was lying to me before, and I'm not about to let that happen again.

As for Ryker... my mate just wants a piece out of Walker for how he carved me up like a piece of freaking meat during the fight.

We go in our fur, our wolves spurring us on to chase after the disgraced Alpha as if he was the most tempting of prey. The other shifters don't even dare try and stop us from joining them. Between me and Ryker, the dominance of our wolves keep them from giving Walker any lead if they somehow planned on it.

He doesn't need one, though. For more than thirty years this has been his territory. He knows every rock, every stick, every dip in the terrain. He knows where to use the river to his advantage, muddying the scent trail so that all we could do was be sure that he'd darted onto the old Lakeview Pack land.

He knows how to escape in one piece.

And, honestly, I expected something like that. When I showed him the tiniest hint of mercy, taking his pack instead of taking his life, my bio-dad would've known that he needed to haul his furry ass as far away from us as possible. If we caught up with him again... well, Ryker hadn't been the one to give him safe passage out of the district.

With a feral snarl, Ryker orders the handful of wolves flanking us to continue the chase. My wolf adds a yip for good measure before the two of us turn tail and head back. At the very least, there are plenty of shocked shifters who just watched their Alpha be defeated. *Our* alpha natures demand we deal with that—not to mention, we still have packmates of ours that need to be rescued.

We pad back to the pit in our fur, shifting to our skin when we rejoin the still-milling crowd so that we can address the worried shifters. Before we do, though, Ryker pulls me to the side, telling me that I should go get ready to leave while he deals with the Western Pack.

He wants us gone by evening.

He also wants to keep me out of sigh to the upset shifters.

Uh. That's going to be a no.

So, as charming as ever, I tell him to bite me. Not the best comeback, especially to a male whose mark I proudly wear, but still. I got us into this mess. I'll stand with him while we do our best to clean it up.

No point dancing around it. The Western Pack needs a leader. I'm the one who has the best claim to it, but I also made it clear during the challenge that I don't freaking want it. But I sure as hell don't want Walker to try and slink back and take it over again, either.

The solution? It has to be disbanded. I know that.

Ryker does, too. The community is too far removed from the rest of the shifter world anyway.

It has to come to this.

Once we're back in Accalia, Ryker will make sure the rest of the Alphas know what happened. Even if we don't disband it now, the Western Pack would never survive once news of the challenge got out. Might as well do something about the situation before we head home again.

Depending on their loyalty to the Wicked Wolf, the shifters in the Wolf District could take their chances and follow him, they could join other packs, go lone wolf, or create their own, new pack. They'd have to leave the district to do so; the territory is free for any alpha to claim, but the Western Pack as it once was will never be allowed to form again.

With the terrifying visage of a naked, bloody Ryker giving them their options, I'm not even a little surprised that not a single one of them choose to pledge their allegiance to Walker.

The both of us stay in our skin longer than we normally would when we have an audience. I barely realize that I'm naked, but it finally dawns on me that Ryker is. The possessive part of me then goes on to pick up on the fact that other females can see him.

I grab the arm of the shifter nearest to me. "Do me a favor?"

It's a teenaged girl with wide hazel eyes and a spattering of freckles across her button nose. I can't tell if she's impressed or terrified that I'm talking to her, and she goes immovably still as soon as I touch her.

At least she answer me.

"Anything for you, Alpha."

Ah, Luna. This was exactly what I was hoping to avoid. It's bad enough that my packmates in Accalia wanted to call me Alpha. Here? It makes me want to snap my fangs again.

Ugh. Maybe Ryker's right. Maybe we need to get the hell out of Dodge as soon as possible.

Not yet, though. And for what I have to do next, I definitely need to cover up...

"Can you go and find a change of clothes for us?"

"Yes, Alpha. As you say."

She immediately darts off. Before I know it, she comes back with a pair of jeans that barely fit Ryker. She offers me a dress that's a size too big, but I don't complain. I just shrug it over my head and wait for Ryker to finish addressing the crowd.

There is so much we still need to do. The Alphas won't meet again until next summer, but Ryker will need to report what happened here. He'll do that once we're firmly in our own territory again and, when he points that out a second time, I don't argue.

Yeah. I'm ready to go home.

But first—

I take his hand, squeezing his fingers with mine. I

see blood smeared past my knuckles and scowl. "I'm gonna get my stuff together. Pack up." I flash him my bloody claws. "Scrub the dickhead out from under my nails. Why don't you go get Trish and Duke? Then we can figure out our next step together."

"You sure?"

Honestly? I am. If there's one good thing that comes out of this disaster of a family reunion, it's how I can finally accept that my bonding with Ryker is absolutely unbreakable. My own jealousy kept me from truly believing that this—what we had—would be for life, that we were forever mates. I know better now.

Besides, now that I also know about Duke's feelings for her, I'm not worried about Trish trying anything funny with my mate.

Fate finds a way, after all.

No one knows that better than me.

I figure that, in the uproar of everything that went down following the challenge, the last thing on anyone's mind would be the captive vampire who has every reason to want revenge.

As I cross to the south side of the district, I'm wondering how I'm going to convince the shifter on guard duty to give me the key to Aleks's cell. One thing's for sure: I'm not leaving without him. If I have to pull rank, I will—and I don't mean playing the "Alpha's daughter" card like I did a couple of times. At the moment, my wolf and I are in complete agreement. If we have to howl and make another shifter obey us, we will.

Turns out it's not necessary. As if the guard had sensed his Alpha's failure, he already abandoned his post when I reach the jailhouse.

The air outside of the structure stinks of fear and piss, the dirt covered in plenty of bootprints. Someone has paced here, and I follow the prints behind the jailhouse. There, I find the tattered remains of clothes and a line of wolf prints running away.

I search through the scraps. Way I see it, either I'll find the key or I'll wrap my hands in the clothes and protect my hands from the silver bars that way. Whatever I have to do, I'm breaking Aleks out.

Luck is on my side. I actually find a keyring that has a single key on it. Hoping it's a master key for the jailhouse, I grab it out of the dirt, then dash inside.

Aleks's eyes are a raging red when I approach his cell. His fangs are fully extended, shoulders hunched in fury as he grips the bars, yanking even as the pure silver eats away at his hands. Before my trip to California, I would've thought that his vampire strength would be enough to bend the malleable metal, but I know better. Silver is deadly to shifters *and* vamps. This really was a perfect cage for him.

He's still tugging away, oblivious to the pain. He desperately wants out of the cell. Remembering the outraged roar from earlier, I bet he's been trying everything he can to escape if only to get to Elizabeth.

And isn't *that* something to think about...

It's only been about an hour. It seems like so much longer, but I'm glad I thought to break Aleks out sooner rather than later. If I left him to struggle with the silver, he'd have stumps where his hands were by the time he finally stopped his assault on the bars.

When I move in front of him, it's like he doesn't even recognize me. He shows his fangs, hissing loudly as he grips the bars, his flesh sizzling.

I don't know what's worse: how sickening the stink is, or how terrifying Aleks is in this moment. For the first time since I met him, I truly recognize what he is: a powerful vampire. A killer.

A dangerous threat.

I shake my head. No. *No*. This is Aleksander Filan. My ex-roommate. My best friend.

I meet his ruby gaze. "Aleks. It's me."

Without warning, he slumps against the bars. His voice is as ragged as his ruined palms must be when he whispers my name.

"*Gem.*"

I show him the key in my hands. "I'm here to let you out. But you've got to get a hold of yourself first, okay?"

With a shudder racking his whole body, Aleks closes his eyes, taking a few pointed seconds to regain control. He retracts his fangs with effort, and when he opens his eyes again, they're back to the pale green color I know so well.

"Better?"

His nod is jerky. "Sorry. I don't know why I lost control like that."

Over the scent of charred skin and burned meat, I catch the sour stink of spoiled milk.

Lie.

And that, more than anything... more than the red eyes, the outraged roar, and the guard who pissed himself in fear... tells me that Aleks is shook. An experienced vampire, I lived with him for a year and never caught him in a lie. Even when he was hiding something huge—like, oh, how me wearing his fang meant I was marked as his mate—I had no idea that he was being less than truthful.

He knows why, and now I'm pretty sure I do, too.

I catch the stink of his lie. Before I can call him out on it, he flares his nostrils. A thread of crimson sneaks back into his irises as he says, "You smell like blood. Walker's." A deep breath and, whoops, there go his fangs again. "And *yours*."

Yeah... a quick splash at the sink to get rid of the worst of the gore hadn't been enough to fool a vampire.

"I'm okay."

"Gem—"

"Seriously, Aleks. I'm okay. Look." I wave the key at him again. "I'm here. I got the key. Everything's okay. You're good. I'm good. Now let me get you out of here."

He doesn't look like he believes me, but he's smart enough not to argue. Instead, he says, "They told me to expect to fight another dog tonight, but they never came for me. And then... something happened. I'm not sure what, but I could tell something was going on. The dog scratching at the door took off. Tell me, Gem. What's going on?"

Tell him?

Gladly.

CHAPTER 22

As I pop the lock on the cell, stepping away from the bars so they don't brush against my bare skin as Aleks shoves them and moves out of the cell, I tell him everything. From how his fight was postponed when Theo challenged Ryker to the reckless way I decided to challenge the Wicked Wolf on the spot.

He mutters something in Polish when I admit that I gave Walker the chance to abandon the district. A vamp would never understand how a shifter's mind works, so I don't expect him to get why losing his pack was way worse of a fate than me ripping Walker's head clean from his shoulders. But it's Polish so I don't understand him either, and I decide to let his muttered comments go.

Then, once I'm done, I go back to the one thing I purposely glossed over. "Oh. I almost forgot. In between the challenges, Walker did something to cause one of the she-wolves pain. You might know here. Elizabeth? The pretty brunette who was sitting by me during the last fight? Poor thing. She shrieked before collapsing into a ball on the platform."

He sucks in a breath, his cheeks hollowing to the point that those sharp suckers could slice through a piece of paper.

Gotcha.

I work to fight my grin. It's probably super inappropriate, but it feels pretty good knowing I'm right. "But you knew that already. Didn't you?"

He doesn't answer me right away. For a second, I'm sure he's going to lie again. Why not? He already tried once.

But he doesn't.

"I felt it," he confesses softly. "I felt her pain. I didn't know what caused it, but I felt. She's alive, but the pain... it would've been excruciating."

I blink. Okay. I knew something weird was going on, but that was the last thing I expected.

For Aleks to feel Elizabeth's pain all the way here, it's not just some kind of empathic reaction because they're both supes. No. That sounds an awful lot like—

"Hang on a sec... do you have some sort of, like, *bond* with her? With Elizabeth?"

The look that flashes across his beautiful face is all the answer I need.

Whoa. I mean, I thought there was a connection, but a mate bond between my ex roommate and the Luna-touched shifter? I don't think anyone saw *that* coming.

"Aleks, that's—"

—nothing compared to what he says *next*.

"Two hundred years ago," he murmurs in his accented voice, "I fell in love with a female alpha wolf."

Aleks's quiet interruption stops me from issuing my congratulations. With my head already spinning at his last revelation, it takes me a second to process what he said, but when I do? My jaw drops.

I shake my head. "Wait... what? I thought I was the only one."

Except for the Luna, of course.

"So did she. Julia." Aleks runs his fingers through his messy curls. He doesn't take his eyes off of me, but that's just like him. From the moment we met, he was never afraid of what I was, and he always stared. "She hid who she was. Just like you did."

"Where is this coming from?" I don't understand. "Why are you telling me this?"

What does this have to do with Elizabeth?

"Because it's time. You see, when you drove into Muncie, your aura... I recognized it immediately. I lost her once. Before we could be bonded, I lost her. And I thought..."

Ah. Now I see. "You thought I was her."

"I told you. She believed she was the only female alpha just as she was the only one for me. My Julia... she was my beloved. My fated partner. And I was her mate."

I still remember the way he said "mine" the first night I met him. Within days, he snapped off his fang, gifting it to me to wear. He told me it was for my protection, but I later learned from Ryker what it really meant: it was a sign that I belonged to Aleks.

I always thought it was strange that Aleks made it more than two centuries without taking a mate. Even if he hadn't found his fated partner—his beloved—two hundred years was a long time. Supes are made to find a partner and claim them. A fated mate was a luxury, but that didn't mean he couldn't have *chosen* one.

He never discussed his romantic past with me. Considering the baggage I carried when I arrived in Muncie, who was I to judge? I had wanted a platonic roommate. A friend. I thought that was Aleks, especially since he made it seem like friendship was all he was after the first couple of months we lived together.

Even when he told me he had feelings for me, I never really thought about why. But if what he's telling me now is true...

"Shifters don't live that long," I point out. "Two hundred years ago... you have to know it wasn't me."

Aleks's lips tug into a crooked smile. "That's logic, Gem. When the heart's involved, you forget logic.

When I saw you, all I could think was that I had my second chance. You were her, returned to me."

Because I was a female alpha. And, if Aleks is right, not the second one ever, either.

I'm the third.

This is insane. I almost have whiplash from how fast our conversation has turned. All I wanted to do was make sure that Aleks wasn't forgotten after the Alpha challenge, and now he's dropping one hell of a bomb on me.

What's worse: finding out that there were more female alphas in the past than the one I already knew about, or that—like so many other males in my life—Aleks was only drawn to me because of my rank?

But is that the only reason why?

When I saw you...

"Did I look like her? Julia, I mean?"

He shakes his head. "My Julia was dark while you're fair. No. It wasn't your looks that made me think you were her, but your wolf."

"What about Elizabeth? She's not an alpha."

Aleks lets out a shaky exhale, all the more notable since—as one of the undead—he doesn't actually have to breathe. "No, but, except for the eyes, she could be my beloved's twin."

Okay. Welp, I wasn't expecting that now, was I?

To be fair, I had thought there was something sparking between the two of them from the moment

Aleks appeared at the pit. When she fell and Aleks's roar shook the district, I was sure of it. There's some kind of bond—but what kind?

Elizabeth is Luna-touched. She can break bonds. She can conceal a shifter's scent. What else can she do?

How old is she? Shifters are long-lived, though two centuries is pushing it. But with her abilities...

"Could she be her? Elizabeth. Could she be your Julia?"

He shakes his head. "No. And if I'd been thinking more rationally when I met you, I would've realized the same thing. Neither of you could be Julia because she died long ago. Before we could even be mated, I lost her. I saw her die."

"I..." Ah, Luna. "Aleks, I'm so sorry. I had no idea."

"You had no idea because I kept it from you. Przykro mi. I'm the one who should be sorry. And I'm sure you're wondering why I'm telling you this." He waves his hand, gesturing around the inner workings of the jailhouse. "Especially here."

A small, awkward grin tugs on my lips. "The thought did cross my mind."

"It's because I really *do* love you, Gem. I don't want you to ever think I only cared because I could tell you were a female alpha like my beloved was. That's simply not true. It might've been why I stopped Gretchen and the others from attacking you that first night, but that's not what made me love you. If you'd chosen me, I would've been the best mate to you."

Oof. And I thought I was uncomfortable before.

"Forget about that." Seriously. I love Aleks, too, but as a friend. If that's what his feelings for me can become in time, I'll be happy as hell. "I have my mate now. Maybe this is your chance to get yours back."

"I don't know—"

"What about Elizabeth? Does she know any of this?" I answer my own question the second I ask it. "No. Walker would've never let you close enough to talk to her. But what about now? Are you going to tell her?"

He hesitates for a moment. "I don't know. But, whatever I do, it's going to have to wait."

"Why?"

With a set to his jaw that gives a hard edge to his supernatural beauty, Aleks says, "The last time I lost my beloved, I single-handedly started a decades-long Claws and Fangs war. Walker was already preparing for another one. I won't be the reason war breaks out among our people again, even if it means I have to stay away from her."

He reaches out, cupping my cheek in his hand. His palm feels unnaturally warm, the flesh still bubbled from where the silver destroyed it. Give him some blood and he'll be back to normal but, for now, he's still dealing with the aftereffects of his time in the Wolf District.

Aren't we freaking all?

Tipping my head back, he meets my gaze. "I lost Julia to an Alpha who had preferred to see her dead than be bonded to a vampire. Two hundred years later, I had to watch as another of my enemy stole you away from me. I don't know if I'm strong enough to love again. Not now. Maybe not ever." He caresses my cheek to my chin, then drops his hand. "I'm content to be your friend. If fortune favors me, maybe I can be hers one day."

I take his hand in mine, careful not to squeeze the blisters. "You're a good male, Aleks. You deserve to be happy."

"Nie mam być szczęśliwa."

"What did you just say?"

His smile is a sad one. "Thank you for coming for me."

Mm-hmm. This isn't the first time that I guessed he was feeding me a phony translation. But I don't call him out on it.

Instead, I return his smile. "You're my best friend, Aleks. I always will."

Even though Aleks leaves immediately so that he can make his report to Roman Zakharov, me and Ryker decide to spend the night in the Wolf District, just in case. For two reasons, too: because we wanted to make sure that my bio-dad stayed away, and because it made sense for us to get a head start in the morning.

Before we turn in, Ryker hand-picks about five or six wolves to form a sentry. It's not a coincidence that most of them were involved in chasing after Walker. Ryker's wolf senses that they're trustworthy and I trust him. If he's willing to leave the overnight watch to them, I'm okay with it.

I'm also really freaking exhausted. Watching Ryker's fight had drained me emotionally while my fight with Walker took more out of me than I had to give. I'm halfway to being healed after a hearty steak dinner, but I need a little rest to be a hundred percent in the morning.

I'm not the only one, either. Ryker released Duke and Trish from their cages, letting them know that her nightmare was over. Duke insisted on leading her to a cabin where she could shower and change and return to her skin on her own while he stood outside as her guard. Not even Ryker could get him to take care of himself first which, to me, was just one more point in the Duke's treating Trish like his mate column.

By the time we meet up in the square again, Ryker's thinking the same thing. And if he looks relieved at that revelation, I don't say a damn word because, in a way, so am I.

We'd be bringing the two of them home with us in the morning, and when Ryker wonders if we'll need room for the bloodsucker, I just shake my head and leave it at that. I'm too tired to go into details, and Ryker is smart enough not to point out that he can smell Aleks on me. When we have time—and privacy—I plan on sharing with my mate what Aleks told me, but, for the moment, he trusts that I know what I was doing.

And isn't that a freaking shock?

Before I knock out, he does ask me what I think about inviting some of the Western Pack to join us in Accalia. On a trial basis until they could prove themselves, of course, but it might be a good idea to bolster our ranks. Who better to help us ward off the Wicked Wolf than the wolves he once lorded over? If they were willing to trade their loyalty from Walker to Ryker, it would definitely help us. Especially since they would know how he thinks, and how we can prepare for his inevitable next attack.

Because there will be one. Whether it's on me or not, I don't know. After my dad beat him, Walker never tried to challenge him again. Would he respect my victory? Or will he use it to fuel his sadistic rage? Good questions, and only time would tell.

So, yeah. Take in more packmates? I'm all for it.

In fact, when Ryker then prods me to tell him what I think, I tell him that—and then mention I was thinking of doing the same thing myself.

The next morning, as soon as Ryker goes out to make his pitch to some of the former Western Pack members, I go searching for one wolf in particular.

It's much emptier in the square. Seems like, overnight, more than half of the disbanded pack already abandoned the unclaimed territory. I don't blame them, either. Shifters, no matter what type, are basically pack animals. We thrive in a community, and tend to go feral more often than not when we're left on our own. With the Western Pack disbanded, they would be feeling the need to find somewhere else to belong.

I'm not sure if the wolf I'm looking for is still here. If I was her, I would've bolted as soon as I learned that Walker was defeated. My tormentor gone? I'd be out like the wind.

And that just proves that Elizabeth is nothing like me. Because while I would've taken the first chance to escape, when I walk up to the abandoned platform, I realize that it's not as abandoned as I thought. She's sitting cross-legged on the floor, hidden in the shadows of the covering, tucked behind Walker's stupid throne.

She's fiddling with her fingers in her lap. Her claws are out. I can hear them scraping against each other as she twiddles them.

"Elizabeth?"

Her head jerks up. For a split second, our eyes meet, then she drops her gaze. "If you've come to challenge me next, Gemma, I don't blame you. A bond is sacred. I learned my lesson and I still tried to break yours. For what it's worth, I'm sorry about that."

Me, too. But that's not why I'm here.

"It's water under the bridge." Look at me. Mature Gem. As pissed as I was yesterday, today I understand that she had no other choice. "Me and Ryker are fine, and Walker's gone. All's well that ends well, right?"

Her dark hair falls like curtains around her face. She hides behind that, too, barely daring another peek up at me. "You mean it?"

"Sure do."

"Oh. Well, then, thank you."

I wave her off. "It's fine."

"Okay. But... if you're not here to challenge me, then is everything else all right? I know the pack's broken up now, but I didn't think we all had to leave right away."

She's not wrong. Staying might be a risk, but the land is unclaimed. Anyone who wants to stay can, and we won't stop them.

"You don't. We're getting ready to head out, though. Actually, that's why I was hoping to see you before I go."

"Oh?"

"Yeah. You were telling me how you wanted out of the district. Now that you can go, what are you thinking? What are you going to do now?"

Elizabeth gets a far, distant look in her strangely silver eyes. "I'm... I'm not so sure."

I understand. The night we had that dinner with Walker, she told me how easy it was for him to trap her here. She was a lone wolf with a gift. No pack. No family. She believed she found a new one when my bastard bio-dad invited her to stay in the Wolf District, but it wasn't long before she realized that his offer came with strings attached.

Maybe if she had somewhere else to go, she could've escaped him long before now. And no matter what happens between her and Aleks, I know exactly what it's like to leave the life you knew behind with nothing but my Jeep and my few belongings.

Aleks had been a gift from the Luna to me when I ran from Accalia and risked death by fang in Muncie. So what if he thought I was someone else? He saved me.

If I can return the favor by helping out Elizabeth, I'm going to.

"Come back to the East Coast with us."

She gives her head a clearing shake, her strange gaze suddenly coming into focus. "What? *Me*?"

I think I know why she's so caught off-guard. For Luna's sake, two minutes ago she was sure I came to challenge her. And, yeah, she did try to break the bond I have with Ryker—on Walker's command. Something like that should probably piss me off... and maybe it would've if Elizabeth hadn't already warned me. She was the one who explained that her touch only worked if one of the mates wanted the bond broken. If it snapped, I couldn't really blame Elizabeth for obeying her Alpha.

Oh, who am I kidding? I totally would have. Good thing it didn't work, though. I like her. I feel sorry for her, and I can't wait to watch as Aleks starts pursuing her instead of me, but I do like her.

And I owe Aleks. He'd never agree, and Ryker would give me a warning nip if he knew I was playing match-maker, but I owe my ex-roomie.

I shrug. "Why not? My mate is Alpha of the Mountainside Pack. He's already invited a couple of your packmates to join us. We've got plenty of cabins. You'd be welcome there."

Elizabeth lifts her hand. Her fingers are slightly trembling as she tucks a lock of mahogany brown hair behind her ear. Her eyes dart away, careful not to meet mine as she admits softly, "I don't know if I'm ready to be part of another pack."

Fair enough.

I gentle my voice. She's not an omega, she's something different, but I figure treating her like an omega is probably the best way to go about it if I want to keep from spooking her.

"I get that. And if you don't want to join our pack, there's always Muncie."

"Muncie?" she echoes. "Isn't that—"

"A Fang City? Yup." Huh. How does she know that? A lone wolf with a strange gift who spent the last few years on the West Coast... how does she know about a vamp settlement three thousand miles away? "You've been there?"

"No. But I've heard of it." She bites down on her bottom lip. "It's not very shifter friendly, is it?"

Most Fang Cities aren't. Then again, after everything Aleks just told me, Elizabeth has nothing to worry about.

"I live there. No one's given me any trouble."

I guess being able to tell when someone is lying to you is an alpha gift, and not one that Elizabeth has because she doesn't call me out on my blatant lie.

"Really?"

I nod, biting back my mischievous grin. "Oh, yeah. And, let me tell you, if you need a place to stay, I know just the spot..."

EPILOGUE

THREE WEEKS LATER

As I park my Jeep in front of the Alpha's cabin, all I can think is: *I can't believe I just did that.*

I probably shouldn't have. Not without running it by Ryker first, at least. As my mate, I owe it to him to be honest and upfront with him about what I do, but when it comes to Muncie… I needed to handle that on my own.

And if "my own" included Jace and Dorian racing alongside my Jeep as I navigated down the twisty mountain terrain, I've given up on fighting *that* battle. These days, my quartet of guards has dwindled down to a trio, but even if Duke is still keeping close to Trish, Bobby, Dorian, and Jace are convinced that I need them to watch my back. Why argue? After everything that happened in the Wolf District, I've finally realized that life's a lot easier when I'm not going lone wolf.

After I ran from Accalia, hiding in plain sight in Muncie, I never thought I'd have that luxury again. Now I have a possessive mate who fought a challenge to the death to cement his claim on me—*twice*. I have loyal guards who would lay down their own lives to protect me. Dozens of packmates who love me, not because I'm Omega Gem or even Alpha Gem, but because I make their Alpha happy.

I have a pack that knows who I am, what I'm capable of, and they welcome me anyway. And if my asshole of a birth father decides to risk his neck by coming after me again, I know that they'll stand behind me.

Even if they didn't? With Ryker Wolfson at my side, Jack Walker will never stand a chance. I proved that in California, and I'll do it in Accalia, too, if I have to.

But not Muncie. The Fang City belongs to the Cadre, and I belong to the Mountainside Pack.

As soon as we crossed back on pack land, Dorian yipped his goodbye before the sleek black wolf disappeared into the shadows of the trees. I didn't see the brindled wolf at my side or in my rearview, but I've gotten a pretty good handle on Jace these last couple of weeks. I sensed him near enough to catch a hint of his dominance the rest of the way to the cabin I share with my mate. Once he gave his word, he stood by it, and if that meant delivering me to the front door, he would.

Another battle not worth fighting. Even though his return to the pack made it possible for Ryker to head out to the wolf district, Jace still blames himself for abandoning me. Nothing short of ordering him to get over it will stop him from brooding, and I can't do that to him again.

It's bad enough that I never mentioned that I kind of, sort of took the choice out of his paws in the first place. Once I gave him the order, his wolf would never let him refuse me. I guessed that from the first time my howl controlled him, then when he and the other three offered themselves up to watch me, but I was always careful to keep the command from my voice.

To save him and get the message to Ryker, I let myself do it. I had to. He was watching my back, but I had to do the same. No way was I going to let him be another one of Wicked Wolf Walker's victims and, if he stayed any longer, I had no doubt in my mind that my bio-dad would've used him against me.

Doesn't mean that I don't think Jace is a powerful protector. I do. He's an asset to Mountainside. It's just... I wish that *I* wasn't the one he felt compelled to protect. As I proved time and time again, I can take care of myself, and if I can't? I've got Ryker. He's all I need, and he's mine forever now.

Mine.

Forever.

A small grin tugs on my lips as I kill the engine and pocket my keys. I start walking toward the front door, waving my hand as I sense Jace heading away from the Alpha's cabin. Now that I'm home, he'll run off to join a patrol, checking in with some of the other wolves that Ryker has watching Accalia's borders.

The Mountainside Pack is smaller than the Western Pack, but we're a tight-knit community that relies on each other. None of our packmates have come out and said it, but I've put a target on our back. First, it got out that I was the only female alpha. Now, the shifter world is buzzing with how I challenged the Wicked Wolf of the West and won. Add that to Ryker's show of dominance when he took down Theo and any wannabe alpha is going to try to rise up against us.

Try being the operative word there, but still. We can't pretend the danger isn't real. And after the way Walker ordered Trish to be grabbed off of pack territory by one of our own, Ryker has made pack security a priority ever since we returned from California a few weeks ago. He's determined to keep his pack safe, and if just the thought that another supe might come after me again has him nearly feral, I give him a pass. I know how hard Ryker is working to rein in his protective instincts when it comes to me, and I get it. Even as tightly bonded as we are, the calculating Alpha keeps waiting for something to wedge itself between us.

Elizabeth Howell and her Luna-touched gift really fucked with him. Even though we now know that even she can't break our bond without consent, the fear I felt pulsing toward me was a wake-up call—because it wasn't just me who was afraid she could do it. After all the times he seemingly rejected me, I was terrified that our bond was shaky at best. Turns out, Ryker had his own doubts when it came to me.

And why wouldn't he? I left him for more than a year, and when he found me, I rubbed my relationship with a vampire in his face. I made him chase me for weeks before I agreed to mate him, only for Ryker to believe I did it as a big ol' "F-U" to Jack Walker. Even after I got him to understand that all I've wanted for the last eleven years was to be his mate, I still made it clear that I had my life in Muncie, he had his in Accalia, and we would just have to make our mating work like that.

I saw it as regaining control. How much do I want to bet Ryker saw it as rejecting him instead?

My trip to the Fang City was a long time coming. The relief coming from my wolf made me realize that I wasn't just fighting Ryker with my insistence to keep some distance. I was fighting my inner self.

I'm so freaking tired of fighting.

It's not goodbye. I made friends in Muncie, and I'll treasure those relationships. But, at the end of the day, I'm a wolf shifter. Alpha or omega, it doesn't matter.

Once we choose, we mate for life. And me? I chose Ryker Wolfson a long time ago.

Reaching inside of myself, I follow the tug of my bond to the back of the cabin. No surprise that Ryker's in the den. I told him earlier that I had to run some errands, and though he would've known instinctively where I went, he gave me a scorching kiss before telling me he had some things he had to take care of himself.

I know what he's doing. He's been looking for any sign that Jack Walker is getting ready to cause us some more trouble. Whether he's building a new pack or licking his wounds until he can issue another challenge, we don't know, but we're both pretty sure that he's not about to slink off into the woods and disappear for good. My luck's too shitty for an easy ending like that.

Oh, and then there's still the whole "Mountainside is without a Beta" issue that's been nothing but a headache for more than a month now.

At least I might have an idea that could take care of *that* problem for us...

As I stride around the side of the Alpha's cabin, I have the strangest sense of déjà vu. Since I've been back in Accalia, this isn't the first time I've taken this path, or even the twentieth, but for some reason, I'm suddenly thrown back to almost a year and a half ago.

I had been furious, heat blazing off of my skin even

though that May night on the mountains was cool. The skirt of my sundress swished against my thighs, my wolf pushing so hard against me that it was all I could do to keep my claws sheathed—and I didn't even manage that considering I ended up sticking all five of them in the meat of Ryker's chest not too long after I burst into the den.

If you had told me that night that, sixteen moons later, I'd be taking the same path with a pep in my step, a smile on my face, and a finalized bond leading me to my mate, I would've thought you were nuts. That I was never going to be Ryker Wolfson's mate.

I've never been so damn happy to be wrong.

I let myself into the den with a lot less aggression than I did that time. Another distinct difference? When I walk into the den, Ryker's the only one inside. He's sitting at his desk—just like then—but his head shoots up as I enter.

He's so fucking gorgeous. You'd think I'd be used to this male looking at me like that, but it's still enough to have my heart racing whenever he does.

And, Luna, he's all mine.

"Hey."

I give my head the tiniest of clearing shakes. "Hey."

He glances at the clock on the wall. "You weren't gone long."

Nope. This might've been a long time coming, but I

decided it was best to treat it like ripping off a band-aid: get it over quick so that it hurts less.

I shrug, still a little in shock that I did it at all. Between Ryker's rugged beauty and my not-so-impulsive decision, I'm a bit rocked right now. "Yeah. I just got back. I figured I'd let you know."

Ryker lifts his eyebrows. From the look on his face, I can tell that he thinks something's up, but he's keeping his suspicions to himself for now. "Perfect timing, sweetheart. I was just about to get started on dinner. You ready to eat?"

I'm a shifter. I'm *always* ready to eat. And even if cooking is one of the few things that doesn't come easily to my Alpha mate, I love how he stubbornly insists on feeding me. To our kind of supe, there's no better way to show your love than to feed your mate.

Which, of course, is why I made a pitstop on the way back up the mountain.

"I'm glad you didn't start yet. I picked up a pizza for us to share." I wait a moment, making my eyes sparkle mischievously as I add, "Sausage and onion."

His lips twitch. "Your favorite."

"You know it."

He does, too. It was the first meal he brought to me, back when he was trying to court me and I wanted absolutely nothing to do with him. He broke into my room in Aleks's apartment, leaving behind flowers and a steaming slice of sausage and onion pizza. Knowing his intentions, I kept the flowers and decided to chuck the pizza in the trash. To eat it was signaling that I accepted his pursuit of me.

I didn't. In fact, I caught sight of him on the fire escape before I even made it to the kitchen. He egged me on, and I tossed the plate with the untouched slice on it like it was a freaking frisbee.

It only seemed fitting that tonight, of all nights, I brought him pizza.

"You wanna eat now?"

The heat in his golden eyes is a sure sign that Ryker is pretty freaking hungry—and not necessarily for food—but he nods. "I was just finishing up in here anyway. Should we eat in the kitchen?"

When he's in the den, any and all packmates have an open invitation to meet with Ryker. As soon as he moves to another room in the Alpha's cabin, it's a sign that he wants privacy. And the kitchen is so much closer to the bedroom than the den is...

My shifter's eyes light up, matching the hunger in his. "I'll grab the pizza from my Jeep and meet you there."

IT'S A GOOD THING THAT COLD PIZZA IS ALMOST AS GOOD as the fresh stuff.

I was already starving when I made it back to

Accalia. The scent of the sausage, onions, and bubbling cheese taunted me the entire drive. I couldn't wait to dig in, but when Ryker Wolfson looks at you like you're tastier than pizza, you throw yourself at him and start shedding clothes without a second thought.

Now that we worked up an even heartier appetite, the two of us are sitting in bed, bare-ass naked and thrumming as we quickly demolish the pie. Ryker wrung three orgasms out of me before he let himself finish, pride pouring off of him when he eventually remembered that I left the pizza box on the kitchen table and left to get it. He came back bearing the pizza like a hunter returning with his kill, nuzzling me out of my post-coital coma so that I could have the first slice.

Once I do, he takes one. Less than five minutes later, the whole pie is gone. I'm full, I've been fucked boneless, and Ryker is staring at my boobs like he's ready for round two.

I toss a crumpled napkin at him.

His head jerks up, meeting my gaze. He's not even a little ashamed I caught him staring, but why would he be? I'm his. I've always been his.

But this is important.

"Hey. My boobs'll still be there in a couple of minutes. Let's talk."

Ryker is immediately on his guard. Don't blame him for that, either. With a courtship like ours, 'let's talk' never meant anything good—but that was before. Now? Everything's different.

"What did you want to talk about?"

"Let's talk about what we did today. I know you were making some calls, talking to some Alphas. Did you hear back from River Run?"

Ryker nods. "Kendall got in touch. Finally. I gave him the head's up about Walker, but he already heard what happened in California."

Of course he did. Even though Ryker was trying to get in touch with as many Alphas as possible before the Wicked Wolf tried to spin exactly how he lost his pack, each pack is its own insular community. Apart from the annual Alpha's gathering, the pack leaders never wanted it to appear like they were answering to another. River Run is the closest pack to Mountainside, and usually one of our allies. If my jerk of a birth father starts shit on the East Coast, he might target Kendall and the River Run Pack. We need them on our side first.

I'm not surprised that he heard what happened. Shifters gossip worse than old ladies, and that's before you factor in Walker's reputation and manipulative tactics. He purposely kept himself away from other Alphas—he refused to go to a single gathering after my mom left him—but that was when he had the Wolf District to lord over.

What is he doing now? No one knows, and both

Ryker and I admit that that couldn't be good. Making sure the packs we thought of as friendly to Mountainside—like River Run, and my real dad's Lakeview Pack—knew the truth was a priority right behind fortifying our own borders.

"And?"

"Kendall liked Trish. Not enough to let her into his pack when he was sure she was still loyal to Mountainside, but he thought she was a good wolf. When he heard that Walker had her in a cage, he stopped pussyfooting around. He'll back us."

That's right. When Ryker kicked Trish out of Accalia, she realized that she wasn't lone wolf material. She needed to be part of a pack, and River Run's the closest. She was in the middle of trying to convince Kendall to let her in when Aleks interfered, telling her to track me and Ryker down in Muncie to beg for forgiveness.

At the time, my ex-roomie was trying everything he could to break me and Ryker up. His motives had been less than innocent, and I nearly went for his throat when my rival showed up in my territory, once again claiming that Ryker was her mate. And, sure, Trish made it clear that she only name-dropped Ryker to the Cadre so that they would let her inside of Muncie, but still. I was a possessive wolf in the middle of the mating dance. Sue me for being a little temperamental.

I'm glad to hear that Kendall is on our side. They're

another level of protection for our pack, and one that we could use.

Good.

"What about the Beta hunt?" I ask next. "Any luck on that?"

"I wish. I swear to the Luna, I don't know how that asshole was able to get a hundred different Betas while he was Alpha. I'd do anything for just one good one."

That asshole... since we made it back to Accalia, the Wicked Wolf has been relegated to "that asshole" by Ryker. I can't say I don't love it.

"You know, I think I've been thinking about it a lot lately." And that was putting it mildly. "What about Jace?"

The way I see it, it's like killing two birds with one stone. Jace gets a promotion that he deserves, I get a little more breathing room when it comes to him acting like my shadow, and Ryker has a loyal Beta who won't betray him. Huh. Make that killing *three* birds.

Not bad, if I do say so myself. Now I just have to get Ryker to agree.

When he scoffs and says, "Jace? Jace can't be Beta," I know I have my work cut out for me.

"Why not?" I demand.

Ryker looks at me like I've asked him why two and two is four. To him, the answer is obvious. "Because he's not a born beta."

"So?"

"Gemma—"

Come on, Ryker. It's not *that* obvious.

"Hear me out. What's a Beta anyway? A title. A position in the pack. The Beta needs to be a right-hand to the Alpha. Someone the pack respects. And, okay, maybe the beta rank is perfect for the job, but there's not that big a difference between Warren's dominance and Jace's. He's younger, devoted to Mountainside, and a good wolf. I think he'd be perfect for it."

Ryker's quiet for a few seconds. And then, almost begrudgingly, he nods. "You're not wrong."

I know I'm not. "You're the Alpha. If you want to choose him to be your Beta, who's gonna stop you? The only one who can even try is me, and since this is my brilliant idea, you know damn well I won't."

My whole life, my dad made one thing clear: nothing is set in stone. While most shifters live and die by fate, he proved that you don't have to. When he became Alpha of the Lakeview Pack, he refused to ask the Luna for the name of his fated mate, deciding that he wanted to choose his mate on his own. That was just the beginning of Paul Booker taking shifter traditions and turning them on their head.

Honestly, I feel kind of silly that it took me so long to remember one of the biggest life lessons he taught me when I was still a pup: the Alpha makes the rules. My dad did. Jack Walker certainly had. Why couldn't Ryker?

He gives me a sly look. "Are you sure you're not just throwing Jace at me because then he'll be too busy to tail you?"

If that was my only concern, I never would've mentioned the idea. Part of being in a pack is looking out for one another instead of covering your own ass; if I was only looking out for me, I could've stayed a lone wolf. If Jace takes the role of Beta, I wouldn't be surprised if he was more determined to keep his Alpha's mate safe, but at least he'd also use his protective urges to watch out for our other packmates.

So, instead of pointing that out, I just ask, "Tail me? Tail me where?"

"Whenever you're in Muncie. Because, remember, sweetheart. Even if Jace is in Accalia, Bobby and Dorian can always stand outside of that blood bar of yours to keep an eye on you when I can't."

"And why would I be at Charlie's?"

I'm still smiling, which usually would have Ryker guessing that something was up. Every time we talked about my determination to stay in Muncie after we were mated, smiling was definitely one expression that I never pulled. Scowling? Sure. Snarling? Oh, yeah. Smiling? Nope.

But I'm smiling now, and Ryker's voice turns hesitant as he says, "Because you work there."

I shake my head.

He blinks.

My smile widens.

Okay. Maybe I should have told him that I was heading into Muncie to officially let Charlie know that I wouldn't be coming back. He had figured as much—even though I was a shifter, not a vamp, the second I got mated, he knew I'd eventually leave—and there were no hard feelings. If I decided to come back, there was always an apron and an order pad for me, and Hailey made me promise that I would keep in touch.

I said I would, and considering I still want to hear about how her fling with Dominic Le Croix is going, I really mean it. She swore she was working her way toward getting her own fang, and I hope she does. Hailey will only be happy when she's settled down with a vampire; even if her forever isn't with the Cadre vamp, then at least with one who deserves an awesome human like she is.

If I was being honest, I think I kept it a secret because—until I did quit—there was always the chance that I could go back to my old life. Ryker stopped pushing me the second I wore his mark, but with our bond cemented, I could sense just how much he wanted to.

A mating is a give and take. I've taken enough. It's my turn to give.

Now, Ryker knew about my plan to let Elizabeth use the townhouse that he had purchased for me before we made our mating official. While she hasn't committed to joining the Mountainside Pack—for now, she's still choosing to go lone wolf—I know that Ryker likes the idea of keeping her close. And it wasn't like I could go back to my old room at Aleks's apartment. I think he thought that I'd keep my job, but return to Accalia whenever I didn't have a shift.

And maybe I could have.

Or maybe I could finally accept that Accalia is my home now.

No. Not Accalia.

Ryker is.

"I'm here now. With the pack. With you. For good."

A slow smile begins to grow. "You're not going back?"

"Maybe for a visit every now and then. Someone's got to check in on Elizabeth if she decides to take us up on our offer, and I still want to keep my friends." And, yes, Aleks is one of them. After everything that happened in the Wolf District, I no longer have to worry about his feelings for me, and I finally have my friend back. "But I'm not going to stay there."

"You mean it?"

"Why would I?" I ask, scooting closer to him. Tipping my chin up, I meet his gaze. "I chose my forever when I chose you."

I was hanging onto my old life in Muncie because I couldn't bring myself to believe that I'd really have a future in Accalia. Even after we performed the

Luna Ceremony, I had my doubts; my wolf might've been all in, but my human side still nursed the pain of Ryker's rejection. And then I had to watch him fight not one, but *two* alpha challenges. For a few awful seconds, I was sure that Elizabeth's touch would snap the bond between us. I was so sure I would lose him.

True, I didn't, but I knew right then that I would never let anything come between us ever again.

And that includes me.

"Gem—"

"I love you, Ryker. I've always loved you. My home is where you are. Muncie. Accalia. The fucking moon… I don't care. I just want to be with you."

"I told you once, sweetheart. We do this, I'm not letting you go."

He did. That fateful full moon, when Ryker's pack council locked me in his basement with him, he made it clear. If I let him claim me while the Luna was out, that was it. No matter how I regretted it, or how far I ran, he'd chase. He'd already spent the last year doing it, and that was before we slept together the first time. Now that he had a taste of me, he wouldn't stop.

Thank fucking Luna.

"Good," I retort, tipping my chin up a little higher. "Because I'm never letting you go."

It's a dare. A challenge. Whatever you want to call it, it's a shot straight at his alpha wolf.

I should've known he could never resist it—and, well, I guess I did.

Before I can react, Ryker grips me by my hips, pulling me onto his lap. Taking me up on my blatant invitation, he slants his mouth over mine, giving me such a dominating kiss that I have my fingers digging deep into the muscles of his back.

When his blood perfumes the room, rising over the scent of sex and pizza, I realize that I've stuck him with my claws.

That only makes him kiss me harder. Following his lead, I kiss him back until I'm almost dizzy.

Suddenly, Ryker is shifting us, tilting me so that I'm lying down again. I cross my ankles behind him as he covers my body with his.

"You're mine," he rumbles, his voice raspy and hoarse and just a touch out of breath.

My chest is heaving. The all-encompassing look in his dark gold eyes has me trembling, my legs quaking even as he nudges the head of his cock against the opening of my pussy.

I've never felt so loved—so *possessed*—than I do at this exact moment.

And I freaking love it.

I jab my claws in his ass, scoring it deep in another mark that, if I know my mate, will be one that he'll keep with pride. He groans in pleasure, and I dig a little harder, pushing him into me.

Only then, when he's buried to the hilt inside of me, do I purposely meet his lust-filled gaze. With a tiny, daring grin, I yank out my claws, clenching my pussy around his cock as he throws back his head in a drawn-out moan. He shudders softly, and I wait for him to go still again before I bring my claws to my lips. Ryker's blood drips from the points. As he stares down at me, I lap at my forefinger. I'm no vamp, but damn if his blood isn't delicious.

His dark eyes go molten at my display. I see his wolf staring out at me, and I know that mine is staring right back at him.

"No, Ryker," I murmur throatily, reaching out to cup his jaw gently with my bloody claws. "You're mine."

Forever.

AUTHOR'S NOTE

Thanks for reading *Forever Mates*!

While this is the last full-length book being told in Gem's POV, this definitely isn't the end of the **Claws and Fangs** series. If it wasn't already obvious, this book sets up the next arc, featuring Aleks and Elizabeth, the Luna-touched shifter who is more than she seems...

That book is coming out in February, so it isn't too long of a wait, but I also have a new series launching this summer! Set in the same world as Gem's books, **Stolen Mates** focuses on what it's like for a few feisty heroines to be captured by another male after being rejected by their fated mates. The first book, *The Feral's Captive*, tells the story of Quinn, a delta wolf who was fated to mate with the Beta of her pack. Unfortunately for her, her fated mate is already in love with someone else, leaving her on the sidelines—until she gets captured by a feral wolf shifter...

AUTHOR'S NOTE

I do also plan on doing a novella featuring Duke and Trish sometime early next year, so even if this is the end of Gem as the POV character, it's definitely not the last you'll see of the feisty alpha she-wolf!

For a sneak peek at Aleks's book, plus Quinn's, keep scrolling/clicking/reading. And don't forget: if you want to find out about exclusives, sales, giveaways and more, make sure to join my newsletter for special subscriber-only information (and maybe a special holiday short available there only *wink*).

xoxo,
Sarah

AVAILABLE NOW
HINT OF HER BLOOD

When Aleks looks at me, he sees his past. Me? I see a future that I just can't have...

For most of my life, being Luna-touched was a blessing—and then I met Jack "Wicked Wolf" Walker and it wasn't long before it became a *curse.*

The powerful Alpha lost his Luna-given mate before I was born, but that didn't stop him from trying to claim me. Only my quick thinking and quicker mouth kept me from being his new mate, but I still ended up locked in a gilded cage.

I thought I'd be trapped in the Wolf District forever—until the Alpha's daughter came, handing him his first defeat in more than twenty-five years. She spared his life, but our laws are clear: an Alpha who loses a challenge is no Alpha. Our pack disbanded, and I was free.

Which... wasn't as great as it sounded. I have no family. No real friends. No money. And a vampire who looks at me like I'm lunch.

Aleksander Filan thinks I'm someone that I'm not. And while it would be too easy to let this handsome, sexy, magnetic vampire take care of me, I reject him if only because I'm terrified of what the Luna whispers to me at night.

No. *No*. He can't be my fated mate. I'm a wolf. He's a bloodsucker. I'm damaged goods, and he's... well, he has his own baggage, doesn't he?

He promises that he wants me. He sees *me*. And when the Wicked Wolf follows me to Muncie, Aleks will have the chance to prove it.

After all, for a hint of my blood, he vows he'll do *anything*.

---

* ***Hint of Her Blood*** is the fourth novel in the *Claws and Fangs* series, and the first in Aleks and Elizabeth's story.

Releasing February 22, 2022!

PRE-ORDER NOW

THE FERAL'S CAPTIVE

There's no escaping him...

Fate sucks.

As a shifter, I've always known that Fate—in the form of our goddess, the revered Luna—would have the final say when it came to my life. That includes everything: my pack, my rank, even my forever mate.

And I hate it.

I want to choose. I want my life to be mine, and if that makes me the odd one out in our pack? Oh, well. A delta, it's not like the higher ranks—our Alpha, his Beta, and the pack council—have much use for me anyway.

Still, even I'll admit I've always been drawn to the Beta of the Sylvan Pack. When I discover that he's my fated mate, it seems like giving in to the Luna's demands might not be such a bad thing after all—until he rejects me for a female he can't even have.

Because, yeah. Not only does Fate suck, it has a twisted sense of humor when it comes to me.

So that's that. I have to pretend like my broken bond isn't a constant ache while watching as my fated mate begs for table scraps from another wolf.

Is it any wonder that I start spending my free time in the woods surrounding our territory?

I wasn't afraid. Even at my low rank, I know I'm scarier than anything else that lurks in the darkness of the trees. But I was wrong—and when I see those insane golden eyes staring at me, I know I'm in deep, deep trouble.

My name is Quinn Malone, and I've just been captured by a feral...

---

* ***The Feral's Captive*** is the first in a new rejected mates paranormal romance. Set in the same world as *Never His Mate*, shifters are an open secret, most humans are off-limits, and a feral wolf shifter male is wiling to sacrifice everything to steal the wolf he believes is his mate. And though it may not be fated, Quinn and Chase's bond is just as undeniable...

Releasing June 28, 2022!

KEEP IN TOUCH

Stay tuned for what's coming up next! Sign up for my mailing list for news, promotions, upcoming releases, and more!

Sarah Spade's Stories

And make sure to check out my Facebook page for all release news:

http://facebook.com/sarahspadebooks

Sarah Spade is a pen name that I used specifically to write these holiday-based novellas (as well as a few books that will be coming out in the future). If you're interested in reading other books that I've written (romantic suspense, Greek mythology-based romance, shifters/vampires/witches romance, and fae romance), check out my primary author account here:

http://amazon.com/author/jessicalynch

ALSO BY SARAH SPADE

Holiday Hunk

Halloween Boo

This Christmas

Auld Lang Mine

I'm With Cupid

Getting Lucky

When Sparks Fly

Holiday Hunk: the Complete Series

Claws and Fangs

Leave Janelle

Never His Mate

Always Her Mate

Forever Mates

Hint of Her Blood

Taste of His Skin

Stolen Mates

The Feral's Captive

The Beta's Bride

Claws Clause

(written as Jessica Lynch)

Mates *free*

Hungry Like a Wolf

Of Mistletoe and Mating

No Way

Season of the Witch

Rogue

Sunglasses at Night

Ain't No Angel *free*

True Angel

Ghost of Jealousy

Night Angel

Broken Wings

Lost Angel

Born to Run

Uptown Girl

Ordinance 7304: the Bond Laws (Claws Clause Collection #1)

Living on a Prayer (Claws Clause Collection #2)

Printed in Great Britain
by Amazon